UNSETTLED GROUND

UNSETTLED GROUND

CLAIRE FULLER

THORNDIKE PRESS
A part of Gale, a Cengage Company

LIBRARY OF CONGRESS CIP DATA ON FILE.
CATALOGUING IN PUBLICATION FOR THIS BOOK
IS AVAILABLE FROM THE LIBRARY OF CONGRESS.

ISBN-13: 978-1-4328-9050-6 (hardcover alk. paper)

Published in 2021 by arrangement with Tin House Books, LLC.

Printed in Mexico
Print Number: 01   Print Year: 2022

For my parents
Ursula Pitcher
and Stephen Fuller

O, will you find me an acre of land,
Savoury sage, rosemary and thyme,
Between the sea foam,
  and the sea sand,
Or never be a true love of mine.

"Scarborough Fair,"
traditional English ballad

1

The morning sky lightens, and snow falls on the cottage. It falls on the thatch, concealing the moss and the mouse damage, smoothing out the undulations, filling in the hollows and slips, melting where it touches the bricks of the chimney. It settles on the plants and bare soil in the front garden and forms a perfect mound on top of the rotten gatepost, as though shaped from the inside of a teacup. It hides the roof of the chicken coop, and those of the privy and the old dairy, leaving a dusting across the workbench and floor where the window was broken long ago. In the vegetable garden at the back, the snow slides through the rips in the plastic of the polytunnel, chills the onion sets four inches underground, and shrivels the new shoots of the Swiss chard. Only the head of the last winter cabbage refuses to succumb, the interior leaves curled green and strong, waiting.

In the high double bed up the left staircase, Dot lies beside her adult daughter, Jeanie, who is gently snoring. Something different about the light in the room has woken Dot and she can't get back to sleep. She gets out of the bed — floorboards cold, air colder — and puts on her dressing gown and slippers. The dog — Jeanie's dog — a biscuit-coloured lurcher who sleeps on the landing with her back to the chimney breast, raises her head, enquiring about the early hour as Dot passes, lowering it when she gets no answer.

Downstairs in the kitchen, Dot jabs at the embers in the range with the poker and shoves in a ball of paper, some kindling, and a log. She feels a pain. Behind her left eye. Between her left eye and her temple. Does the place have a name? She needs to go to the optician, get her eyes checked, but then what? How will she pay for new glasses? She needs to take her prescription to the chemist, but she is worried about the cost. The light is wrong down here too. Lowing? Owing? Glowing? She touches her temple as though to locate the soreness and sees through the curtains, in the gap where they don't quite meet, that it is snowing. It is the twenty-eighth of April.

Her movements must have roused the dog

10

again because now there is a scratching at the door at the bottom of the left staircase and Dot reaches out to unlatch it. She watches her hand grasping the wrought iron, the liver spots and crosshatching seeming peculiar, unlike anything she's seen before: the mechanics of her fingers, the way the skin on her knuckles stretches over bone, bending around the handle. The articulation is alien — the hand of an impostor. The effort of pushing on the tiny plate with her thumb seems impossible, a bodily weariness worse even than when her twins were three months old and didn't sleep at the same time, or the terrible year after they turned twelve. But with great concentration she depresses it and the latch lifts. The dog pokes her snout through, the rest of her body following. She whimpers and licks Dot's left hand where it hangs against her thigh, pushes nose into palm, making the hand swing of its own accord, a pendulum. The pain increases and Dot worries that the dog might wake Jeanie with her whining, Jeanie asleep in the right-hand dip in the double mattress, first made by her husband, Frank, long dead, and on the rare occasions when her children were out of the house, by that other unmentionable-at-home man, who is too long for that old

11

short bed so he cannot stretch out, and then hollowed further by Jeanie even though she is a wisp of a thing and ate only a tiny slice of the Victoria sponge they made for when Dot herself turned seventy last month and had at the little celebration here in the kitchen with Bridget taking telephone pictures of Julius on his fiddle and she on her banjo and Jeanie on the guitar all singing after a drop of port to lubricate the vocal cords Julius always says and how the sensation Dot has now is similar to the way she felt following her third glass clumsy and blurred with her thoughts diffuse dizzily leaving the remains of the cake on the table so that dog naughty stood on her hind legs and yumphed it down and them scolding and laughing until her sides . . . yurt? kurt? . . . all her loves but one, there with her, and the dog barking and jumping and barking too excited and noisy like she'd be in the snow waking Julius who sleeps so lightly and stirs at any noise.

All these thoughts and more, which Dot is barely aware of, pass through her mind while her body slows. It is a wet coat she wants to shed like the chickens with their autumn moult. An unresponsive weight. Leaden.

Dot falls back onto the kitchen sofa as

though someone had reached out a palm and pushed on her breastbone. The dog sits on her haunches and lowers her head onto Dot's knee, nudging her hand until she places it between the animal's ears. And then all thoughts of chickens and children, of birthdays and beds, all thoughts of everything, vanish and are silent.

The worries of seventy years — the money, the infidelity, the small deceits — are cut away, and when she looks at her hand she can no longer tell where she ends and dog begins. They are one substance, enormous and free, as is the sofa, the stone floor, the walls, the cottage thatch, the snow, the sky. Everything connected.

"Jeanie," she calls but hears some other word. She isn't concerned, she has never felt such love for the world and everything in it. The dog makes a noise that isn't like any noise a dog would make and backs off, so that Dot is forced to remove her hand from the bony head. She shuffles on the sofa, she wants to touch the animal again, put her arms around the dog and fall inside of her. But as Dot leans, she tips, her left foot turning on its side and sliding along the floor. Her balance is upset, and she pitches face-forward, her right hand going out to break the fall, while the other catches under her chest, the finger with her wedding ring pinned beneath her. Dot's head goes down and her forehead hits the edge of the hearth where a flagstone has always been slightly raised, shifting it so that the fire irons, which hang beside the range, fall. A last lucid fragment of Dot's mind worries that the clatter of the metal pan and brush might shock her daughter's heart from its regular rhythm, until she remembers that this is the biggest lie of all. The poker, which has fallen too, rolls away under the table, rocks once, twice, and then is still.

2

Jeanie is woken by Julius shaking her arm, at first gently and then more roughly. She flies down the stairs after him, her night-dress flapping out behind, even though he has said she must walk. It's gloomy in the kitchen, curtains drawn, lights off, only the orange glow of the fire in the range. Their mother lies face down on the floor, not moving. Jeanie puts her hands to her mouth to hold in her noise.

"Help me turn her over," Julius says, and as Jeanie touches their mother, she knows she is dead. Dot's arms remain by her sides and her ankles cross, slippers coming off, and although she has her dressing gown on, Jeanie thinks she looks as if she were sun-bathing, something her mother would never have done; if you were outside, you were working. Jeanie keeps her eyes averted from the wound on Dot's forehead and then to save herself from seeing any of it, puts her

15

hands over her face. Strips of pinkish light, showing the kitchen and segments of her mother's body, filter through her fingers. When she and Julius were twelve, up in Priest's Field, she also hadn't been able to look away. The dog, who has been cowering under the kitchen table, comes forwards with a whine and Jeanie takes her hands from her face.

"Maude!" She clicks her fingers and points and the dog slinks back under the table.

"Her neck, press against her neck. Feel for a pulse," Julius says. He's crouching the other side of Dot in only his pyjama bottoms — Jeanie hasn't seen him without his work clothes on for years — grey hairs on his chest; arms and torso muscled from manual work.

Out of habit, and without even knowing she's doing it, Jeanie presses her fingers to her own neck, and then touches her mother, quickly on the cheek. "She's cold. It's too late."

"I tried to call for an ambulance but my phone's dead," Julius says.

"We don't need one. It's too late."

"Must have been a power cut. The electric went off last night. I'll check the fuse board."

16

"She's gone, Julius."

"What about that chest-pumping thing?"

"She's dead."

"Christ."

Julius's face is solemn, and the situation so surprising that Jeanie wants to laugh. A guffaw of disbelief is rising like a belch inside her and again, she clamps her hands to her mouth to contain it. Julius spreads his large palms over his head, across his receding hairline, and his body convulses, jerking; his sobs like the call of some exotic animal. Jeanie watches him with fascination. They were born nearly a whole day apart, him first and Jeanie second — unexpected and unprepared for — delivered by their panicked father after the midwife had gone home. "My little runt," Frank had affectionately called his daughter. Jeanie often thinks that those twenty-three hours account for her and Julius's differences: the way he embraces the world and shows his emotions, open to people and situations; while she, Jeanie, craves home, quiet, and security.

She reaches awkwardly across the body of their mother and hauls Julius to his feet and guides him to the sofa, where they sit. Maude looks up as though waiting for an invitation to join them, but Jeanie gives a

17

quick shake of her head and the dog rests her snout on her paws.

"I must have heard her fall," Julius says when his sobs have subsided. He wipes his hand under his nose, rubs his palms across his eyes. "Or the poker and brush, at least. I thought it was Maude playing silly buggers with something. I went back to sleep."

"It's not your fault," Jeanie says, although she doesn't yet know if she really feels that. Her brother, and their father before him, said many times that they would re-lay that flagstone. When your mother is dead on the kitchen floor is someone to blame? She holds him and they stay like that for a few minutes until Jeanie looks over his shoulder and through the gap in the curtains. "It's snowing," she says.

They cover Dot with a blanket. Jeanie wants to lift her onto the sofa, but the sofa is too short. She boils the kettle on the range and makes tea and they sit at the table to drink it with their mother's body behind them on the floor, as though, like a child in a game of hide-and-seek, she has found a particularly poor place to hide and they are pretending they can't see her.

"She was a good woman," Julius says. "A fine mother."

Jeanie nods, murmurs into her tea.

"Are the trestles still in the old dairy?" she says, knowing that Julius will follow her train of thought like he always has.

In the parlour, she rolls up the rug and pushes the chairs to the edge. She could be preparing for a dance in a room which has never seen dancing. Julius lays an old door on top of the two trestles and goes back to the kitchen to lift their mother with a heave and a groan. He won't let Jeanie help. There is a long list of things she regrets never having lifted because of her weak heart: boxes, hay bales, babies, tractors. He carries Dot through to the parlour. It's chilly in here; much colder than the kitchen. An antimacassar lies on the back of an overstuffed armchair; a Toby jug and a framed photograph of Dot and Frank on their wedding day, in front of an Italian landscape they never visited, stand on a low polished chest; a tapestry screen hides the fireplace which is never used in this half of the cottage.

Newly married, Dot and Frank lived in the single-bedroom semi-detached cottage for a year, but as soon as the twins were born, Frank negotiated renting the mirror-image right-hand side. He knocked the two cottages together and blocked up one of the front doors so that from the gate the place has a lopsided look about it, while inside it

19

still has two staircases, each leading to a small landing and a bedroom.

Julius lays Dot on the old door and Jeanie swaps the blanket for a clean sheet.

Both dressed now, sister and brother sit again at the kitchen table, teapot refilled. Julius has checked the fuse board in the scullery; nothing has blown but the electricity won't come back on no matter how much he fiddles with the wires.

"I suppose we have to tell a doctor. Isn't that what you do when someone dies?" Julius says, almost to himself. There was a process followed when their father died which Jeanie and Julius knew nothing about and now can only guess at.

"Doctors are for people who are ill," Jeanie says.

"But we'll need a death certificate."

What for? Jeanie thinks but doesn't say out loud.

"So we can bury her," Julius says as though answering. "I'll get a doctor and he'll give us the form, and that'll be that."

Jeanie shakes her head. Dot wouldn't have wanted a doctor to come to the house, certificates, forms, authority. None of them has seen a doctor in years.

But Julius is up, pulling on his work boots. "I'll have to walk to the village," he says.

The village, Inkbourne, has a GP surgery, a village hall with public toilets, a fish and chip shop, and a small supermarket with a post office counter. There is also the old grocer's which has been bought by a young man from London with a waxed moustache who has turned it into a deli selling posh bread, cheese, and olives, as well as some vegetables and eggs supplied by Jeanie and Dot. The owner, Max, serves fancy coffees and pastries at aluminium tables on the pavement outside, catching passing trade from walkers following the long-distance path which goes through the village, or Lycra-clad men on bicycles with ten-pound notes folded into the little pocket in the front of their leggings. "I won't be able to cycle," Julius says, and Jeanie remembers the snow. "If the surgery is open, I'll tell Bridget, she'll definitely want to know, and she can tell one of the doctors. If it's closed, I'll go on to her house." He takes his coat from the hook on the back of the door. Maude stands, wags her tail.

"Aren't you meant to be finishing that plumbing job with Craig today?" Jeanie says.

"I'm not going to help lift a cast-iron bath upstairs into some bathroom on the day my mother dies."

"How will you let him know?"

21

"He'll realize soon enough that I'm not coming."

"Isn't he meant to be paying you today?"

Julius pauses. "I'm not going to leave you here on your own all day."

"I've got to feed the chickens. There are things to do in the garden that won't wait." She comes towards him. "You should go, get paid. We need the money."

Julius's hand is on the front-door catch. "I'll see. If I can't cycle there, I'm going to be late anyway." There is irritation in his voice, perhaps he notices too, because he comes back into the room and puts his arms around her. "We'll be all right," he says into her hair. "It'll be all right."

"I know it," she says, pushing him away. "Get going."

She watches him leave from the cottage's front door, Maude by her side, expectant and then disappointed at being held back. Jeanie sucks in the freezing air. April's mud is hidden, the snow showing only the bumps and dips of the plants like the sheet laid over the body in the room behind her. Maybe the shock of the snow so late in the year made Dot fall. If she saw it, she would have worried about the vegetable seedlings out in the cold, and about the time and the money they'd lose. Later, Jeanie would have come in from the garden to see her mother sitting at the kitchen table with a scrap of paper, chewing on the end of her pencil while she calculated one column of numbers and another.

For half a mile, the track curves through a small wood and then between the hedges of two fields. On any other day Julius would have stopped at the place where the view opens out and climbs, up the steep and sinuous scarp with Rivar Down on the right and, leftwards, the three-mile stretch of the high chalk ridge all the way to Combe Gibbet. Clusters of trees on the slopes — beech, oak, and conifer — are white, the snow thick and the sky low on the grazed common land. But today he keeps his head down, not noticing the tracks of small mammals and birds who have gone before him through the snow. He rolls a cigarette and smokes it while he follows the ruts which his feet know from fifty-odd years of walking or cycling along them, even if today the ruts are hidden. Towards the end, the track straightens, and he goes past the back of the dented sign that says *Private, No Public Right of Way* before the farmyard. Here, he passes a large barn made of planks stained black, concrete sheds with open sides filled with forgotten machinery and surrounded by nettles. Around the corner is the Rawsons' brick-and-flint farmhouse and their manicured garden, the topiary like giant snowmen. He could walk four more miles to the village or he could knock on the Rawsons' door and ask to use their landline or a mobile. Pepperwood Farm has been in the Rawson family for three generations; Rawson was twenty when he inherited it after his father died of a heart attack. Its 120 acres include the arable land from the bottom of the ridge to the bank of the Ink, the muddy stream which gives the village its name. It includes the beech wood on either side of the track and the meadow behind the garden, and officially, it included the cottage and its land. Julius sometimes works on the farm when they need an extra pair of hands, but the jobs are always arranged through the farm manager. If Julius ever sees Rawson, in his country squire get-up of tweed jacket, waistcoat, and corduroy trousers, he keeps out of the man's way. But four miles walking on the morning your mother has died is another four miles walking. He goes up to the farmhouse door.

3

Julius falters over the lion's head knocker. He has never stood on the front doorstep of the farmhouse before. As a child, he often went to the farm with Jeanie and their father and played in and around the disorderly collection of barns and outbuildings which are mostly tucked around the back. They spent time roaming the fields, picking blackberries and watching badgers at night as if the land belonged to the Seeders and not the Rawsons. From the back door inside, Julius has only ever been as far as the pantry, when he and his sister were invited in by the housekeeper for a glass of lemonade.

He lets the door knocker fall. The snow has stopped and already there are steady drips from the trees and bushes. Someone has driven in and out of the driveway, scoring and muddying the ground, but the early morning sun is shining, and where the snow is still clean, the shadows are sharp-edged and blue.

There are no sounds from inside the house and Julius is turning to go when he hears the door being unbolted. It's opened by Rawson, dressed in trousers and a white shirt, his feet bare. Julius realizes he's been expecting the housekeeper from his childhood, a large, kind, and aproned woman, who would surely be dead by now. Like his mother, he thinks. Dead. Rawson is tall, a whole head taller than Julius, and about his mother's age, with brilliant white hair, black eyebrows, and a white moustache which flows down either side of his mouth. This morning he has also grown a crop of white stubble across his jaw and cheeks. The whole effect is that of a polecat, like the one Jenks, Julius's drinking friend, once caught in a trap and brought into the pub: supple and lean.

"Julius," Rawson says, stepping back, surprised, and Julius in turn is surprised that Rawson remembers his name. "Is everything all right?"

"I need to use your phone." Julius's own mobile, which he put into his coat pocket out of habit, is a basic model, not a smartphone like everyone seems to have these days, and he didn't think to bring his charger.

26

"Of course, come in," Rawson says in his educated voice, and steps back. The large hall has a carved fireplace, a tiled floor, and panelling. A blocky wooden staircase turns up the wall. Arts and Crafts, Dot used to call it, but Julius hadn't known what she was on about and wasn't interested.

"Is your electric working?" Julius wipes his feet on the mat.

"We've no problems here. Have you had a power cut? Checked the fuse box?"

Julius rolls his eyes as Rawson turns away. "Now where's that handset? Caroline's forever using it and not putting it back in its holder." He goes through a doorway into a room that overlooks the front garden, a red-brick fireplace and two white sofas facing each other, a baby grand piano behind. It's like a room that no one uses: no dogs on the furniture, no feet on the chairs, no wet spoons in the sugar. "Shall I look up the number of the electricity company? Who are you with?"

"I need the number for the GP surgery," Julius says, coming into the room. He has an urge to take off his cap which he forgot to put on anyway. Fuck that, he thinks.

Rawson glances at him and looks away. Too stuck up, Julius supposes, to ask why he needs that number. The man bumbles

27

around, finding the telephone handset on an armchair, pressing one button and then another to make sure there's a dialling tone. "Who would have expected snow at the end of April?" Rawson says, making conversation and not waiting for an answer. He gives Julius the handset. "No problem up at the cottage, is there?" Rawson is searching on his mobile for the surgery's number, walking about the room and back to the hall. Julius follows.

"My mother's dead," Julius says bluntly, just to see if he can stop the man's mumblings, but the words shock Julius too. She really is dead. The two men stare at each other and Julius sees his own expression mirrored on Rawson's face.

"What?" Rawson puts a hand out to the wooden mantelpiece.

A woman's voice comes from above: "Who is it?"

"Julius," Rawson calls while looking at him. "From the cottage."

"What does he want?"

Rawson continues to stare at Julius, and Julius looks back, waiting to see what he will say, until Rawson raises his eyes to where the wooden banister turns squarely out of sight, and then back to him. "It's nothing," he shouts. "I'll tell you later."

Nothing, Julius thinks. That's what the Seeders are to the Rawsons.

The woman — Rawson's wife, Julius presumes — doesn't reply or come down and in that moment, Rawson seems to catch and compose himself. "I'm so terribly sorry. What happened?"

"She fell, hit her head. Early this morning. I need to call the doctor."

"Of course, of course." Rawson fumbles some more with his smartphone, saying, "My wife always uses Alexa for phone numbers, but I can't get the hang of the thing."

Julius wonders if the man is going senile; he has no idea who Alexa is. Rawson reads out the telephone number and while it's ringing he goes back into the sitting room, but Julius is aware of his presence just the other side of the door, most likely listening. A receptionist answers the phone — a different one from Bridget — who makes sympathetic noises and takes the details. She searches for Dot on their computer system and Julius thinks that perhaps she won't be registered with them any more, but the receptionist finds her name and says that Dr. Holloway will visit this morning as soon as he is able. When the call is finished, Rawson comes back into the hall. His eyes are bright, shiny.

"Okay if I make another?" Julius says.

"Go ahead. Can I get you a cup of —" Rawson starts.

"No."

"Of course. I'm sure you've got lots to sort out."

"Thanks," Julius says, although he doesn't mean it. This man owed my mother, Julius thinks. And now Rawson owes him and Jeanie. "I need another number. A bathroom fitter. I'm supposed to be working for him today."

When he has the number, Julius phones Craig while Rawson shifts a vase of flowers on a table a centimetre left and pretends not to listen to this conversation too.

At the front door as Julius is leaving, Rawson says, "Hang on. I've got some post for you." The postman won't come up the track after his van got stuck one time and had to be towed out by a tractor. Julius isn't sure how or when his mother collected the post. He doesn't look at the envelopes, just folds them in half and shoves them in his coat pocket.

"Have you thought about . . ." Rawson starts, stops, and begins again with, "Will you be having a thing for Dot? A wake? I'd like to pay my respects."

"No," Julius says. "We haven't thought about any of that." On the drive, he turns to look back. Spencer Rawson is standing in a patch of snow in his bare feet, watching.

4

Two hours later, without Julius having returned, the doctor arrives at the cottage. His large stomach, wide shoulders, and bull head fill up the kitchen and block out the light. The first thing he says to Jeanie after introducing himself as Dr. Holloway is that he doesn't have long. He asks where Dot was found, why the electricity is off, and where the body is now. "You probably shouldn't have moved her," he says as Jeanie shows him to the parlour and the shrouded figure. She doesn't stay to watch his examination. When he returns to the kitchen, she's relieved that he declines her offer of tea.

The doctor rubs his hands to warm them. In front of the window his features are indistinct and Jeanie can barely see his mouth move while he explains that he is certain that Dot died of a stroke and that there is a procedure which involves him telephoning the coroner before he can give Jeanie a particular certificate which she needs before she can get the green form. She has no idea what he's talking about and at the mention of the word *form,* her fingers flutter to her heart and press there without her realizing and she can no longer focus on Dr. Holloway's sentences about Dot's illness, warning signs, and medication.

At the door, he says, "I'll see you at the surgery for the medical certificate," and clamps a meaty hand on her shoulder, adding that Dot was a good woman, and he's sorry she's gone. And then he's gone too, revving off in his jeep, leaving Jeanie wondering how he knew what sort of woman her mother was and why he wasn't able to give her the death certificate then and there, if that's the form she needs.

After another hour, in which Jeanie moves aimlessly and unseeing through the cottage, and Julius doesn't return, she assumes he must have somehow got to the work he has with Craig. She turns on the portable radio and listens to a couple of minutes of a woman talking about how she walked the Appalachian Trail in America, but her voice is too grating even at a low volume and Jeanie switches it off. She finds herself staring out of the scullery window at the chickens high-stepping through the snow, without knowing how or when she got there. Finally, she decides that it is the death certificate they need and for some reason which she doesn't understand she has to pick it up from the surgery. She clicks her tongue at Maude, and they walk through the snow to the village.

The GP surgery is a series of purpose-built, low-level boxes set in the middle of a car park near the edge of Inkbourne. Jeanie knows that three doctors work there including Dr. Holloway, but she's never been to see any of them. She last saw a doctor when she was thirteen for a final routine check-up after her bouts of rheumatic fever ended. Then, the surgery occupied one of the double-fronted Victorian houses overlooking the village green. It was a year or so after her father died, when her mother was still listless, still forgetting to cook dinner, to shop for food, or to round up the chickens at the end of the day. They lost six to foxes that year. Her mother had taken Jeanie to see a GP whose name she no longer remembers. His consultation room was cold and frost patterned the window. He told her to lie on the high bed in the corner and lift up her vest. Behind him, her mother nodded her encouragement, and although shy,

Jeanie lay down and revealed her narrow ribcage and the sore little swellings that were developing behind her nipples. She remembers the grey hairs growing from the doctor's nostrils and the chill of his stethoscope as he pressed it against her chest. When he took the thing out of his ears, he shook his head, and her mother started crying in a way that Jeanie thought might never end. Dot got her handkerchief out from her handbag and covered her face with it, rocking back and forth where she sat on the chair next to the doctor's desk. He called for the receptionist to come in, and Jeanie was led by the hand back to the waiting room. There, heels on her chair and arms hugging her knees, she stayed until her mother came to fetch her. Was it then, when they got home, that Dot explained that the fever and the aches Jeanie had suffered from when she was younger had weakened her heart and made it fragile, or was it later? Either way, her mother said, "Think of your heart like an egg. You know what happens if you drop an egg?" Jeanie was worried her mother was going to start crying again and if she did Jeanie wouldn't know what to do. Perhaps the doctor had given her mother a pill to stop her crying when Jeanie had been in the waiting room. As her mother spoke,

Jeanie imagined something within her chest the size and shape of a duck's egg but with a pinkish tinge and its shell so thin that the creature inside was visible: curled, bloody, and featherless, it knocked and scraped on the shell's inner layer. What mayhem would it cause if it broke free?

Added together, the amount of school she'd missed from rheumatic fever was probably a couple of years, and after the diagnosis of her weak heart she missed more, but Dot was happy to keep her at home tucked up on the sofa or helping out with the easy jobs in the garden. Dot might not have expressed it clearly, but the message Jeanie received was that an education for the kind of people they were — poor people, country people — would only steal her away from where she belonged — at home. Even Julius left school at sixteen having sat and failed two exams.

Outside the surgery, she takes the dog's lead from her pocket and ties Maude to a metal pole. The dog protests, whimpering at being abandoned, but Jeanie shushes her. At the set of glass doors, she hesitates, her heart jumping at the thought of going in, the way people will look at her, but a woman comes out and holds the door open, and Jeanie enters. The waiting room is filled with rows of chairs with upholstered seats, some of them occupied. The place smells of disinfectant and furniture polish. Easy listening pop music plays over a loudspeaker and a baby is crying.

Bridget, her mother's best friend, is sitting behind the low desk beside another receptionist, and when Bridget sees Jeanie, she rushes out, her moon-face crumpling and her eyes filling.

"Oh, my love," Bridget says, opening her arms, and Jeanie lets herself be embraced. Bridget's hold is soft, different from Dot's, which was quick and bony, or Julius's, which is enveloping and tight and expels the air from Jeanie's lungs. Bridget smells of cigarettes and Polo mints. When she lets go, she says, "Has Dr. Holloway been out to the cottage yet? I was going to come over as soon as my shift finished." The other receptionist shoos Bridget away and Bridget mouths a thank you. "Let's go into one of the nurses' rooms."

They walk beside the back of a row of chairs where a young man with dirty blond hair and large lips is flicking through a magazine, his boots resting on the chair opposite. As they pass, Bridget gives him a shove on his shoulder. "Feet off!" she says near his ear, and while Jeanie is shocked that Bridget might be this rude to a patient, the man lifts his feet one by one off the seat and puts them on the floor. When Jeanie looks at him over her shoulder, the man gives her a grin — a wide, cheeky smile — and she hurries on.

In the nurses' room, Bridget says, "Why didn't you call me? Julius phoned and spoke to one of the women here who was opening up. I couldn't believe it. I still can't believe it." She puts her hands either side of her face and opens her mouth, squashing her cheeks like a cartoon character. Jeanie wonders where Julius phoned from; perhaps he used Craig's mobile. "Was it a stroke?" Bridget continues. "Oh, I hope it was quick." She sits heavily on a swivel chair. "Was she taking her medication?"

Jeanie has forgotten how much and how fast Bridget can talk. Just listening makes her tired and she can't help speaking in a voice that sounds as if she's falling asleep. "I didn't know she had any medication to take."

"I bet she didn't collect it from the chemist, did she? I kept telling her that it would be free because she's over sixty. Was over sixty. Oh God. It wouldn't have cost her anything."

"Mum didn't like being given things for

free." Jeanie sits on the chair beside the desk, the patient's chair she supposes. Behind Bridget are rows of kitchen cupboards and in the corner a high bed similar to the one Jeanie was examined on. Being in this room is making her anxious. "I didn't even know she was ill or had been to see the doctor."

"Oh, my love," Bridget says again, and leans forwards to touch Jeanie's knee. "She'd had a couple of mini-strokes a month or so ago. I'm so sorry. She didn't tell you? No, I can see she didn't. I'm sure it was just that she didn't want to worry you and Julius, it would have only been that. But she should have got the prescription at least. Aspirin, that's all it would have been. God, I could do with a fag. Let's go out the back."

They stand shivering against the windowless back wall of the surgery and Bridget takes a packet of cigarettes from her uniform pocket. "Snow at the end of April," she says, shaking her head and lighting up. There had been girls at Jeanie's school who stood outside the back gates smoking and talking about boys, but she had never been one of them.

"I'm sorry I didn't make it out to the cottage before you walked all the way here to tell me," Bridget says. "Well, anyway, the other receptionist told me."

"I didn't come here to tell you," Jeanie says. "I came to get the death certificate."

"Oh, okay," Bridget says, her voice tight. She drops the match by her feet where it joins a few others and a number of scuffed cigarette butts mashed into the dirty snow. "Well, it'll be the medical certificate you need from Dr. Holloway first, but he probably has to phone the coroner. Did he mention that? He has been, hasn't he? Then you'll have to take the certificate to the register office in Devizes."

"Devizes?"

"To get the death certificate and the burial certificate — the green form."

Jeanie puts her hand on the brick wall to steady herself. "Can't the doctor give me those?"

Bridget stares at her, draws on her cigarette. "You have to register a death, Jeanie. At the register office." She speaks as if Jeanie were a child. "That's how these things work. You'll need the certificates for the vicar, or the crematorium, and you'll probably need the death certificate for other things too."

"Other things like what?" Everything is

beginning to jostle for space in Jeanie's head.

"Like Dot's bank account —"

"Oh, she never had a bank account. None of us ever had a bank account. We keep all our money in a tin in the scullery." Jeanie laughs, a mad-sounding laugh, knowing she shouldn't have said this, and wondering how it was only yesterday that she and her mother were out in the garden weeding the onion bed. The wall she is pressing against seems soft, as though if she leaned harder, she might be able to fold herself into it and be gone.

"I can take you to Devizes."

"I'll catch the bus."

"Don't be silly."

"I'm not being silly. I am capable of catching the bus."

"Look." Bridget scrapes the lit end of her cigarette against the wall and the falling sparks melt pinpricks into the snow. "You're going to have to get through a lot in the next few days. I know — I buried my father last year, remember?" Jeanie has forgotten this and feels bad for it. "It's not just the certificates, but there's the funeral, the wake."

"Wake? I don't want a wake." The thought of people milling about the kitchen, the babble of them, the way they would stare at her and Julius: pitying the weirdos who still lived with their mother at age fifty-one.

"Of course you want a wake."

"Mum didn't know many people. I can't think of anyone who'd want to come."

"Well, me and Stu, for a start." Bridget sounds put out.

"Apart from you and Stu."

"And anyway, your mum knew loads of people. What about Kate Gill from the B&B, and Max? I know Dr. Holloway will want to come. The Rawsons, or maybe just him."

"Rawson? Why would he want to come? I'm not having either of them in the house. It's not about trying to make up numbers, is it? It's not like it's a party."

"Julius might want to invite Shelley Swift."

"Shelley Swift?" Jeanie struggles to place the name.

"Aren't they friends? I'm sure I saw them together." She says it with a rise of her eyebrows.

The woman comes to mind: pretty with downy cheeks the colour and shape of apricots, thick limbs, a secretary at the brickworks. "For goodness' sake, he's doing a job for her. Something to do with a stuck window. He barely knows her."

42

Bridget pops a Polo into her mouth and rolls it around. "All right. How about I drive you to the register office on Wednesday afternoon? I'll see if Dr. Holloway has the medical certificate for you yet, and then we can phone and make you an appointment."

"You don't need to do everything," Jeanie says crossly. She's never liked the way Bridget bosses people around and gossips. Bridget has been Dot's friend since Jeanie and Julius first went to school, when Bridget's first job was in the infant school office. She's been one of the surgery's receptionists for years, partly, Jeanie thinks rather meanly, so that she'll know what everyone in the village has wrong with them.

Bridget lets out a puff of exasperation. "You're as stubborn as your mother. I'm trying to help. You just fill out a couple of forms and it'll be done. Simple."

Jeanie imagines it will be anything but simple.

5

In the afternoon, Jeanie stares out of the scullery window again but sees nothing; the radio is on but she doesn't hear it. Her thoughts move from one thing to the next, unable to settle. She remembers sitting on the grass at the top of Ham Hill with her father, watching starlings turn in the autumn dusk, moving together like a black cloud. A murmuration, he called it. "I'll write the word down for you when we get home," he said, "and you can copy it out." But when they got home he had the paper to read, and there were jobs to do and she didn't remind him. She thinks about the bird scarers she and Julius made from old CDs they found beside a dustbin in the village. He read the labels and they laughed at *The Best of Burt Bacharach* keeping the crows away from the lettuce. And she recalls her mother waking from a nightmare in the bed they shared after Jeanie's father died.

In the dream, Dot told her, she was in the village shop delivering tomatoes and salad leaves but the place was empty — there was no one there, and somehow she knew there was no one in the pub or any of the houses. And then, Dot said, she was at home, suddenly transported as you can be in dreams, and Jeanie and Julius were gone too, and her mother realized that she was utterly alone.

Now, Jeanie becomes aware of the knocking on the front door only when Maude barks in the kitchen.

"Sit," she says, and reluctantly Maude obeys. Perhaps it's the doctor returned for some reason, or Bridget — although she comes in through the back and never knocks. When Jeanie opens the door, Mrs. Rawson is there, with her husband coming up the path behind her. Maude trots to the doorstep, gives a couple of toothy barks, and then shoves her nose in Rawson's crotch until Jeanie gives a whistle through her teeth, marginally later than she could have, and the dog retreats behind her legs to flop in front of the range.

"We were so sorry to hear about your mother," Mrs. Rawson says. She leans as though to kiss Jeanie or hug her, but at the last moment holds back.

45

"Jeanie," Rawson says, a little awkwardly, showing his white teeth under his white moustache. He holds himself like he knows he's attractive — for an older man — upright, taller than the doorway, joints loose.

Jeanie feels she has no choice but to hold the door wide and invite them in. She turns off the radio. Mrs. Rawson is younger than her husband by a good few years, and everything about her, from her tight, cropped trousers and high-waisted jacket to the sunglasses on top of her hair — deliberately dyed grey and stylishly cut — says money. Jeanie keeps her own naturally greying hair held back with an elastic band and every couple of months pulls it forward over one shoulder and slices off the ends with the kitchen scissors.

She watches Rawson stare with curiosity around the kitchen, taking in the range and the fire, the piano with the guitar propped next to it, the shadowy corners and the central table scrubbed to brightness, the tidy dresser hung with flowered mugs. She sees it through his eyes, unchanged since he was last inside maybe forty years before. His gaze stops on Jeanie. "Julius called in earlier to use our telephone and he told me what happened. I just can't believe it." His head is bent as though he's bowing in pity or sorrow, but she realizes it's just that the ceiling and the beams are too low for him.

"We can't believe it," his wife chimes in.

Jeanie is surprised to learn that Julius decided to go to the Rawsons' but says nothing.

"We wanted to come and pay our respects," Mrs. Rawson continues. She pushes the tops of her fingers into the tight front pockets of her trousers, hunches her shoulders. Her voice is gentle, solicitous. "It must be such a shock. So sudden. Julius told my husband it was a fall."

"A stroke," Jeanie says, and hates the word, too soft and beautiful for something so terrible.

Rawson, who is moving towards the piano, stops, and says, "A stroke? Not a fall?"

"A stroke," Jeanie repeats.

"I'd heard she'd been ill for a little while." Adding, "Hadn't she?"

Jeanie wonders how everyone, with the exception of her children, seems to know Dot had been ill. Mrs. Rawson cocks her head and the atmosphere in the room is suddenly dense with something unsaid.

Rawson lifts the piano key lid. "Was this your mother's?" he asks.

Mrs. Rawson's sympathetic smile tightens, and Jeanie can see the woman wants to get

47

out of the cottage as soon as it is polite to do so. Jeanie wants them gone too; she needs to be alone with her random thoughts which now, with these people in the house, she must try to keep in order. Rawson, though, seems unaware, deliberately or otherwise, of what his wife wants, and sits on the piano stool — the leather split and the horsehair showing — and plays part of a tune with his right hand, a trill of a song that sounds like it comes from an old-time musical. Immediately Maude is up and barking and Rawson looks down at the dog. "All right, all right," he says, and smiles.

"Maude!" Jeanie calls the dog back and she goes under the table. "It was my father's," Jeanie says, and Rawson lifts his fingers quickly off and puts his hands down, almost appearing to wipe them on his trousers.

"Well —" Mrs. Rawson starts, readying them to leave.

"Did you get the electricity sorted out?" Rawson says. He stands, puts one hand on the top of the piano.

"No," Jeanie says sharply. She has no time for this man; she despises him. She shouldn't have let him in, her mother would never have let him put one foot in the cottage.

"Julius told me your power's off."

"We're managing. We've got the range."

"Of course," Rawson says. "Of course." Jeanie can tell he has nothing else to say and yet he is lingering.

"Well," Mrs. Rawson says again. She has taken her car keys out of her bag and is holding them. "Please do let us know if there's anything we can do."

"Can I see her?" Rawson says. "That's if she's still here. Her body, I mean." His words stagger out, one over the next. He touches his white moustache which brackets his wide mouth, first one side, then the other.

It's the last thing Jeanie expected to hear, and from his wife's expression, hers too. "Darling," she says, like a warning.

"See her?" Jeanie says.

"Sorry, forget it." He shoves his hands deep into his pockets, clinking his loose change. He coughs, turns away.

"I think we should go," Mrs. Rawson says. "Let you get on." Her voice is mechanical and she doesn't look at Jeanie, only at her husband.

At the door Rawson turns back once more. "Will you let me know about the funeral, the wake?"

When she doesn't answer, he follows his

wife down the path.

As soon as Jeanie has closed the door, she goes to the kitchen window. She doesn't care if they see her watching. Mrs. Rawson climbs into the driver's seat of the Land Rover and before she turns the engine on, Jeanie can hear her shouting. The woman backs the vehicle into the opening to the field opposite, making short, sharp jerks forwards and back, and then the Land Rover roars off down the track towards the farm.

From outside the cottage, Julius can hear Jeanie playing the guitar and singing. He flattens his ear against the front door, and she sings the start of "Polly Vaughn": *"I shall tell of a hunter whose life was undone."* He isn't surprised; this is what they do when things are good and when they aren't — play music. He pauses, key in the keyhole, remembering that so recently he would have heard a banjo too and his mother's voice. Now it is Jeanie's, alone.

The warmth of the kitchen after his walk hits him as he enters — uncomfortably thick and airless. Jeanie is sitting on a kitchen chair, her guitar on her lap. She is tiny, he thinks, like a child, and she stops playing and looks up at him, desperately hopeful, as though he might tell her that it's a mistake; their mother is alive and nothing is going to change. He can't come up with anything that will bring her consolation, but because something must be said in the room's silence, he tells her: "Snow's almost gone. Nippy though." He pats Maude, who has risen to greet him, and scratches behind her ears.

Jeanie puts down her guitar and he knows something is coming, something bad. Still she doesn't speak.

"The doctor's been then?" he asks. He saw the tracks of a large vehicle up the lane.

"The doctor said it was a stroke. She died of a stroke. Not a fall. I went to the surgery and Bridget said that she'd had two mini-strokes. Or more. I don't know. I can't believe she didn't tell us. That's what the doctor said she died of, a stroke."

Julius pulls out a chair and sits. "Christ." He wonders again if she was alive for any length of time on the kitchen floor, and whether she'd be alive now if he'd gone down when he'd heard the fire irons falling. He knows that Jeanie is thinking this too, he can see it in her face. He knows her face, knows what she's thinking, he always has.

They are silent, neither of them looking at the other, both aware of the body in the

51

house, in the room next door. Julius drags off his work boots without unlacing them, and he thinks about the number of times his mother told him not to do that with his shoes, that they would be ruined, and where was the money coming from for new shoes? He removes his socks, a hole in a heel, and massages his feet which ache from walking.

"I haven't made anything for tea. I haven't even thought about what to cook for tea." Jeanie stands. Food has always been ready when he's got home from work, being dished up by Dot or Jeanie as he walks through the door. Every day of his life except this one.

"Sit down. Don't worry about tea," he says and his stomach growls so loudly that Jeanie hears it and smiles, and he laughs and the tension in the room is defused.

Jeanie sits and puts her guitar back in her lap, her fingers making chords, plucking at strings out of habit. "Did you go to the bathroom job after all?" she says.

He knows it's the money she wants to ask about and that she won't say it directly. It's always the bloody money. He balls up his socks and throws them at Maude, who's lying on the sofa on her back with her legs splayed. With an easy twist of her neck she catches the socks in her mouth but lets them drop and goes back to sleep.

He brought the dog home as a surprise for Jeanie a year ago. They'd had one of their rare arguments about something silly — he can no longer remember what started it, but Dot was out of the house, gone to the village or somewhere, and Julius had told Jeanie that one day he was just damn well going to leave. Sometime, or when their mother died, he'd be off. He was sick of living here, worrying about her, why was it even his job? She shouted back that he should go now then, she didn't need him. And through his teeth, almost hissing, he'd said, "One day you'll come in from the garden and I'll be gone." For a few days they were quiet around each other, the words they'd said making them tender like a bruise knocked again. Their mother asked them over and over what had happened until eventually he snapped, "Leave it, Mum." A week after that he was working for Craig at a dog breeder's place ten miles away, running water pipes from the house to the outdoor pens. Too many dogs, too much shit and barking to make it a pleasant job. Maude barked alone in a pen by herself, tipped over her water, trod in her own mess. He heard that she was going to be put down: she'd been sold to a family who hadn't been able to control her, had no idea of training, and had returned her. She was wilful and bitey, the breeder said, and it was too late now to sort her out. When Julius brought her into the cottage, his mother had said, "Not another dog," but this time Jeanie and Julius had overruled her.

In the kitchen, Jeanie asks, "How did it go?"

"Okay," Julius says. "We got the bath upstairs. Took four of us. Bloody heavy. I spent years ripping those buggers out and now they all want them put back."

She carries on playing her guitar quietly while his stomach growls again.

"I found out about funerals today," he says. "I used Craig's phone to call an undertaker."

"And?"

"And Christ." He sweeps his hand through his hair. "They're bloody expensive. Thousands. They didn't want to give me prices over the phone, kept umming and ahhing and trying to get me to make an appointment to come and look at some coffins. 'So sorry about your loss' and crap like that, when all they want is your money. They said there was some social fund, but you've got to be on benefits."

"Thousands?" Jeanie says.

54

"Do you remember a few years ago having that conversation about how we all wanted to be buried?" Julius says.

"No."

"Yes, you do. We were sitting round the table, here. You'd heard something on the radio about green funerals or some other rubbish. Said you wanted to be buried in a wicker coffin and put under a tree."

"I would never have said that."

"Well, you did. I remember. And Mum said, 'You must be joking. I want the full works. Proper comfy silk-lined coffin and one of those carriages pulled by black horses with black plumes, all the way to the church.' "

"And everyone in the village had to come out and stand on the pavement while she went past."

He knew she remembered. "Hats off, heads lowered."

"And hymns, she wanted, didn't she? Hymns and then weeping. Lots and lots of weeping."

They smile and Jeanie puts her guitar behind her, propped in the corner between the wall and the piano. They don't look at each other, taking in the information about the cost of a funeral. They've never had thousands, never will. Jeanie feels queasy with it, thinking about money.

"How much is in the tin?" Julius says.

In the scullery, Jeanie searches behind the sink skirt, behind the box of ant powder, groping for the housekeeping tin. It's circular and rusted, with a picture of a Spanish dancing woman on the top, and once must have been filled with biscuits. Jeanie has never opened it herself before. Dot was the keeper of the household income and in charge of all outgoings. Each week Jeanie handed over whatever cash she'd collected from the honesty box screwed to an old table at the bottom of the lane where she put odd vegetables — the carrots with many legs, nibbled turnips — and surplus eggs, although people often weren't very honest. And Julius handed over his money from the bits of work he managed to get — helping with removals, farm jobs, a few days of tiling or decorating — all of it paid in cash. Jeanie knows he keeps some money back for beer and tobacco, and to top up the credit on his phone. Dot contributed the money that Max gave her for the produce they supplied to the deli, as well as the cash from Kate Gill who took their eggs and fruit for breakfasts at the B&B. Money was always watched, especially when Dot had to pay the council tax and other bills at the post office counter in the village shop. But there was never anything Jeanie wanted that Dot didn't agree to save for, although there wasn't much that Jeanie wanted. Before Maude, all she'd have asked for was another dog — the one they'd had died of old age when Jeanie was fifteen — but Dot had always refused, saying they were too much trouble, too expensive. They'd managed with very little money, and Jeanie has always assumed this was because years ago Rawson had agreed not to charge them rent for the cottage.

At the kitchen table she prises the lid off the tin. She doesn't know how much she expected to find but certainly more than the change rattling around in there now. Julius puts his finger in and stirs the coins, counting. Jeanie has always struggled to understand columns of numbers and the mathematics that was taught at school which required her to do written calculations. *Show your workings* — the phrase would make her feel exposed, in danger, and to avoid doing maths she acted up in class and was often sent out to the corridor or the headmaster's office. Jeanie has never had a problem with money or mental arithmetic. She can see that the tin contains three pounds and fifty-four pence. The price of four loaves of sliced bread from the village shop.

"Three pounds and fifty-four pence," Julius says. "That can't be right."

Jeanie moves her fingers to her opposite wrist, presses, and counts. "How will we pay for the funeral?" she says.

Julius shakes his head. "There must be more money somewhere." He puts the lid back on the tin.

"The cost of the coffin? Getting it to the church or wherever?"

"I don't know," Julius says.

"And the rest of it? Flowers, whatever else it is we have to do."

"The wake."

"Why does everyone keep going on about a wake?" Jeanie snaps. "The Rawsons were here earlier, acting all weird, asking about a wake."

"I used their phone this morning."

"So I gather. Anyway, we don't need a wake."

"We've got to have a few drinks after."

"Who says?"

"It's the right thing."

"We don't need anyone else. Traipsing in here, smoking, pitying us."

"I've already told people." Julius is leaning against the dresser. His feet are incredibly white and bony. The way he's standing, what he's saying, is irritating her like it's never done before.

"Who? Who have you told?"

He comes forwards and now takes his fiddle from the top of the piano. "Aren't we going to play?" He tunes the instrument quickly, and with his bow starts the accompaniment to the piece Jeanie played earlier. "Bridget will want to come," he says.

Jeanie's blood pulses in her neck. She breathes long and deep through her nose. "Who else?"

"I shall tell of a hunter whose life was undone . . ." Julius restarts the words to "Polly Vaughn" and plays the long sad notes on his fiddle. *"By the cruel hand of evil at the setting of the sun."*

"Shelley Swift?" She tries to sound casual.

"Shelley Swift? Why'd I invite her?" He continues to bow the fiddle, slowly. "I barely know her. I'm going round tomorrow to do her window."

"And it went well with Craig today?"

Julius removes the fiddle from under his chin and holds it by the neck, the bow in his other hand. "He docked seventy-five quid because I threw up in his van."

"Oh, Julius." She goes to him, but he takes a step backwards, won't look at her. It's been a long while since he was sick in a car or a van, but then it must be a long while since he's been in one for any length of time.

"I had no choice but to go in the van. I couldn't cycle in the snow. It's too far to walk and Craig was kicking off about lifting that bloody cast-iron bath."

"You told him about Mum?"

"Of course I told him. And he started going on about how the job was booked in with the customer, and how I'd be letting down the other guys, all his usual crap. I had no choice. And anyway, didn't you tell me I had to go to work?" The tendons in Julius's neck are standing proud. "He picked me up outside the Plough. I managed just about on the way there, got him to stop the van. Chucked up by the side of the road." For the first time since their mother died Jeanie feels tears come to her eyes, but not for Dot; for Julius and what he saw — what they both saw — when they were twelve. "On the way back, I don't know. It took me by surprise, I suppose. Happened quicker than normal. All over the door and the edge of the seat and down the side. Hardly touched me." He gives a sour laugh. "Craig reckoned the van will need an industrial clean and he's probably right. They'll have to take the passenger seat out."

Holding the bow and fiddle with one hand, he fishes in his back pocket. "I should go and change, but here's the money. He had to stand me lunch too, because I didn't take any with me." Julius puts a twenty-pound note on the table. Twenty pounds for a day's work.

"Don't worry about it. We'll manage." Jeanie knows that neither of them believe it. They look at the money.

"Nothing is going to change," he says.

"Really?"

He puts his fiddle to his jaw and runs the bow across the strings. "It's always been the three of us, here. Hasn't it? Now it'll be the two of us."

She sits, crosses her legs, settles the guitar, and plays.

6

The half-acre garden is bounded on three
sides by scruffy hedging with assorted
pieces of salvaged wood — planks, panels,
another old door — filling the gaps. Behind
the compost heaps, the polytunnel, and the
large greenhouse, rabbits are digging, and
here the ground and the perimeter are
continually threatened with collapse. On the
fourth side, facing the cottage, the picket
fence built to keep the chickens out of the
vegetable garden is better maintained. A
central gate opens to a long strip of paving,
mostly brick, interspersed with the odd
piece of concrete or flint where the bricks
have crumbled. Heavy-duty scaffolding
planks lie in between each bed, coming off
the central path at an angle, positioned like
ribs extending from a spine. The garden
slopes gradually uphill so that it is possible
to sit on the bench at the top and look out
over the rich brown beds and the plants, to

the apple and cherry trees behind the old dairy, and onwards to the track and the beech wood beyond. Rosemary and thyme grow close to the house, lovage and angelica, and in the summer, basil and tarragon. Up against the western boundary is the fruit cage, filled with raspberry canes, blackcurrant bushes, and gooseberries. The garden is south-facing and sheltered, and the plants, which have never seen chemical fertilizers or insecticide, thrive in the loamy soil. Julius often tried to persuade Dot and Jeanie to consolidate and grow just two or three crops over the whole garden. He would say that the opportunities for better sales outweighed the risk of a whole crop failing because of some pest, but the women always grew many different vegetables and fruits, and never let Julius grub any of it up.

Jeanie spends the morning resowing the gaps where the snow killed off some of the tender plants, but most have survived, and where the garlic has pushed up its green spikes, flowers are already forming, spearheaded and trapped in their paper cocoons. Her knees ache from the crouched position she has been in for an hour and from the cold. Her joints are getting stiffer, prone to pain in the mornings; she's noticed it more in the past year. As she works, she wonders again why Dot didn't tell her and Julius that she'd been ill. She was stubborn and proud, it was true. She'd taught them not to take anything from anyone, because as night turns to day, they — especially if *they* were the government — would come knocking and asking for it back, or more. Jeanie isn't surprised that her mother hadn't claimed her free prescription, neither is she too shocked that there's so little money in the tin, but still she can't help calculating expenses in her head: the funeral or cremation, a coffin, funeral directors, a hearse, and flowers. What are you supposed to do if you can't afford any of it — bury your mother in the garden?

Beside the back door she snips off four rosemary twigs and rubs them to release the scent. The bush has become leggy and will need to be replaced soon and she reminds herself to take some cuttings. She holds the twigs under her nose and inhales.

In the parlour she places the rosemary around her mother's body and another piece she tucks into the neck of her own dress. She's kept the door closed so Maude can't get in and the window closed too because she's worried about flies entering and about what would happen next. Her breath steams with the cold and it isn't so much that there is a smell but more that she's afraid of smelling something. She cuts up the middle and sleeves of her mother's nightdress with the same scissors she used to snip the rosemary. The body is the colour of newly picked mushrooms and she washes it with care, warm water in a bowl which she places on the small chest in the corner. She starts with Dot's face, and then her breasts and belly where the skin is soft and loose. The limbs are already stiff and unwieldy. When she's finished, she goes out to the front garden and tosses the water onto the flower bed. Upstairs, she chooses one of Dot's dresses, an everyday summer dress but pretty, of pale yellow with a pattern of ivy. At some point she knows she will have to go through it all — her mother's clothes, her belongings.

In the year following the death of her father, Jeanie had been given the task of removing her father's things from the bedroom he'd shared with his wife for thirteen years. Dot wasn't up to it, wasn't capable of much that year besides sitting in the kitchen or following her daughter around. Any suitable clothes had already been passed to Julius, trouser bottoms taken up, cuffs shortened, Frank's good suit and his coat mothballed for when Julius was older. Other clothes, Jeanie gave to the Salvation Army, the shoes too — though he was twelve, Julius's feet were already half a size larger than his father's. Only the chest of drawers on Frank's side of the bed remained to be cleared. When Jeanie opened the top drawer the spicy smell of his favourite boiled sweets wafted out, mixed with something oily, male. All sorts of things had been shoved in the top drawer: the newspaper he must have been reading in bed the night before he died, nail clippers, his razor and spare blades in a paper packet. In a copper bowl were pennies from his pockets heaped together with screws, a piece of flint with a sharp edge, fasteners and washers. Dot wanted Jeanie to throw it all out and move her own clothes over from the room she shared with Julius. She lied and told her mother that she'd got rid of Frank's stuff, but instead she placed her vests and jumpers over the top of the last of her father's things, so that for a while — a few months at least — her clothes smelled of Winter Mixture and the nuts and bolts of her father.

When Jeanie hears a knock on the front door, she goes to the bedroom window and tries to see who it is, but the visitor is just out of sight. If she opens the window they'll hear her and look up, and then she'll have to go down. She sighs, leaves the yellow dress on the bed, and goes down.

Mrs. Rawson is on the doorstep and twice Jeanie has to order Maude to stop barking and go back into the kitchen. Mrs. Rawson is wearing cream leather trousers, a kind of silky top with what looks like drawings of shops on it, a camel-coloured raincoat with a big collar, and sunglasses. She has a large handbag over her arm. "I need to speak to you," she says, and Jeanie is so taken aback that she opens the door wide and for the second time in two days lets the woman in.

In 1979, at age twenty, Caroline May was crowned Wiltshire Young Farmers' Dairy Queen, and a few months later married the man who presented the prize. This, Jeanie overheard Bridget tell Dot, and she knows that there were problems early in the Rawsons' marriage — babies lost or unconceived. Bridget would say this with a slow shake of her head as though not having a child were the worst a woman could suffer. Mrs. Rawson has always been pleasant to Jeanie when they've met on the lane or passed each other in the village. Civil, if not friendly, and that has suited her fine. It is her husband whom Jeanie actively dislikes.

Mrs. Rawson doesn't take off her sunglasses even though the kitchen is lit only with oil lamps and the little natural light that comes in through the low front window and from the scullery at the back.

"I'm sorry to call around again so soon," Mrs. Rawson says. She smiles and then the smile is gone.

"Would you like to sit down? I'll put the kettle on."

"No tea. Thank you. This won't take long." She remains standing, the two women in the kitchen with the table between them.

"Unfortunately, I've come to talk about an outstanding debt," Mrs. Rawson says coldly.

"What debt?" Jeanie says.

"On the cottage."

"What do you mean?"

"An unpaid debt."

"On the cottage? There can't be a debt on the cottage. We don't pay any rent. We have an agreement." Jeanie doesn't let her emotion show. She can be as icy as Caroline Rawson if she needs to be, but the animal in her heart is stirring.

"Indeed. An understanding. Which meant that your mother and you and your brother could stay on in the cottage after your father died, and she paid —"

"Was killed," Jeanie corrects her.

Mrs. Rawson talks over her: "— and she

was paying weekly until a few months ago, when I understand from my husband she started slipping into arrears."

"What?" Jeanie grips the top of a kitchen chair.

"She was finding it difficult to keep up." Mrs. Rawson speaks as though reciting lines she learned earlier.

"I'm sorry," Jeanie says, although she isn't sorry at all. "There's no rent to pay, and there never was." Her heart is knocking but she tries to take the same level tone, concentrating on her breathing. If she looks too hard, she can see herself, warped and murky, in Mrs. Rawson's glasses. "The agreement, the understanding, whatever you want to call it, was that we could stay in the cottage rent-free even after our mother died." She emphasizes the *rent-free.*

"Your mother —" Mrs. Rawson says *mother* as though she is about to complain about Dot letting Maude shit on the Rawsons' front lawn — "has been paying for the cottage for thirty-eight years. More or less. She started a year after your father passed away. I'm surprised, although of course it's nothing to do with me that she didn't tell you."

Jeanie wants this woman gone. Filling up the kitchen with her perfume. She wants to say that she has more important things to do than to discuss this stupidity. The chickens need gathering in, there are plants in the greenhouse and polytunnel that need watering. She has to work out what to cook for tea. Without electricity, the fridge in the scullery is starting to smell rancid even though it contains only half a packet of butter, half a pint of milk, and a small lump of cheddar. She can make an omelette, bake a couple of the old potatoes. She must finish dressing her mother. Her dead mother. A day or so dead and here they are discussing ridiculous debts which aren't due.

"That's just not possible." Jeanie folds her arms.

Mrs. Rawson laughs as though she is the most good-natured person imaginable. "There's a receipt book if you'd like to see it, back at the farm, with your mother's initials beside every payment. She hadn't paid fully for at least a few months because of her illness, or so my husband tells me."

"How much is it you think we owe?" Jeanie has picked up, again from overhearing Bridget's conversations with Dot, that Mrs. Rawson does charity work, organizing fundraisers for a premature baby charity, and has nothing to do with the farm's finances. Their money — including a large

70

inheritance — is managed by Rawson.

"Two thousand," she says quickly, as though it is a figure she simply made up that moment.

"Two thousand pounds?" Jeanie can no longer keep the shock out of her voice.

"Yes," Mrs. Rawson says. "I was surprised too when I found out how behind she'd got. It's unfortunate, but of course, if you want to stay on in the cottage . . ." She takes her car keys from her bag, jangling them. "I'm sure you can work something out with your brother."

When Julius gets home, again there is no tea cooking and no hot water on to boil for his wash. Jeanie is sitting in the same chair as yesterday, head down over her guitar, playing. Only Maude looks up to greet him. This time, rather than the surge of sympathy and sorrow he felt yesterday, he has a burning irritation that she hasn't done anything with her day while he's been working, earning them money. Why is it she hasn't ever had a job?

Jeanie says something too quiet for him to hear.

"What?" he says, sitting on the sofa, pushing Maude along roughly. The dog's eyes widen and Julius bends to put his forehead

71

to Maude's as an apology.

Jeanie stops playing, looks up, and he sees that her face is flushed. "Caroline Rawson came this morning."

"Again?" He's confused.

"She said we owe them rent."

"What rent?" He rests his elbows on knees.

"You know — rent, rent." Her voice is rising.

Julius holds his hands up to calm her. "What do you mean?"

"For the cottage."

"It's ours. There's no rent."

"I said that to her, but she said Mum had been paying rent since the year after Dad died."

"You must have got it wrong."

"I haven't got anything wrong. You weren't here." Jeanie is shouting now.

"Well, it's a lie. What about the agreement? Rawson gave us the cottage in return for . . ." He doesn't finish the sentence. He doesn't understand what Jeanie is saying. Or he understands it, but it doesn't make any sense.

"Caroline Rawson knew that Mum had been ill. Just like Bridget and Dr. Holloway. The whole bloody village probably knows our business before we do. She said Mum couldn't keep up with the payments. She was horrible, Julius. So horrible and frosty. Like a different person."

"Calm down, Jeanie." Julius sits on the edge of the sofa and takes off his boots and then his socks. He loves the feel of the cool floor on the soles of his feet after a day's work. "It's not good for you. Please. Rawson didn't say anything about any rent when I used his phone. There'll be some mistake." He chucks his balled-up socks at Maude and they bounce off the top of her head. She doesn't stir.

"I don't think so. She said we owed two thousand pounds."

"Two thousand pounds!" Julius shakes his head. "None of this is right. You think Mum's been paying rent for what, thirty-eight years?" He laughs sarcastically.

"*I* don't think it! This is the Rawsons, not me."

"Well, if Rawson thinks I'm going to give him any money, he'd better think again."

"Don't shout," Jeanie says.

"Sorry, I'm sorry." He sweeps a hand through his hair and blows out his cheeks.

"You'll have to go and speak to him," Jeanie says.

Julius stands. "What?"

"Have a word with him." She puts her

73

guitar down and lowers her forehead onto the kitchen table. Her voice is muffled. "You're right. It must be some misunderstanding."

"Why should I go?"

She snaps her head up, her voice sharp now, impatient. "Because you're better at these things. Talking to people."

He sighs. He's just got in, taken his boots off, he's not going to go out again now. It'll just be a stupid mistake.

"I wish you wouldn't do that," Jeanie says.

"What?"

"Throw your socks at the dog."

The electricity is still not working, despite Julius fiddling some more with the fuse board. Jeanie lights two oil lamps and carries them through to the parlour. Maude is again shut in the kitchen.

"I can ask Bridget," Jeanie says.

"No." Julius stands the other side of their mother's covered body. It's good that it's the two of them doing this, he can manage, it's his duty. Still, he can hear his pulse in his ears and his mouth is dry.

"Ready?"

Julius nods and Jeanie draws down the sheet. His eyes move over the body's surface, not lingering on any single point. He is adept at not remembering the details of the first time he saw a dead body. The images of it have blurred like a photograph smudged by the rain, and there are no smells that bring it back, no human noises. It is only the sensation of an engine on his bones — the way its bass note resonates through him — that he can't extricate from his physical reaction.

"I couldn't get her nightie or dressing gown out from underneath," Jeanie says. "We have to roll her."

"Towards me," Julius says. He pulls the body over, while Jeanie tugs at the nightclothes. The flesh is cold, of course, and the body stiff, the muscles hard.

"Get them out," Julius says, holding the body. He closes his eyes and thinks of Shelley Swift. He went to her flat today above the fish and chip shop. The sash window in her wedge-shaped kitchen which her cat uses for coming and going was jammed open. The rope was broken on one side, but he greased the parts of the mechanism he could reach without removing the whole window and got the thing moving again. Shelley Swift made tea while her cat purred and sat on the counter. As Julius checked that the window slid smoothly, he watched Shelley Swift from the corner of his eye while she squeezed teabags against the sides of the mugs, flinging the bags into the sink, and when she thought he wasn't looking adjusting the elasticated neck of her peasant-style blouse, so that it sat below her shoulders and showed her freckled skin. She dragged the cat off the counter and into her arms, cradling it like a huge hairy baby. "Pixie, Pixie, Pixie-pie," she crooned, rubbing her cheek against the cat, which without moving its mouth or its eyes wore an expression of bored tolerance. Shelley Swift came closer to Julius, rocking the cat and saying, "Meet Julius, Pixie. Isn't he a nice man, mending your window?" The cat purred up against her breasts, the tops of which showed above her blouse, and when she let the cat go it leaped away, unexpectedly light-footed for its size. Shelley Swift looked down at herself and picked a couple of cat hairs off her skin, tutting. He watched and he knew Shelley Swift knew he was watching. She talked about her flat and the whiff of the public toilets which drifted up sometimes, outdoing the fish and chip shop, the thrillers she liked to read, and her job — stories about her manager and how even if she took her sandwiches in a plastic box, they tasted of brick dust by lunchtime. "It gets everywhere." She pulled at the elastic

76

of her top and looked down again, laughing, a husky grate, which he found he liked. It was good to hear Shelley Swift laughing the day after his mother died.

He wasn't planning on telling her what had happened, but she winkled it out of him and they stayed in the kitchen for an hour or more after he finished the window. Her expression of tenderness and sympathy had been almost too much for him to bear.

Jeanie pulls at Dot's nightie and dressing gown and this time they come free, and Julius lowers the body. She ruches up the knickers, high-waisted greying cotton, which Julius finds more embarrassing than his mother's nakedness. Jeanie tugs them over the feet, and by dragging one side and then the other she gets them above the knees, but there they stick.

Brother and sister stand back. "If only she'd worn underwear to bed," Julius says.

"Best to let things breathe," Jeanie says in an impersonation of their mother.

"Really?" Julius says. "Is that what she told you? I was told pyjamas, always. To stop any fiddling, I reckon."

"Julius!" Jeanie laughs. She looks at the knickers. "What are we going to do?"

"Maybe the dress will cover them?"

"We can't bury her with her underwear

half on." Jeanie puts her hand over her mouth to stop herself from laughing again. "Can we?"

"Inappropriate." Julius is laughing too.

"Indecent."

"She's never been seen naked. We can't start now."

The words spill out as they laugh.

"Not even Dad?"

"Especially not Dad."

"Not on their wedding night?"

"No, surely not."

And then, just as suddenly as it came, the laughter is gone.

"Poor Mum."

"It wasn't much of a life, was it?" Julius says.

"She was happy, I think. She had us, the garden, the cottage. Music."

"Was that enough?"

"Of course it was enough. It's enough for me."

They're silent, until Jeanie says, "I don't know how we're going to get the dress on her."

"Doesn't she have one with buttons down the front?"

"They all do up at the back, apart from her house dress which ties at the side. But she did the housework in that. It wouldn't be right."

"An apron?"

"Buried in an apron." Jeanie starts laughing again.

"We'll have to cut them," Julius says. "The knickers and the dress. Cut them all the way up the back, and the sleeves of the dress, and then we can lay them over her and tuck them around the sides so it looks like she's wearing them. It's only us who'll see her. And the undertaker."

Jeanie is still then, and silent.

"And God," Julius adds.

Jeanie flaps her hand dismissively. She knows Julius is joking. None of them has ever believed in God or gone to church. "He doesn't care what the dead look like."

"Even if their knickers are around their knees?"

"Especially then." Jeanie pulls the knickers off. "I've been thinking. What about if we don't have a funeral or a service? What if we dress her, wrap her up, and bury her in the garden?"

Julius frowns. "Can we do that?"

"Who says we can't? It's our land. She's our mother. There's a patch near the apple trees which would be nice. What do you think she'd have wanted? To be next to her vegetable garden or some burial place full of people she doesn't know? Or worse, burned into ash and chucked somewhere? I heard on the radio once that 98 percent of the ash in one of those little boxes doesn't come from the person who's been cremated. The ash from all the bodies that have been burned that day gets mixed up and shovelled into pots and handed to the families. We could be scattering anyone's ashes."

She is thinking of their father whose body was cremated and ashes scattered on the fields that he loved, and from the way that Julius looks back, she knows he is too. There was never going to be an open coffin or a lingering moment over Frank's body. And his cremation, Jeanie considers now, might have been Dot's attempt to erase what her children saw.

"If we do it the way everyone else does it, we still don't know how we're going to pay for it," she adds.

"Okay."

"What?" Jeanie says. She didn't expect him to agree. She hadn't really thought about the spot near the apple trees until she said it.

"Okay, let's bury her in the garden. We don't need to tell anyone. We can say we're having a private ceremony."

After that decision, so quickly and easily

made, Jeanie cuts the knickers, and while she is laying them over the body, Julius cuts the dress.

"At least it was fast," he says. "She didn't suffer."

Jeanie makes a croak of agreement although she's not sure how fast it would have been. She tries not to think about how long their mother may have lain on the cold flags alone and conscious, but unable to move or cry out.

"She wouldn't have wanted to spend the rest of her days sitting in a chair, staring out the window and not even able to wipe up her own drool."

"No one would want that," Jeanie says.

When they've finished tucking in the clothes, Julius says, "What about her wedding ring?"

"What about it?"

"We should take it off, don't you think?"

"But it's hers."

"She's not going to need it."

"Will we?" Jeanie's question comes out more forcefully than she was expecting. "Besides, she never took it off when she was alive, so why should we take it off now?"

"Yes, she did."

"No, she didn't." Jeanie is suddenly angry that Julius should think he knew their mother better. "Not even when we were gardening. I would remember."

"She used to put it in that flowered china dish on the windowsill behind the scullery sink."

"She never took it off."

"Well, what do you think we should do about it now?"

"Take it, if you really want it. If you think you'll have a use for it."

"You might have a use for it." He winks.

"Why would that be? Don't be ridiculous." She refuses to smile.

"You never know. How about . . . Doug Fletcher? He always seems jolly."

"From the fish and chip shop!"

"What's wrong with that? Free batter bits at the end of an evening."

"He's married for starters."

They cover Dot's body.

In the morning, after Julius leaves for work, Jeanie looks again at their mother, lifting back the top half of the sheet. The ring has gone.

7

Jeanie opens her handbag and checks that the medical certificate is tucked into the side pocket. Next to her, Bridget keeps one hand on the steering wheel and with the other flips open a packet of cigarettes and takes one out. She feels in the compartment below the dash and her hand draws out a box of matches, searches again, and finds a lighter which she flicks alight, holds to the end of the cigarette. Bridget smokes too much, Jeanie thinks as she moves her feet amongst the mess of empty crisp packets, old leaves, plastic water bottles, and the dried crumbs of mud from the soles of boots which fills the footwell. She prods her window down and then up, and jabs at it twice more to keep it cracked open. They are driving so slowly, every car that comes up behind overtakes them.

"I could have gone on the bus," Jeanie says. In truth, there is only one bus a day to

83

Devizes and it would have got her there too late to leave her enough time to catch the one back. And, of course, she is grateful that she can save the bus fare. She's not sure there was enough in the tin to cover it.

"It's hard managing these life-changing events on your own," Bridget says. She sounds like she's speaking the words from the leaflet Jeanie was given by the doctor, along with the medical certificate. Julius read some of the leaflet aloud in the evening at home and chucked it on the fire. Jeanie watches the cows in the fields, and the hedgerows, and the lines of oaks go past. Her mother is dead and yet oak trees are still growing, cows continue to eat grass. Bridget pushes her window down and taps her cigarette on the edge of the glass. The ash blows into the car, and the wind whips it up and flings it about. She takes another drag and lobs the cigarette out of the window.

"It's kind of you to offer to come in with me, but thinking about it, I'd rather do it on my own." Jeanie grips her handbag, determined.

"Don't be silly," Bridget says. "I don't mind. I had to do it when Dad died, so I know how it works. Stu went on his own when Nath was born, I was in the hospital.

He wanted to wait until I was out so we could go together but they kept me in for two weeks. Women's problems, you know. That's why we never had any more." Bridget moves her hand above her stomach, indicating Jeanie doesn't know what. "I thought it was sweet that he wanted us to go to the register office together, he was so excited about being a dad."

"No," Jeanie cuts in. "I can do it. Thanks."

Bridget looks over at her and the car moves towards the verge, bumping along the shoulder until Bridget straightens the wheel.

"Suit yourself."

They're silent until they reach the town and begin circling the parking area in the main square. Bridget is too hesitant, indicating first one way and then the other, missing a couple of spaces and going round again. She only learned to drive a few years ago. "I suppose you'll carry on living in the cottage?" She pulls into a space without indicating, narrowly missing a car already parked.

Jeanie doesn't know how to answer. What does Bridget know about what Caroline Rawson claimed? About how little money they have in the tin? Jeanie makes a non-committal *hmm* which could be taken either way. Bridget yanks up the handbrake and puts her fingers on the sleeve of Jeanie's coat. Jeanie looks at them — the wedding and engagement rings, the nail varnish, a chipped red the colour of Winifred, a rose which grows in the cottage's front garden. "I know about your mum and the thing with Rawson," she says softly, as though testing whether Jeanie knows it too.

"The agreement, do you mean?" Jeanie says. Of course Bridget knows about the agreement, this isn't a surprise. "Nothing changes it now Mum's dead. It was always supposed to apply to me and Julius too. We can stay in the cottage for the rest of our lives without paying any rent."

Bridget examines her closely, her eyes flicking from one pupil to the other. "The agreement, yes," she says, although there's something false about her tone. She turns off the engine. "Is that what you want, then? To stay on in the cottage?"

"Why wouldn't we?"

Bridget reaches into the back seat for her handbag. "You don't think it's a bit un-natural?" She takes out a tube of Polos, puts a mint in her mouth, and offers the packet to Jeanie.

Jeanie shakes her head. "Unnatural? What's unnatural?"

"Well, I don't know. Living with your brother when you're fifty-one. Gardening. That cottage." Bridget shudders. Jeanie knows she doesn't like the place, finds it dingy and claustrophobic. She won't ever use the privy when she visits. Says it's full of spiders.

"It's our home. We've always been there."

"Exactly," Bridget says. "Look, I'm just saying you should live a little. Get a proper job maybe. Earn some real money. Buy some new clothes."

"New clothes? My mother has just died. I don't care about new clothes."

"That came out wrong." Bridget folds the packet of mints away. "I'm sorry, it's just, what if you can't carry on living there? You need to think about that."

"Of course we'll carry on living there. That was the agreement." Perhaps Bridget does know about the rent that Mrs. Rawson says they owe. She and Julius haven't talked about it since Jeanie told him that Caroline Rawson came round, and he hasn't yet been to see her husband like she said he should. Nothing has happened. Nothing is going to happen. Still, as much as she tries to dismiss that outrageous amount, it flies around inside her like a bluebottle at a window, making her heart buzz with anxiety.

Bridget seems to think for a moment, starts to say something and then dismisses it. "Well, if you're going to stay, you must get that man to put in some decent plumbing, a bathroom with an inside loo, get it re-thatched. The place needs sorting out." She takes her purse from her handbag and pokes through the coins. "Do you have a pound? I think that's what the car-park machine needs."

Jeanie would like to put her fingers to her heart to keep the creature from escaping but she looks in the compartment in her own purse where she keeps her coins. She knows there is exactly three pounds and fifty-four pence in there — all the loose change from the tin. Julius took back the twenty pounds he put on the table, and she knows he will have bought tobacco with it, rolling papers, matches, maybe topped up his phone. She needs the change in her purse to buy bread and margarine and milk, some cheese if she can make it stretch that far. Bridget peers over and takes the fifty-pence piece. "That'll help," she says, and goes to buy a ticket.

When they're standing on the pavement Bridget checks her phone for the time. "Your appointment's in fifteen minutes, so you should be fine." Bridget has telephoned and got her booked in. Jeanie and Julius discussed whether they needed to register the death if they're going to be burying their mother in the garden and decided they did. Jeanie feels sick at the thought of the forms and would have preferred Julius to do it, but Devizes is an hour in the car, and he would never have made it without throwing up.

"I'll meet you back here at half past," Bridget says.

The waiting area in the register office is empty of people. Tinny classical music is playing and on the wall there is a large painting of flowers in a vase — lily of the valley and roses — flowers that don't bloom at the same time. She gives her name to the woman at the desk and sits in a chair. They are the same chairs in style and upholstery as the ones in the surgery waiting room. Perhaps waiting room chairs are the same across the country, across the world; perhaps one company has a corner on the sales of waiting room chairs. Apart from the awful music — something that is meant to cover all three situations she supposes: birth, death, and marriage — it is quiet until she hears a roar coming from behind a closed door, cheering and whooping like a football crowd, and the waiting room fills up with people in bright clothes, streaming out and congratulating and clapping a couple who hold hands and laugh. Jeanie stands and smiles too, caught up in the celebration. The group leaves, their chatter fading down the street, and Jeanie is bereft, holding her breath so that she won't cry at being left behind while the party carries on elsewhere, as always. The tinny music is audible again, and her name is called.

After the registrar has sat on one side of the desk and invited her to sit on the other while murmuring noises of sympathy, he looks from his computer screen to the document which Jeanie has passed to him. He asks her for Dot's full name, her age and address. These are things Jeanie can answer easily, and gradually as he types, she relaxes, thinking now that there will be no forms for her to fill in. When he spells out her own name and address for her to confirm, she nods. His two index fingers peck at the keyboard and Jeanie watches his expression, wondering at his concentration and the mechanism that transfers her voice to his head, then to an instruction which travels down his arms, making his fingers move, which creates words on the computer, and which other people, perhaps years from

90

now, can look at and comprehend in their own heads. The registrar asks if she has brought Dot's birth and marriage certificates, but it doesn't seem to matter that she hasn't. All the time the man smiles and nods until Jeanie leans back in her chair and releases the tight grip she has on the handles of her handbag.

"What funeral home are you using?" the man asks, looking at her over the top of his glasses.

Jeanie stares at him, seeing Dot in her sliced dress on the table in the parlour.

"If you haven't decided yet, that's no problem. Do you know which crematorium or church?"

She thinks of the plot near the apple trees which she and Julius marked out the night before, and which he says he might be able to start digging today.

"I can put it down as undecided, but you do need to let us know as soon as you've reached a decision. I'll be giving you a green form today which you must pass on to the person who buries or cremates your mother's body, and they must return the bottom part to us."

He touches a few more keys on the keyboard while Jeanie waits, until eventually he says, "I just need you to check that everything I've entered is correct." A printer behind the desk starts sucking in paper. He puts the sheet in front of Jeanie and she stares at it, the words incomprehensible. Surreptitiously she presses the fingers of her right hand under her left breast, feeling for the tapping of the creature. Can she be suddenly ill? she wonders. Unexpectedly indisposed? A mist gathers in between the paper and her eyes and she blinks to refocus.

"Sorry?" Jeanie says.

The man points and reads, upside down. Upside down! thinks Jeanie. He goes through each line and she nods. "If you're happy with that, I sign here." He takes the paper back and signs, and then turns it to her once more. "And you sign here." She peers at the page and then back up at him. He is holding out his ink pen. "Careful with it, it can be temperamental."

"Sorry?" Jeanie repeats.

He moves the pen towards her, and she takes it. She looks again at the page: the printed words, the man's signature. They swim around, dancing and merging. She puts the nib on the paper, conscious of the watching registrar. Her fingers are too far back, the pen held too lightly; it slips but before it can fall she moves her hand, pressing so that the ink spits, and from the corner of her eye she sees the registrar wince, but a line comes out which zigzags and sputters across the page. She keeps her head lowered and lifts the pen from the paper, waiting to be accused of incompetence, but the registrar takes the pen from her and turns the paper back to himself. He makes no comment about the signature.

"Would you like a copy of the death certificate?" he asks.

"Isn't that what I came to get?" she says, confused.

All Jeanie hears is that a copy of the certificate costs eleven pounds. She doesn't have that on her. Julius might have some change from the twenty pounds, and doesn't Shelley Swift owe him some money? He's working today, cleaning gutters, but when will he be paid? A trickle of sweat runs down her back, her thighs and buttocks are hot, she's afraid that when she stands, she will leave a line of condensation on the seat. She wants to get out of there, her mother was right about officialdom always trying to get something out of you. The registrar explains that another form which doesn't cost anything will do the same job. And then he says it's all done and hands her a folder containing various bits of paper and shows her to the door. She is on the pavement outside breathing real air, high on her success, as though she has got away with it, escaped, and then someone calls her name. When she turns, the registrar is coming towards her with a glossy leaflet in his hand. "I forgot to include this in your folder," he says. "It's about what you need to do next. Do you have someone at home who can read it to you, or we could —" She snatches the leaflet, and without looking at him, she shoves it in her bag and strides away.

When she gets back to the car a bird has made a mess on the windscreen and Bridget isn't there. Jeanie hovers nearby but not too close, worrying that a traffic warden will come and tell her she needs to drive away or buy another ticket. Bridget finally arrives, trotting in bursts and breathlessly apologizing, carrying bags. Jeanie hasn't managed to do her food shopping. In the car, Bridget puts the windscreen wipers on, and the bird shit smears across Jeanie's side, worsening with each swish of the blade.

"I was thinking about getting a job," Jeanie says when they're on the road home.

"What about the garden and the chickens?" Bridget says, sucking on a Polo.

"Didn't you tell me I should get a job?"

"I don't see how you're going to manage that enormous garden on your own. All those vegetables. I never knew how you and Dot did it, the weeding, the digging, it's no wonder —"

Jeanie stops her. "Something that pays more regularly than supplying vegetables to the deli and the B&B."

"Is it the cost of the funeral you're worrying about?"

"We're not having a funeral," Jeanie says, but Bridget isn't listening.

"I couldn't believe the cost of Dad's. Bloody rip-off, if you ask me. I could send Stu round. He'd help, sort out a decent coffin and transport maybe. His mate Ed helped with Dad's. I'd have to ask Stu though about having a body in the back of his van. That'd be a new one." She gives a gruff laugh and then looks at Jeanie apologetically.

Jeanie is offended — the thought of her mother in the back of Stu's van. Tins of old paint and his other rubbish pushed to the side.

"A local job," Jeanie says. "If you hear of anything."

"I heard the brickworks were looking for someone to help with admin. You'd be in the same office as Shelley Swift, though. Can you type?" She laughs and then looks horrified, the implication of her question betrayed on her face. Now that Dot is dead, only Julius openly knows that Jeanie struggles to read and write. But she is sure Bridget must suspect it.

"No," Jeanie says, nettled, remembering the registrar's fingers pecking at the keyboard. "I can't type."

Bridget stares straight out through the windscreen.

Occasionally Jeanie sees these problems as her own failings and is ashamed, but most of the time she is cross that the world is designed for people who can read and write with ease. When she recovered from one bout of rheumatic fever and returned to school, it seemed that the children in her class had suddenly learned to pick up a pencil and make patterns of circles and lines that everyone else understood. She was put in the remedial class for reading and writing, but the patterns and the process never stayed still for her, and after a while she couldn't be bothered to keep trying. History she liked, learning about how the Great Fire of London started, colouring in pictures of the houses along the Thames, her red crayon worn to a stub. At home, when she told Dot about it, her mother replied, "When I was your age I knew how to start the fire in the grate *and* how to bake a cake without it burning. That was good enough for me."

A few times the school bobby came around asking questions about Jeanie's poor attendance when her couple of days' absence had lengthened to ten without a note from the doctor. Each time Jeanie had managed to be on the sofa tucked in under a blanket, and after a few words and a wagging finger the school bobby had gone away. There weren't any books in the cottage, although occasionally her father read the newspaper, the old pages of which were used to stuff the window frames in winter. He tried to encourage her a few times: sitting her on his knee and holding the newspaper out in front of them. She enjoyed being enclosed in their papery tent, but she had no desire for the words, and he had little patience. Other parents may have read to their children before bed but in the Seeder cottage they played music together before she and Julius brushed their teeth at the scullery sink and went upstairs. Jeanie left school as soon as she could, at sixteen, without any qualifications.

In the car, Bridget says, "Jobs are all advertised online these days. Catering assistants and whatnot. You could always pop into a library, they'd help you do an internet search."

Jeanie looks out of the window; they're coming into the village. She has never been into a library and she never will — all those books snapping at her. She can't use the internet, go online, search for work, complete an application form, send an email. Not even, and perhaps especially not, with a librarian's help. The keeper of the words. And besides, she would have to buy a ticket and catch the bus into Devizes or Hungerford to get to a library.

"Shall I take you back to the cottage or do you need to pick anything up from the village?" Bridget asks.

"The cottage. Thanks," Jeanie says quietly. She's too drained to think about what groceries they need and what they can afford.

When they're outside, Bridget says, more kindly, "The shop has some of those cards up in the window. Old people selling stuff, like those great fat tellies that no one wants any more. Sometimes there are adverts for cleaners or gardeners."

Jeanie knows she should invite Bridget in, to thank her for taking her to the register office, for all her help, but she also knows that if she were to make Bridget a cup of tea the milk would separate in the hot liquid and form into lumps because the fridge is no longer cold, and she doesn't want Bridget to see the hole that Julius will hopefully have started digging. Bridget doesn't show any inclination to get out of the car.

Inside, Jeanie calls for Julius and when she gets no reply she collapses on the sofa. Maude jumps up beside her, licking her face and hands, until Jeanie catches the dog and wraps her arms around Maude's neck, pulling her in close, breathing in her doggy-rivery smell.

Jeanie builds up the fire in the kitchen, boils the kettle on the range, and makes herself a cup of hot water. She takes it into the parlour, the dog following. Her mother's covered body lies on the table and the room is chilly and smells of rosemary.

"What are we going to do?" she says. She might be addressing the body, or Maude. One of them doesn't reply, the other tilts her head and stares, waiting for Jeanie to provide the answer.

8

In the shop, Julius dithers. He's low on tobacco and rolling papers and he wants — no, needs — a pint in the pub. What to do with the money from the guttering job? If he wants to get any work, he'll need credit for his mobile phone. He buys ten pounds' worth and some tobacco. In the pub he plugs his mobile in to charge. He sits at the bar next to Jenks, sips at a pint of bitter to make it last, and rolls a thin cigarette.

"Heard about your mum." Jenks, a scrawny Scotsman, whom Julius has rarely seen out of the public bar of the Plough, tips his glass towards his mouth and Julius sees his top lip reach out to the beer like a snail feeling its way. "What a bummer," Jenks says when he's swallowed.

"Yup," Julius says, licking his cigarette paper, sticking it down. "Thanks." He waves the cigarette at Jenks and goes out the back to smoke. He has a blister on his palm from digging and he rubs the bubble of it across his lips, feeling the fluid move beneath the skin. He considers if there's a legal requirement for the depth of a grave; he wonders again whether they're allowed to do what they're doing. Sod it, he doesn't care if they aren't. He's taken off the turf and has gone down a spade's depth, which isn't enough. Won't be enough for Jeanie, and it would be an utter cock-up if the foxes started digging, or Maude. He rubs the bristles along his jaw, smokes his cigarette, thinks about what the Rawsons say is owing, again sees Rawson shout *nothing* up the stairs to his wife, remembers the contents of the envelopes in his coat pocket. Fuck it, he thinks. Fuck it all.

When he's back at the bar and another ten minutes have passed, Jenks says, "You got a text. From that bit of totty who lives over the fish and chip shop. Something about a boiler."

"Bloody hell, Jenks. Read everything why don't you? Shall I bring in my diary next time?"

Jenks smirks, and after checking his phone, Julius finishes off the rest of his beer in one open-throated gulp.

Boilers aren't his specialism — he doesn't really have a specialism — and he doesn't have his tool rucksack with him, but he wheels his bike through the village to Shelley Swift's.

She's wearing a leopard-print top and a denim skirt when she answers the door, and lilac lipstick that she surely doesn't put on for work.

"Bloody boiler. There's no hot water," she says as he follows her up the stairs.

The boiler is on a wall in the kitchen, and as soon as he inspects the hole in the cover, he sees that the pilot light has gone out. He pushes two buttons, the gas ignites, a tiny blue flame shows through the hole, and they hear the boiler kick in. "You're amazing," Shelley Swift says and when he turns, she doesn't move back. Her nose and mouth are out of focus, but her eyes, lashes clotted with makeup and hazel irises with a circumference of a deeper brown, catch him and hold him. He wants to kiss her but feels he is too tall, too stooped, all elbows and knees. He is unused to an encounter like this, out of practice.

"Can I use your toilet?" he says, and she laughs that husky laugh and lets him go. In the bathroom under the window is a shelf unit crammed with books. He pulls one out. *Just Like Her Mother* the title reads in raised silver letters. Behind the words is a close-up of some scrubby bushes and a patch of bare soil. Just visible in the earth is a woman's ear with an earring through the lobe. He shoves the book back.

On the landing at the top of her stairs, as he is saying that she should text him if anything else goes wrong, Shelley Swift kisses him, her mouth slightly open, her tongue touching his lips, and he's aware of the waxy greasiness of her lipstick. He doesn't exactly kiss her in return, too shocked by the feel and the taste of her. When they pull apart, she laughs once more, and he almost runs down the stairs and out through the door. All the way home he rides his bike without holding on as though he were thirteen again, using his knees to steer so that he can hold his fingers to his nose and smell the lemony scent of Shelley Swift's bathroom soap.

When Julius is still in the pub, Jeanie is at the end of the garden scything nettles from around the bench. She has sharpened the blade to a shine and has just bent again when she hears someone calling. A man. She stands up straight, arches her back the other way to stretch the tightness out of it, and sees Stu coming towards her. Christ, she hadn't thought that Bridget would actually send her husband. He is already through the yard and the gate, passing the apple trees and the cherries, whose blossom has fallen in the last few days, precipitated by the snow, spreading pink and white confetti over the vegetable beds. Near the oldest apple tree — a Cox's orange pippin which is gnarled and almost white with lichen — Julius has cut away the top layer of rough grass turf, placing it upside down in a heap. It will make fine compost. The hole is a foot deep so far and the reddish ends of the tree's roots feather out from the straight sides. To Jeanie, it is clear that the earth hole is a grave.

Stu is a big man. Once, she'd had the misfortune to see him up a ladder with his belly, swarthy with black hair, overhanging the waistband of his shorts. He only ever wears shorts, even in winter. As he approaches, he removes his baseball cap, revealing his high forehead, the top half of which rarely sees the sun and is glaringly white. What remains of his hair sticks out at crazy angles. The cap, which Jeanie knows has *Stu Clements Painter and Decorator* printed across it, is greasy around the rim. Stu doesn't only keep to painting and decorating, he will do most things if the money is right. Now, he dips his head and says he's sorry to hear about her mother, and he doesn't mention the plot of bare soil, it's probably just another vegetable bed to him. Maude gets up from where she's lying, sniffs at Stu's hand, and then goes back to her place — she knows Stu.

"Bridget asked me to call in," he says.

Jeanie nods. She doesn't want to have to talk to this man, wants to get rid of him as soon as possible. Leaving the scythe behind, she walks to the house, keeping him on her left so that he won't see the grave.

"I'll be able to get a coffin to you on Friday if I can take the measurements now. It's my mate Ed who sells them, but I can sort it for you," he says. "She's here still, isn't she?"

"I'm not sure —" Jeanie starts.

"Or tomorrow if that works better."

"We might use a funeral director after all," she says. She takes him through the gate into the yard, a couple of chickens clucking and scattering. "Sorry if you've had a wasted journey."

"Is that right?" he says from behind her. "Only, Bridget said you're having some problems. She said things are a bit tight, what with the funeral and everything."

Jeanie feels her cheeks flush at the thought

105

that Bridget would discuss their financial situation with anyone, including her husband. Who else is she telling that they can't afford to bury their mother? The whole village must know. Jeanie presses her thumb to her opposite wrist and pushes down hard. "I don't know what she meant by that," she says, not turning. She was planning on taking Stu round the front of the cottage and showing him on his way, but now, affronted and needing to prove that she has no idea what he's talking about, she goes in through the back door, Stu following and Maude coming along behind.

"She's in the parlour," Jeanie says, taking him through the kitchen and past the front door. For a moment she watches him standing beside the covered body, and then she returns to the kitchen. After a few minutes she hears a cough in the doorway.

Jeanie is stabbing at the fire with a stick — they have mislaid the poker — so that she appears busy when Stu comes in and not as though she has been listening and imagining him with his tape measure. She stands upright.

"Ed's got a nice bit of pine in his workshop," Stu says, tucking a small notebook and pencil into a back pocket of his shorts. The soft part of his baseball cap is stuffed into the other. He comes to stand beside the range to warm himself.

Jeanie screws up her face, shakes her head, she doesn't want a coffin.

And as though he thinks she's shaking her head about the type of wood, he says: "Or I could get you an oak one, if that'd be better. It'll be a bit more expensive than pine but it has a lovely finish."

"Oak?" she says.

"Although, of course, there's some outstanding already."

"Some of what outstanding?"

"The money your mum borrowed."

"Mum borrowed some money?" The animal in her chest thumps its shoulders against her ribs. Stu stares at her and is about to speak. "Oh, that," she says. "Of course." The pulse is in her throat, her bile rising. She wants to ask if he knows why Dot borrowed it, whether she was going to give it to the Rawsons for the overdue rent.

"I can add the cost of the coffin on to what's outstanding if you like," Stu says gently. "You don't want to be worrying about money at a time like this. Ed says it's a fine piece of oak." Stu has always been a salesman. "Well seasoned, it's not going to warp or split open." He clears his throat, disconcerted perhaps by the image he's conjured. "Of course, it's harder to work than pine, but it's quality wood."

Jeanie goes into the scullery and fills a glass with water. She can't believe that her mother borrowed money from Stu. Dot, who always told them never to accept or borrow anything from anyone, whether it was the government, charity, or neighbours. Getting the cottage rent-free from Rawson didn't count after what he did. Stu follows her in, crowding her in the narrow room. She can smell the fabric conditioner which Bridget must use for their clothes, floral and artificial.

"How much will the coffin be?" She drinks some water.

"Normally, Ed would charge two hundred and fifty for a handmade coffin, but I know he'll be happy with two hundred, on account of the fact that your mother was a good woman. A very good and honest woman, Dot Seeder. I can give you some time to have a chat with Julius if it's your brother who needs to decide. When's the funeral arranged for?"

"No," Jeanie says. "I can decide."

"If anyone sees that oak, they're going to snap it up. It's not going to hang around for long."

"Okay, oak," Jeanie says firmly. He's too

close, she needs him out of the house. Julius will just have to dig a bigger hole.

"There'll be a bit extra to take her to the church or the crematorium. Ed and I can put on suits, you know, make it a bit fancy."

"We won't be needing that." Jeanie sets her glass down and Stu raises his eyebrows. "Julius is sorting something out," she says.

"I didn't think Julius liked going in vehicles." He pronounces it *vee-hic-culs*. "Don't they make him sick?"

She folds her arms. Stu knows very well that going in anything with an engine makes Julius throw up after fifteen minutes and he damn well knows why too. "I said he'll sort something out."

"Okey-dokes," Stu says, backing out of the scullery and putting his baseball cap on, tugging the peak down. She walks behind him like she's herding an animal towards the front door. "What about beer for the wake? I can get you a few crates for a lot less than the Plough would charge."

"We're not having a wake," Jeanie says firmly.

At the front door, when he is out on the threshold, she says, "I've forgotten how much Mum borrowed. Can you remind me?"

Stu narrows his eyes and she wonders

whether he's trying to work out if she knows the amount or not. "Eight hundred pounds," he says.

After he's gone, Jeanie searches the house for the money. Stu can be unscrupulous, she can imagine him upping the amount Dot borrowed by fifty pounds, or a hundred, but not even Stu would completely invent the debt. Perhaps she should argue that this isn't in fact her and Julius's debt, why should they take it on. But she knows this will never wash with Stu or Bridget. She leafs through postcards and articles and pictures cut from magazines stuffed into the dresser's drawers, she opens the storage tins in the scullery and looks inside, searches through the clutter under her and Dot's shared bed, and stuffs her hand under the mattress and claws about. She sits at the kitchen table and thinks of the places her mother could have hidden an amount of cash. If she borrowed the money to pay the Rawsons and it never reached them, then her mother, this good and honest woman, must have hidden money in a place she thought Jeanie would never look. The old dairy is full of broken objects and ancient gardening equipment, baskets and boxes, there is Julius's bedroom and the gaps beneath every wonky floorboard in the house. There are too many places.

9

Jeanie is making a rabbit pie from a recipe she knows by heart. Julius shot the animals on the meadow yesterday, this time in anger, after she told him that their mother borrowed money from Stu. When Julius asked how much it was, she lied and said it was a thousand pounds, adding that Stu was including the coffin for free. She isn't sure that Julius believes her, but he raved about the amount and where it could be, pulling out the drawers and looking in cupboards which Jeanie had already searched. He didn't understand why she had ordered a coffin — now he'd have to dig a bigger hole. She tried to calm him but he took two creased envelopes from his coat pocket and slammed them on the table, his big thumbs pinning them down. The crinkle of the see-through address windows as he flattened them worried her.

"What are they?" she asked.

"This" — he picked one up and waggled it at her — "is a notice to say that our electricity is being disconnected. Dated more than a week ago. And this" — he picked up the other — "is a letter from the council to say that our latest council tax bill is late. I paid some of it at the post office counter with the money from the guttering job, but there's still loads owing."

"You paid the council tax bill but not the electricity? And here I am cooking by sodding lamplight on a range that hasn't been used in thirty years."

"You weren't there. I had to decide. There's a reconnection fee to get the electricity back on. Admin charges or something, and that's before you start paying off the bill. I had to make a choice."

"Okay," she said. "Okay."

Julius leaned forwards, shaking his head. "Christ, Jeanie. These debts. I'm out of ideas. What are we going to do?"

Julius has always been the one with ideas, hare-brained, ridiculous — building an oven in the garden and starting a business delivering cakes, leasing the meadow from the Rawsons and turning it over to asparagus, or putting a yurt on it and renting it out as an Airbnb. Schemes that failed before they started because he needed a computer, the internet, a website, so he could send emails to those beardy types in London. Julius has never stuck with any of his schemes. But this brother without an escape plan frightened her.

"Craig will give you more work," she said.

"Craig isn't going to give me any work, ever again," Julius shouted. He fished in his trouser pockets, brought out his loose change, and slammed it on the table. Three pound coins and three pennies. "This is it."

"We can contact the electricity company. Pay in instalments or something."

"What with? How will we pay the next instalment and the one after that? How will we do that, Jeanie? And what about Stu? How are we going to pay Stu back?" His hands became fists, the knuckles white. "Fuck." He picked up a kitchen chair and thumped all four legs on the ground. "What was she thinking?" Neither mentioned the Rawsons' debt, and Jeanie hadn't asked where he had been all afternoon and evening because she had been able to smell the beer on his breath and the perfume on his coat.

Now, in the kitchen, Jeanie guts, skins, and joints the rabbits, checking for any gun pellets. Julius is usually a good shot, getting them in the head and killing them instantly. But this time the pellets have gone into the meat and she has to poke at the holes with a pair of old tweezers to remove the lead. She stews the rabbit pieces with an onion and a wrinkled apple which she unwraps from last year's newspaper. At the kitchen table she makes the pastry, bringing the flour and suet together with tablespoons of water, all the time aware of her mother's book of recipes behind her on the dresser. For years she's seen Dot's finger move under each ingredient and instruction as she read them out, hesitating over her own cramped letters. Without needing to think about what she is doing, Jeanie shreds the cooked rabbit meat from the bones in the way she would have done if she and Dot were working beside each other, speaking about everyday things while conscious of the other's economical movements as they reached for bowl or spoon or knife. Jeanie rolls out the pastry, lays the lid on the pie, and cuts out rabbit shapes from the scraps. As she works, she thinks about another rabbit pie she ate, years ago.

She last saw Nick when they were eleven and now of course he must be her age — fifty-one. As she brushes the pastry with beaten egg, she laughs at the idea of him as a middle-aged man, grown up. Where might he be? Nick arrived in her class at the very end of the last year of junior school, without the right uniform, his shirt grubby and his knuckles grazed. He slouched sullenly in the seat next to hers at the back of the room. Jeanie didn't see the point in that final month of school — the teachers weren't bothered about teaching and the pupils brought in games from home. If they weren't sitting around the classroom chatting, they were playing sports out on the field. She didn't go in to school often, but one day when she and Nick were loitering at the back of a group hoping not to get selected for rounders, he said, "Bugger this, I'm going home. Wanna come?" and they moved quietly away without being seen. He lived in one of the four caravans which were parked in an old chalk pit outside the village. Jeanie knew about them because she'd heard Bridget complaining about the mess, how things went missing from sheds when gypsies were about, how it wasn't normal to always be moving — disruptive for the children's schooling for starters. Dot had replied that travellers had always been scapegoats, and travelling was their way of life, like living in houses was ours. Bridget didn't answer.

Jeanie and Nick threw sticks for the dogs and rummaged through the rubbish that lay in the nettles at the bottom of the white cliff. Most of it seemed to have been there for years. Nick's mother brought them slices of cold rabbit pie, the meat set in a savoury jelly — Jeanie wasn't invited into their caravan although she would have liked to see how a family of three people and four dogs fitted. They sat on a chalk rock and ate the pieces of pie — better than her mother's — and then drew white stickmen on the side of a rusting tank. She went back several times to the caravan site, and she and Nick pulled things out of the under-growth, messed around, ate whatever his mother gave them sitting outside, although never the rabbit pie again.

The last time she went in to school after a few days away, something in the classroom had changed. Nick had been made to sit at the front of the class and wouldn't catch her eye. A girl on the next table leaned on her chair, tipping on the two back legs, and announced to all who could hear that Jeanie was "Nicko the gypo's girlfriend."

"I am not," Jeanie said, knowing that the denial in some way was a betrayal of her and Nick's friendship, even while she didn't want a boyfriend, didn't understand what they were for. The next day school was over, and when she finally went back to the travellers' site, the caravans and the dogs were gone.

The front door bangs open before Jeanie is finished preparing her own rabbit pie — Stu and Ed with the coffin, oak, as she'd agreed. Ed is a small man, heavy bags under his eyes and a lipless mouth which draws back in a leering smile. Jeanie thinks she's seen him about the village, but she's never spoken to him before. "All right?" he says to her. "In here, is it?" Stu, Ed, and Julius carry the coffin between them into the parlour, tipping it up to get it through the narrow doorways and around the corners. It's much bigger than Jeanie expected, and as they manoeuvre it past her, she sees four tiny holes in the lid where a plaque was screwed to it and removed. A cancelled order. They have bought a second-hand coffin.

Ed says, "Put it on the floor, lads. Careful, careful." The man's tongue sounds thick, too big for his mouth, so that every word is lisped. Stu's eyes slide away from the shrouded body on the makeshift table. But Jeanie has grown used to it being here in the house with them. Since Dot has been in the parlour, the feel of the cottage is different, the air denser, her and her brother's actions slower, as though they were moving

118

through smoke, feeling their way with their hands outstretched in a house that once was familiar. They are quieter when they're in opposite ends of the cottage: neither of them call to the other from a different room or let a door slam. She knows that Ed and Stu will think they are odd, keeping their mother at home, but she doesn't care. She is used to people considering them odd, it's pity she hates. She starts to complain about the coffin and to tell Stu and Ed to take it away, but Stu says, with his back to the body, "Bridget was asking about when and where the service will be."

Julius, behind the two men, shakes his head at Jeanie. "Monday," he says. "But we've decided it'll be just the two of us. Mum wouldn't have wanted a lot of fuss. Tell Bridget thank you, though." Julius raises his eyebrows and jerks his head at Jeanie, like when they were children and she was supposed to back him up on some minor lie.

"Yes," Jeanie says, folding her arms. "Please thank her. And you, of course." She directs this to Stu; she would like to shove Ed into his own bloody coffin, made for a person twice the size of their mother, but Jeanie returns to her rabbit pie. She sings to herself about the dead Polly Vaughn being wept over by the lover who killed her, her voice not quite loud enough to hide the sounds of a hammer nailing the coffin closed in the parlour next door.

When Stu and Ed have gone, Jeanie and Julius stand beside the coffin.

"You can't dig a hole that big," Jeanie says. "We won't even be able to carry it out. I'm not going to let you take one end. I don't want you dead as well." She knows these words are his apology for shouting.

Over the weekend Julius finishes digging the hole, and without them discussing it, they decide to bury Dot on Monday morning, as they told Stu they would. It feels to Jeanie that only when they get this momentous task done will they be able to focus on the money. Julius can visit Rawson and sort out the misunderstanding, she can search the cottage thoroughly for the cash Dot borrowed, and she can telephone the electricity company to see what can be done about the overdue bill. In the afternoon she will take some vegetables to Max. Nothing will seem impossible once their mother is in the ground.

In the chest in the parlour there are tablecloths and other linen which have never been used. Folded for so long in the damp, they are sprinkled with rust stains and have creases and wrinkles that no hot iron will ever eradicate. On the old treadle sewing machine, Jeanie stitches them together into a sheet large enough to wrap Dot in several times, while Julius levers off the coffin lid with a crowbar, cursing with the effort. But it is getting the body out of the coffin, when it is so deep and on top of the door on top of the trestles, that is the hardest thing. Jeanie tips and Julius heaves and swears until the body is in his arms. There is definitely a smell now. She follows him out through the yard, moving ahead to open the gate into the garden. Beside the grave he falls to his knees and the body almost rolls in, but he catches himself in time and, nearly lying flat, perpendicular to the grave, he lowers their mother inside. Jeanie lays twigs of apple blossom on the wrapped body, but neither know what to say. They stumble over the words and, in the end, Julius says that Dot always put them first, and Jeanie adds how much she loved this garden and this cottage. Neither of them say that she has gone to a better place.

10

Together, Jeanie and Julius hitch Dot's small wooden trailer to her old bike. It's been a long time since Jeanie has cycled — preferring to walk with Maude. She loads a basket into the trailer, filled with boxes of eggs and the vegetables she's picked. There aren't many — bundles of asparagus, bulbs of fresh garlic, and lots of radishes and spring onions from the polytunnel. Max's customers seem to buy a little of everything, rather than be able to cope with gluts, and he pays only for what he sells, a deal that her mother arranged when he first opened the deli, which Jeanie has always thought unfair.

Julius makes her promise that she will go slowly and won't exert herself. He has a hatchet in his hand, ready to chop up the coffin for firewood. She cannot allow herself to think about how much this firewood will have cost; instead she enjoys the feeling of the air on her face as she wobbles past Pepperwood Farm and down the lane. The produce that was on the table at the bottom has gone, and the honesty box contains two pounds fifty-one, as well as a farthing — a coin that hasn't been in use since before she was born. There is no one about in the village; the fish and chip shop is open only in the evenings and no one is sitting at the tables outside the deli. Max is inside wearing his brown apron, doing something on his phone. There aren't any customers.

"Jeanie," he says when he finally looks up. He comes out from behind the chiller cabinet where expensive cheeses, pâtés, and tubs of salad are displayed. Behind him on a tall rack are loaves of different shapes. "I heard the news about Dot. I can't believe it. I'm so sorry." Max moves his arms about a lot, his hands fly together as though he's praying. "Is there anything I can do?" He puts his fingertips under his chin.

"I've brought some asparagus and other things," Jeanie says. This job — delivering vegetables to Max — was something Dot did; Jeanie has been in the deli only a few times.

"Today?" he says. "You didn't need to come today of all days."

She thinks for a second that he must know

they buried Dot in the garden a few hours ago. She frowns. "Well, I'm here now." She has the basket in her arms, and he looks in it.

"More radishes," he says. "I can put them out, but most of the last lot didn't go. It's a bit early in the year for people to want salad." He takes the basket from her and puts it beside the chiller cabinet. "The asparagus, though, is wonderful. I can take as much as you can bring." There isn't any asparagus left in the garden, but plenty more radishes, and if she doesn't pick them soon, they'll become mealy and dry. "Let me make a note of everything," he says. He counts the bundles in the basket, holds his thumb to a screen which he gets from behind the counter, and flicks it, touching various areas with his index finger, all too fast for Jeanie. When he finishes, he looks up and smiles. "There we are then. Can I get you a coffee?"

She'd love a coffee, but she isn't sure whether he'll charge her for it or if it will be free and she doesn't want that floundering moment of confusion. "No thanks," she says.

"I really am so sorry about your mother. Such a wonderful woman."

There is a pause and Jeanie knows he is

expecting her to leave but they both continue to stand, waiting. Finally, she clenches her belly muscles and says quickly, "Is there anything due, any money for the last delivery?"

"Oh," Max says, and she sees that he's embarrassed too. They don't look at each other. "No, well. Dot didn't say? I gave her a little in advance, just to help her out, you know. I've kept track of it, all above board." He lights up his screen again which Jeanie sees has some contraption attached to the back to allow him to hold it with one hand. "I can show you if you like?"

"It's fine," she says, backing out, past the jars of fancy piccalilli, the mustards, the bags of pasta sealed with cardboard and a single rivet. "I'll be back on Thursday or Friday with whatever's ready." She's through the open door, Max following.

"But I'll see you later," he says, and she is already pushing the bike and trailer across the road. "Up at the cottage." She has no idea what he's on about.

In the village shop Jeanie concentrates on keeping the prices steady in her head, making them add up. They are low on lots of basics: toilet paper, flour, soap, bread, pasta, tea. Her periods haven't stopped yet and she needs tampons. The butter has gone off and there's no shampoo or dog food. The oil for the lamps is nearly finished, although she has found two boxes of candles under the sink. She hooks a wire basket over her arm and cruises the three narrow aisles. She has five pounds and fifty-five pence in her purse. A bottle of basic cooking oil is more expensive than a tub of margarine, although the latter will do for both frying and sandwiches, but how long will it last without a fridge, and it's only worth buying if she can also afford a loaf of bread. The tins of dog food are beyond her budget so she decides on a container of Bisto gravy granules — she can make some up and mix them with cooked vegetables and an egg for Maude. She and Julius can eat this dinner too. She recognizes the Bisto packaging, but there are two sorts: red and orange. She runs her finger under the word on the orange container, sounding out the letters at the start: *ch.* Chicken. The beef flavour is likely to upset Maude's stomach less, but the chicken variety seems to have extra included, and is cheaper. Jeanie puts the chicken Bisto in her basket. She can't decide between a packet of four toilet rolls and a bottle of washing-up liquid which would also do for soap, clothes washing, and maybe even shampoo. There is a stack of old newspapers in the dairy they can use for toilet paper if they must; she selects the washing-up liquid. A loaf of bread and a single pint of milk, and she's reached her limit. With longing, she walks past the aisle stocked with bars of chocolate, trying not to breathe in. At the till she prays she has added up the price of her five items correctly. The total comes to five pounds and thirty-five pence.

Beside the door on her way out she sees a large box with a sign above it, full of random produce: dried pasta, tins of beans, a box of tampons on top. She walks past this too.

11

Bridget and Stu arrive first at the cottage with two large carrier bags of food and a crate of beer. Julius tries not to think about how much Stu will charge for the bottles of IPA. He has changed into a clean shirt and an old jacket which had belonged to his father but sees brown crusts of soil under his fingernails. Bridget hugs him and when she lets him go, she has tears in her eyes.

"How was it?" she says. "I wish you'd let me come." She flaps her hand at herself, wipes her cheeks, and gives half a laugh.

"It was fine," he says, and when she seems to want more, he adds, "Nice."

"A cremation?"

"No," he says, and then thinking that she'll ask where Dot is buried, immediately says, "Yes." He pulls the corners of his mouth down. "Sorry, it's been a long day."

"I expect you don't know if you're coming or going." She puts the carriers on the table. "I know, I know, you didn't want me to bring much, but . . ." She shrugs and takes out a plate of sandwiches covered in cling film and unwraps them, as well as three large pork pies. "Where's Jeanie?" Bridget slices the pies and puts the food out on the table. Stu has gone back to the van for more beer.

"She went to deliver some vegetables to Max," Julius says.

Bridget stops in the middle of sliding a quiche lorraine out of its packet. "You didn't tell her, did you?" He looks away. "Oh, Julius. She's not going to be in the village for long, surely? She's going to come back and find her house full of people."

Did they have a wake for their father? Julius can't remember, but as Bridget is laying out slices of buttered malt loaf he remembers Frank's birthday cake: badly iced in pink by Jeanie. Julius had piped a blue *Happy Birthday Dad* in barely readable script on the top. The cake sat beside the sink in the scullery for more than three weeks after their father died. None of them ate it and none of them could throw it away. The icing hardened and crazed like the frozen puddles Julius liked to break with the heel of his shoe in winter. The cake grew a grey speckled rash and a sage-green moss sprouted from the cracks. Bridget took the cake away in the end while their mother had sat in a dull, unseeing silence at the kitchen table.

"Jeanie wouldn't have let me have a wake," Julius says to Bridget. "She was dead set against it."

Luke Emerson, the roofer from East Grafton, Richard Letford, who sometimes hires Julius when he needs an extra hand with fitting a kitchen, and Jenks arrive at the same time. They gather beside the beer and hem Julius in, between the dresser and the table.

"She was a fine woman all right," Luke says as though continuing a conversation. Bottles of beer are handed round. Jenks, his cigarette in his mouth, shakes Julius's hand. "I appreciate the invitation," he says. Julius isn't certain that he did invite Jenks, or that Jenks ever met Dot. "I remember your mum," he says, and seems to be thinking about what should come next. Julius tries to pull his hand away but Jenks grips it tighter and shakes it some more. "Vegetables," he says, and lets go. "Carrots," he says, removing his cigarette and taking a swig of his beer. "Those posh ones with the leaves on. Don't know why, it's more work, slicing them off. Should be cheaper."

"And beetroots," Luke says.

Jenks swings round. "Potatoes with mud all over them, like a muddy spud is supposed to be better for you."

"Can't go wrong with a few brussels sprouts," Richard says.

"On the stalk though," Jenks says. "What's that about?"

Julius leans in towards Richard and asks, "Got any work coming up? I'm a bit short at the moment."

"Sorry, mate," Richard says. "It's all pretty quiet. No one's booking any big projects."

"Me neither," Luke says. "Too bloody quiet. It's those Eastern Europeans, working for peanuts."

"Sooner we're out of there, the better," Richard says.

As the conversation moves on, Julius looks behind him and sees that the room has filled with a dozen people. Through the mass of bodies, he spies Shelley Swift in profile beside the door to the left staircase, talking to the man who sets up the stalls at the Tuesday market. She has had her hair cut, and whereas the rest of her skin that he's already seen — her face and shoulders, cleavage, arms, hands, and legs from the knees down — is a reddish colour, the back of her neck is a milky white. He remembers the feel of her tongue on his lips, the smell of her lemon soap, although it has gone from his fingers.

As though she knows he's watching, Shelley Swift turns and smiles straight at him, takes a sip from her glass, and turns back to the market stall man. Julius is suddenly parched and he tips up his bottle, finishing his beer. Jenks hands him another and Julius edges between the people and the rising volume towards Shelley Swift.

"I'm so sorry about Dot." Julius frowns at the woman with her hand on his arm, trying to bring her name to mind. He knows she runs the B&B in the village.

"Kate Gill," she says.

"Kate," he says, embarrassed that he forgot, although delivering the eggs had been Dot and Jeanie's job. Bridget must have told her about the wake. Kate is saying something and he refocuses his attention.

"Will Jeanie look after them on her own now?"

"Look after who?" Julius says.

"The chickens. Only it'll be a lot of work, won't it? The size of the garden — Dot showed me round it once. I suppose you'll be able to help."

Julius stares at his bottle of beer and sees that it's already empty. "Can I get you another drink?" he asks and takes her glass before she can reply. He slips away just as Stu comes up. Julius opens another bottle and moves counterclockwise around the table, heading once more for Shelley Swift. Bridget intercepts him.

"This is Dr. Holloway," she says, introducing a large man. They shake hands.

"How was the service?" the doctor asks. Julius knows he should have prepared himself for this question — everyone is going to ask it.

"Fine, fine," he says. He looks at his hands, picks a rind out from under a nail. "It was simple. Nice. Nice and simple."

"Just the two of you, was it, Julius?" Bridget says, and he wonders if she's only upset that she wasn't invited or whether she suspects something.

"Julius," the doctor says. "Julius Seeder!" He laughs, deep and booming. "I get it now."

"Wasn't that down to Frank?" Bridget says. "Dot told me that he thought your name sounded grand, important, and neither of them realized what they'd done until you were five and started school."

Julius no longer minds about his name. In the playground, as soon as he'd learned to punch, no one teased him much about it.

"In the end, it is impossible not to become

what others believe you are," Dr. Holloway says.

Julius is only half listening, one eye and one ear on the corner of the room between the sofa and the left staircase.

"Something Julius Caesar said. I find the words truer the older I get." There is a gap in the conversation and then the doctor says, "How's your sister doing? Is she about?"

"Excuse me," Julius says. "Just got to . . ." He points vaguely across the room and inches himself past the doctor and Bridget, knocking the plate of malt loaf with his hip.

"Careful there," says a man coming the other way, catching the plate before it falls. It's the bloke who sets up the market stalls. Julius tries to see who Shelley Swift is talking to now.

"Do you know the thing I always remember about your mum?" the man says.

Julius shakes his head. He can't remember this man's name either.

"In winter, on those mornings when it's cold enough to freeze your bloody bollocks off, so cold that if you've got damp fingers, they'll stick to the metal poles, Dot would arrive with a couple of hard-boiled eggs in her coat pockets. She gave me them, once. Hot. Said they'd keep my hands warm and give me something to eat later. That's a woman with her head screwed on right, I thought. A sensible woman. A good woman."

What will they say about him when he's gone? Julius wonders. Lived with his mother, and then his sister. Worked hard, but never made enough money. Never did anything with his life. Never went anywhere. Engines made him throw up. His thoughts drift away from the conversation and then Shelley Swift is beside him. She's wearing a dress that his mother would have said was too low-cut for a wake, curving around her body. Christ, what does it matter what his mother would have thought? She is in the ground, under the apple tree. What would they say if they knew? He almost laughs. He feels light-headed, on his way to being drunk but at that easy, slack stage. He bends towards Shelley Swift, looking at her tremendous breasts swelling at the top of her dress, and inhales the smell of her lemon soap.

"Thanks for coming," he says, and she smiles up at him. "You're right. She was," he says to the man who puts up the market stalls.

Jeanie is past the farmhouse, cycling faster

135

than she knows she should, the trailer rattling along behind. Anything could happen: she could fly over the handlebars or the animal in her heart might burst out, but right now she doesn't give a monkey's. If Rawson or his wife appeared, she would run them both down and not stop. Past the large barn, across the concrete slabs and the bumps where they were poured and joined, she turns the bend onto the track, where she sees the first parked car, and then another and another, pulled up in a row along the verge. Half a dozen or more. Stu's van is there but she doesn't recognize any of the others — she never remembers cars, they are only ever silver or black or some different colour. Immediately she knows that Julius has invited people over while she was out of the way. The track is too narrow now to stay on the bike with the trailer joggling along behind. She gets off and pushes. At the front gate she sees a few people moving about in the kitchen, their bodies cut off below the thighs and their heads and shoulders vanished because of the low window. She won't go in, instead she storms around the back of the cottage, up the garden where Maude has been put, and into the greenhouse.

In the warm, scented air she scoops compost into a dozen clay pots, the soil running between her fingers, much looser than the clotted pile of earth she stood beside a few hours before. Did Julius finish filling in the grave before he was stupid enough to let these people into their house? She dibs a hole in the compost, turns a young tomato plant out into her palm, and buries its roots in the earth. Like cooking, it is a job she did beside her mother for nearly fifty years, and now the lack of her, the empty space, is tangible: the way Dot shifted from one hip to the other when she had to stand for long periods, how she flicked her head when her hair fell in her eyes, the way she would catch a bee in her cupped hands without being stung.

The greenhouse is the place where mother and daughter talked or were contentedly silent. It is the place where they stood side by side while Dot explained things when Jeanie was young. It is here that Dot taught her how to listen to her own heartbeat, how to take her pulse with her fingers on her throat or wrist, to breathe slowly.

Now, Jeanie works angrily, potting on the tomatoes, shoving the delicate roots too hard into the soil, knowing they will grow crooked, and not caring. Pot after pot she rushes until she picks one up, ready to hurl it through a pane of glass, but with her arm raised, she hears a bray of voices as someone opens the back door of the cottage and goes into the privy. She puts the pot down. She lifts her head, listening, wondering if she can simply walk out of the garden, down the lane, and disappear. Then she wipes her earth-blackened fingers on her skirt, leaves the greenhouse, and goes into the cottage.

Through the scullery, she slips into the dark end of the kitchen, letting Maude in with her. The dog looks at the people, turns around, and slinks out. The room is more crowded than Jeanie anticipated: a dozen or so people crammed in around the kitchen table and sitting on the sofa, the buzz of multiple conversations, the haze of cigarette smoke turned orange by the oil lamps; the oil they can't afford to waste. No one was allowed to smoke in the house when Dot was alive.

In the gaps between the bodies she sees the bottles of beer on the dresser, as well as a half-empty bottle of port, and when she sees the label, she realizes that someone must have taken it out of her own dresser. On the table are plates of food — Bridget's involvement she presumes. There is the big brown teapot they never use, and on the end closest to her, the remains of the rabbit pie. Maybe, with any luck, it will make someone ill — it was baked three days ago and hasn't been refrigerated. She wants to shout for them to leave, to drive them out like cattle. She wants only the fire, the dog, and her brother. The packed room and the people are overwhelming; sweat prickles her hairline. Bridget is talking to Kate, and Jeanie tries to hear what they are saying, thinks it might be something about fifty-one-year-olds still living with their mother, until recently, of course; never having a proper job; never learning to read or write as well as everyone else. But it is something about life being too short and how you should accept love from wherever you can find it, no matter what other people think. Jeanie watches the doctor, standing with Max and eating a piece of pork pie. A crumb falls onto his lapel and then to the floor.

Julius is in the corner by the left staircase, a cigarette between his fingers, talking to a woman with her back to Jeanie, and it takes her a moment to recognize Shelley Swift with a new haircut, showing her thick neck and chunky shoulders, done up like she's at a wedding, not a wake. Nobody notices Jeanie as she edges forwards, ready to bolt, like the dog. She grabs for her guitar and sits on the piano stool, bending her head over the strings so that no one will speak to her, and she tunes it. It's only Julius she's calling to. When she looks up, his hand is on Shelley Swift's arm. Someone, Stu, gives him a glass, and he takes a swig, grimaces. They don't usually drink alcohol at home, only on birthdays and Christmas and then just a drop of port, although she knows Julius goes to the pub, but he has never come home drunk. She plucks harder at the guitar to make him look over.

"We roamed through the garden, down the green avenue," she sings quietly. Bridget and Kate stop talking and see her, and Jeanie lets the room and the people go out of focus. *"Felt the ground start to harden, saw the sky turn its blue."* The knots of people nearest to her also stop talking and look around, shuffling backwards to give her some space. And then she is aware of Julius beside her, his fiddle under his chin. His notes carry further than hers, and the people nearest the front door quieten. She and Julius sing:

"Like a morning bird's song
Or a light summer's rain
Like a place to belong

140

That you cannot sustain
Do you know? Where, then we'll go."

When they finish the song there is a collective sigh and Jeanie imagines the breaths of the people, some of whom she knows have come only for the beer and the food, rising above their heads and mingling with her mother's last breath, settling around the beams and into the cracks in the wood and plaster so that a part of them, like a part of Dot, will remain.

They start another song and Julius's playing is looser than usual, less controlled, and his head movements more pronounced, like one of those nodding toys on a car's dashboard. Jeanie hears their mother's banjo like a vacancy in the music; the sparring and the blending between the three instruments is missing, her voice absent. Perhaps this is how it happens: eventually, after every activity has been carried out at least once without Dot's presence — the potting on of tomatoes, the making of a rabbit pie, the playing of each song — Jeanie will no longer notice that her mother is gone. She isn't sure this is what she wants.

Julius untucks his fiddle and drinks from a glass he's put on top of the piano. Jeanie smells whisky.

"One more!" someone calls.

"Play us another, love," says a man with bleary eyes and a Scottish accent. He leans so far towards her she thinks he might topple. She glances at Julius, who shrugs and plays a long trembling note, teasing her so that she can't guess what song it will be until he lets it roll gracefully down into "Polly Vaughn" — a peace offering, perhaps, for arranging the wake.

"I shall tell of a hunter whose life was undone," Jeanie sings. Her voice is smoky and melancholic.

> "By the cruel hand of evil at the setting of
>   the sun
> His arrow was loosed and it flew through
>   the dark
> His true love was slain as its shaft found
>   its mark."

And in harmony, Julius joins in, his words running together:

> "She'd her apron wrapped about her and
>   he took her for a swan
> And it's so and alas, it was she, Polly
>   Vaughn."

Jeanie puts her guitar in the corner behind her and, as she turns to the room, through a brief gap between the people she sees someone beside the window, head bent below the ceiling, the dull afternoon light catching the side of his face, his body drooping as though the air inside him has been released. Rawson, she thinks. The people shift and her sight of him is lost, and when they move again a different man is there — one of Julius's friends — not Rawson at all. Then Dr. Holloway is in front of her, saying, "Have you and your brother ever performed in public?" His voice is loud and a couple of people glance over.

"In public?" Jeanie says.

"You know. A gig."

"We never play outside the house."

"But you must, you really must. You're both terribly good. Your mother told me she played too."

Someone chimes a piece of cutlery against a glass, the room quietens and Jeanie sees Julius across the length of the table, glass and fork in hand. When the room is silent, he lifts his head, swaying slightly and steadying himself on the back of a chair.

"I wanted to say thank you." His words are slurred, and he struggles to find them. "First off, to Bridget and Stu for helping to organize this little get-together. For the food and for the beer!" He swings his bottle and

143

some beer foams over the lip. The people in the room raise their glasses and bottles, and drink. "My mother, Dot Seeder, was a good woman, a good and loving mother to me and to Jeanie, over there." He gestures with his bottle towards her and she shrinks back as people turn to look. "There was always home-cooked food on the table and the fire to keep us warm. She was a hard worker and a loving mother." Jeanie can't help but roll her eyes and when he comes to a stop she wonders if that is it, is that all there is to say about Dot? "When my sister Jeanie and I were twelve we were up in Priest's Field . . ."

You can't tell them this, Jeanie thinks. This thing is theirs alone.

"When my sister Jeanie and I were twelve, our father was murdered —" Julius's voice cracks. He trails off, swaying where he stands, his chin trembling and tears falling. "Murdered, in a bloody field," he says, barely lifting his head.

They've never shared what they saw with anyone and it has tied them together for thirty-nine years, and now with a little drink in him and their mother dead, Julius is prepared to share it with anyone who will listen. She is disgusted.

A man who might have been a friend of

their father's, although he looks much older than Jeanie remembers, pats Julius on the back and steers him towards a chair. Her brother resists, rolling his shoulder to remove the man's hand.

Jeanie sees something glint under the kitchen table. She gets down on her hands and knees and, ignoring the questions from Bridget and the looks from Kate, crawls underneath. Julius is still speaking, but other people are trying to hush him now. Lying on the stone floor amongst the crumbs and dust that she hasn't had the inclination to sweep up since their mother died is the missing poker. She picks it up and shuffles out backwards, and before she can hear any more of what Julius is saying she is out through the scullery and up the garden with Maude to the strip of bare soil. Where a gravestone might have stood, were they ever able to afford one, she stabs the poker into the ground. A late afternoon sun that is pushing through the cloud stretches the shadow of the poker across the earth, slicing the grave in two. "Where did you put the money, Mum?" Jeanie says out loud and Maude looks up at her. She goes with the dog to the greenhouse and sees the chaos she made of the tomato plants, compost, and pots. They will have to be done again.

She turns a wooden crate upside down for somewhere to sit and sees that fallen behind it are her mother's gardening gloves, which she misplaced months ago. The leather is dirty and stiff, and the stubby fingers are slightly curled and set into the shape of Dot's hands. Jeanie slips her fingers into where her mother's had been and lowers her face into the palms and cries, racking sobs which heave her body and make Maude nuzzle against her in confusion. The gloves become wet and the dirt smears across Jeanie's forehead, and she weeps until her nose is full, her eyes puff up, and she hears the people leave.

12

The day after the wake Julius stays in bed all day and Jeanie doesn't go up to his room, angry with him for adding to what they owe Stu, for drinking, for letting those people into the cottage, and for saying what had happened in Priest's Field. She hopes he didn't manage to finish the story. When he finally makes it downstairs, instead of picking up their instruments and playing as they would have done in the past, they talk about the agreement. Julius says that out of principle he won't do any more jobs for Rawson, even though the few he was given were organized through the farm manager, Simons. Jeanie, holding tight to her opinion, had hoped that any work he did on the farm might have reduced what the Rawsons said they owed — if it was owed at all. Again, they return to the questions: How could money be due on a cottage that was rent-free? If the money Dot borrowed from Stu was to pay the Rawsons, why didn't she hand it over? And where is it? They don't have any answers. They rarely discussed money in the past and it comes awkwardly now, and they never talked in any depth about the agreement, they know it simply as an arrangement that was negotiated between Dot and Rawson a year after their father's death — an event that was only ever alluded to, all of them orbiting an incident so horrific they were unable to shift themselves closer.

Frank died the day before he turned thirty-two. Now, Jeanie is amazed at how young he was, how much life was before him, but when she was twelve, she thought her father ancient, and wise. She hadn't yet reached the stage where she might have challenged him or grown irritated by his views and sloppy ways. Every day of the months leading up to the harvest that year — 1980 — was full of chatter about the imminent arrival of Rawson's new tractor. It was all Frank and Julius talked about at the tea table. The old one was temperamental and liked to stop in the middle of a field and would start only when Frank had spent an hour or two tinkering with it. The new Massey Ferguson was delivered too late to pull the trailers for the harvest, but it arrived soon after, together with a new plough.

Jeanie didn't remember the tractor and plough being delivered, but she was left with an impression of them both: the top of the back tyres with their raised treads higher than her head, the shiny red body, the black vinyl seat with its wrap-around arms, and the sharp shine on the blades of the plough. Frank and Julius took turns sitting on the tractor seat, and Rawson started it up for them to admire. There was a day's delay, some problem with hitching the new plough to the tractor, but finally it was ready to go out.

They — Frank, Julius, and Jeanie — were up in Priest's Field ploughing the first line of furrows. Frank said that ploughing wasn't girls' work, but he let Jeanie come with them, telling her that she wouldn't be allowed on the tractor. She walked in the long grass at the edge of the field, arms crossed, furious that she could only watch while Julius sat between their father's legs, his hands on the steering wheel, whooping with pleasure. She kept up with them for a while, trailing alongside, seeing the plough's blades slice and turn the sod. The smell of new earth had a sweet dread for her in those days: the end of the summer and the start of the school year. Soon she became bored

— it was hot out in the field that September and she hated the stink of the exhaust, the unending din of the engine — and she let the tractor, with her father and brother on it, lumber on ahead. She sat and watched a hoverfly dance around some teasel heads. The tractor's hoarse rattle reached the end of the field. She was drowsy and thinking about lying down when there was a bang, the burst of an explosion moving past her, immediately followed by the engine screaming. When she stood and shaded her eyes, she couldn't see the tractor, but the screaming didn't stop and as she began to run, the noise, continuous and high-pitched, was worse even than when one of Rawson's horses kicked a farm dog and sent it flying. The screaming was no longer machine, but human.

She slowed when she saw the tractor tipped on its side, the engine still running but the plough somehow unhitched and underneath. It was Julius who was screaming, thrown so hard into the hedge that the hawthorns had him pinned there.

"Where's Dad?" she shouted.

Her brother struggled and twisted, the thorns catching his skin and clothes. "Don't look, don't look!"

Jeanie saw her father's hand, his arm

150

trapped beneath a wheel. She recognized the long, piano player's fingers, the pared nails. "Dad?" she called. In the hedge Julius struggled more and shouted at her to keep away, to go and fetch someone. But Jeanie crouched and saw the top of her father's arm, saw the white of his shirt streaked with the mud of the field, and a crimson flower blooming. She called for him again. She couldn't make sense of the mess of tractor, man, and plough until she noticed the buttons up the front of his shirt, his shoulders and his neck, but this ending, bloody, as though he had pushed his head deep into the ground. And then she saw and understood. She put her hands to her eyes and finally Julius was quiet and still.

For Julius that moment was all sound and light: the tractor or Jeanie screaming, the sun so bright it hurt his eyes, burned his face, seared the image in his mind. The image is in a box he rarely opens. The memory that has stayed with him most is from a time after the accident. It might have been days later, except that the wheat was halfway grown and the hawthorn was again full of petals, and by then there must have been police, an ambulance, a health and safety investigation of the farm, a delayed funeral, an inquest: accidental death. This day too was hot, and Dot took him and his sister to Priest's Field, to the spot where their father died. At school he had earned some awed respect for using the word *decapitated* without flinching. He said it so often it lost its meaning.

That afternoon he was bored. His mother and sister — recently diagnosed with a heart condition — sat on a blanket with a flask of tea and slices of cake in a tin. Jeanie picked a bunch of red campion to lay on the spot where Frank died but Julius thought this was a stupid idea: the grass they were sitting on was full of the stuff. He wouldn't sit with them, instead he tramped up and down between the lines of wheat, the sun burning the back of his neck. Every now and then he picked up a broken flint, testing the sharpness of its edge against his thumb. His mother called that they were leaving, and then he saw an object glint in the dry soil. When he bent over it, he realized it was, or had been, a large bolt, its nut gone and the metal shining where it had been bent out of shape by some terrific force. He imagined it might be a meteorite or, better, part of an alien spaceship which crash-landed and the authorities hushed up. If he dug down far enough, he might find the spaceship itself buried in the earth and he could bring his friends from school to the field and charge them fifty pence each to take a look.

"What have you got there?" his mother asked, and he went to hold out his hand to her and Jeanie, proud of his find. His sister exclaimed over it, as excited as he was, but their mother said, "Dirty rubbish," and snatched the bolt from him.

Sometime after that, at about the anniversary of Frank's death, Dot told him and Jeanie that the tractor and the plough were delivered without hitch pins — the pieces of metal that couple the tractor safely to the plough — or else they were lost, and new ones had been made from nuts and bolts. She told the story in such a roundabout way, while refusing to answer questions, that the twins were never clear about the details. But three times Rawson came to the cottage late at night after Jeanie and Julius were supposed to be asleep. On the first night when Julius heard Rawson's voice, he crept downstairs and tried to listen to the conversation through the parlour door. On the second and third nights, Jeanie also listened, sitting on the left-hand stairs. In the morning on their way to school they discussed the snippets of talk they'd overheard, finishing each other's sentences, piecing the events together: the year before,

Rawson, excited to get his new tractor and plough but frustrated about the missing pieces, had fashioned them out of bolts; something homemade and so unsafe, the nuts had been sheared off with the consequences that neither Jeanie nor Julius could now unsee. They talked until they decided that Rawson must know he was guilty — of manslaughter, of murder — and out of shame and remorse, or terror that Dot would finally tell the police what he'd done, he consented to the agreement and they were allowed to stay on in the cottage, rent-free. They never saw Rawson visit their mother again.

Jeanie is in the garden digging up baby carrots. Max says that his customers like them finger-sized, which Jeanie thinks is a waste of bed space and growing time. When she stands, back aching, she sees someone in the scullery. Since Dot died, she has tried to remember to lock the front door when she is up the garden, but sometimes she forgets. This person isn't Julius — he has gone to Wheilden Farm to help take down a chicken shed. She bends to get a better look and see whether it's Stu or, God forbid, one of the Rawsons. She imagines using the garden fork to pin them to the cottage wall,

154

the tines piercing lime render, wattle and daub.

The figure — she can see only the torso through the low cottage window — seems to be moving back and forth as though examining items in the scullery. She takes the garden fork with her, prongs forwards, and goes in through the open back door. The person has gone from the scullery and when she gets to the kitchen, a young man is peering up the left staircase.

"Can I help you?" Jeanie says in a tone that she hopes will suggest outrage but not fear. The man jumps and turns at her voice, and then takes a step back when he sees the fork pointed at him. It is the same young man whom Bridget cuffed in the waiting room of the surgery a week or so ago. He is wearing different clothes now: a cheap suit, the material shiny and too tight for his muscled frame.

"Jeanie?" he says, and smiles, and she realizes that it's Bridget and Stu's son, fully grown, his blondish hair gelled sideways and upwards as though a wind is coming at him from the bottom left. The shape of his head, his chin, his cheekbones, make him surprisingly handsome. Did Stu look like this when he was younger? She can't imagine it. She remembers that there was some trouble with drinking on the village green late at night, making a nuisance of himself at home, and Stu kicked him out. Jeanie hasn't seen him for years.

"Nathan." She lowers the garden fork. "What are you doing here?"

"Is your brother home?" He licks his full lips.

"No," Jeanie says, although as soon as the word is out, she thinks she should have pretended Julius was ill in bed or up the garden. There's something about Nathan and his veneer of confidence that makes her uncomfortable. "Can I help?"

He hesitates and then says, "I've come to give you a warning of eviction."

"Pardon me?"

Nathan leans against the dresser. "You're going to be evicted." His smile becomes a grimace with the effort of keeping it going.

She almost laughs. "Don't be ridiculous."

"I have to put the notice on the front door on Monday, and then you'll have a week."

"A week? A week for what?" Jeanie's voice is rising. She still has hold of the fork and her hands grip it tighter.

"To get out." Nathan crosses one ankle over the other. Now that he's said what he came here to say, he seems to relax.

"We have an agreement with Rawson that

we can stay. This is crazy. This is our house. And if he or his wife thinks some money is owing, they have to give us some bloody time to pay it back." She thinks that she or Julius should have tried to go and see Rawson. Sorted this problem out.

Nathan stands upright and goes past her with a practised swagger and puts a hand on the top of Dot's banjo case. "I was sent to tell you about the eviction notice. Give you some warning. I don't know nothing about any agreement or payback times."

"Is this your job now, working for Rawson? Does your mother know what you're up to?" Jeanie leans the fork against the table and lifts the banjo case out from under his hand and hugs it, an urge to fight firing through her like electric sparks.

He doesn't answer but picks up a framed photograph of Jeanie and Julius as babies lying at either end of a pram. He turns it over, examines the back and the frame as if assessing its value, before replacing it on the dresser.

"He's not a man of his word and you ought to be careful, Nathan, doing his dirty work. I have to get on." She is shaking inside but she holds one arm out, inviting Nathan to leave.

"Monday," he throws over his shoulder

157

once he's on the doorstep. "I'll be back on Monday with the notice."

From the doorway she watches him walk down the path, a loose-jointed amble, aware, she thinks, that she's watching. When he gets to the gate, she shouts, "This is our house. It will be our house until we're carried out in our coffins. You can tell Rawson that." She slams the door and rests a palm against it, controlling her breathing, slowing her pulse.

When she tells Julius about Nathan's visit, he rages around the kitchen, like he raged when she told him about Caroline Rawson coming over. He shouts that he'll go to Bridget's and demand that she and Stu control their son, or he'll go and see Rawson and give him a mouthful. She lets his anger roll over her, agreeing, commiserating, calming. She can't see that either of these plans will do any good in the state that Julius is in. And the sum of money that the Rawsons say they owe — the size of it — is so far beyond the pence and pounds Jeanie's used to dealing with that it seems fanciful, made up. They could owe two million and it would be the same. But every night she can't sleep, and tonight, during their dinner of spaghetti mixed with a tin of condensed mushroom soup and whatever vegetables there are to hand, Jeanie twirls the pasta on her fork and doesn't ever bring it to her mouth.

Jeanie has twenty pence remaining from the money she spent at the shop. Julius adds the change from his pockets and the thirty pounds from his wallet that he was given for helping with the chicken shed. There is nothing to add from Dot's purse, they've already searched it and her handbag for the missing money.

"I heard there's a food bank in Devizes," Julius says without looking at her.

"We're not going to a food bank, Julius. We have a whole garden full of food." She points outside and doesn't tell him about the box she saw in the shop.

"When are you going to realize that there's nothing wrong with asking for help, or taking it when it's given? All those middle-class kids who can just ask the bank of mum and dad when they need some help. This isn't any different."

"But we aren't kids any more."

"No, we're fifty-one and we need a hand. It doesn't mean there's something wrong with us."

"Anyway," Jeanie says, "who have you been telling that we're short of food?"

Julius shakes his head, doesn't answer. "I

159

asked Wheilden if he's got any more work, but he doesn't."

"I'm sure not everyone has paid you what they owe." Jeanie means Shelley Swift, but she isn't going to say the name. "You need to ask for it."

"I will."

"When?"

"When you stop acting like my mother and telling me what to do."

"What about money for your tobacco? I suppose you kept some back for that and for your pints with your drinking mates in the Plough."

"And you're not going to spend anything on that bloody dog?"

Maude, on the sofa, lifts her head as though she knows she's being talked about.

"I don't think you understand. We're going to lose the cottage." Jeanie puts her palms on the table. The creature is in her throat. If she opens her mouth wide enough and screams, it will come sliding out, newborn and slippery, ready to fight.

"I understand! I bloody understand." He shoves the edge of the table towards her and she moves back from it. "We don't owe any money to Rawson, and he can't evict us. I'm going round there. I'm going round there right now."

"Now? It's after ten." In the mood Julius is in, she's worried he might make the whole situation worse.

"Now." He pulls his coat and cap from the peg, jams his feet into his boots, and grabs the thirty pounds from the table. For a second he looks at the money; then he slaps down a ten-pound note and leaves before Maude is even off the sofa.

For five minutes Jeanie sits at the table and then, in an act of economy which gives her a momentary boost, she extinguishes the three oil lamps and, lighting a candle, resumes her search of the cottage for the missing money.

In half an hour Julius returns. Jeanie is on her knees putting rarely used crockery back into a dresser cupboard. "Well?" she says.

"They weren't there." He sits heavily on the sofa next to the dog. "No lights on, nothing. I went and woke Simons. He wasn't too happy. He said they've gone away. Ten days, two weeks, he wasn't sure. Greece or somewhere. They don't even need our money."

In the morning Jeanie spends nine pounds fifty-seven in the shop, buying most of the necessities she couldn't afford on Monday: more pasta, toilet rolls, tins of baked beans, toothpaste. Outside she stares at the few handwritten advertisements slotted into a plastic sleeve hanging on the inside of the window, trying to puzzle them out. In the shop, a young man with acne peppered across his forehead is placing glossy magazines along the shelves.

"I was told there was a card in the window advertising for a cleaner," Jeanie says to him, waving her hand vaguely towards the front of the shop. "But I couldn't see it."

"Probably thrown away," he says, carrying on with his work. "They're only up for a couple of weeks."

"My friend said there was definitely one there about a cleaning job."

The man huffs and, holding his stack of magazines to his chest, goes outside and Jeanie follows. He scans the cards. "Nope, must have been chucked out." He starts to go back inside.

"Is there one about gardening?" Jeanie leans in and squints. "Did you write these? The handwriting is shocking."

He comes back and looks over them again, taps the glass. "That's it." He reads it without enthusiasm: "Female gardener required by female householder, for lawn mowing and other basic gardening. One to two afternoons a week."

"Have you got a pen?" She feels around in her handbag.

"Take a picture on your phone," he says.

"Maybe you could write the phone number down for me?" She knows there's no pen in her handbag, what would be the point, and besides, the numbers won't stop jumping. The young man has already gone in. After a moment she follows him and pretends to browse the newspapers on a stand beside the window. When his back is turned, she reaches over and takes the card out of the plastic pocket and slips it into her handbag.

13

On her way home, Jeanie takes a detour up Cutter Hill. She gets off the bike and wheels it slowly, aware of the speed of her heart; making sure she pauses when she thinks she needs to. It's a couple of miles out of her way, but just as she remembers, the red public telephone box is outside the Rising Sun Inn, which last closed its doors two years ago. As a young child, when she was off school, she would have to come with her mother to this phone box which smelled of wee and old cigarette breath. Dot brought a little bag of twopence pieces and used them to make boring telephone calls about bills and appointments, sometimes lifting Jeanie up so she could press the coins into the slot. The calls seemed to last for ever and most of the time Jeanie squatted beside her mother's legs, blowing hot air onto a glass panel and drawing pictures of animals in the condensation. After her mother finished these calls, she usually had a conversation with someone called Sissy, which Jeanie thought was a funny name. There was one conversation with Sissy which she remembers even now, where her mother said, "I can't," again and again, and Jeanie drew her own *I can't, I can't* onto the glass as little crosses. "Because of the children, because where would we go, because how would we manage? Because he's a good man, because I took a vow. That means something, doesn't it?" Her mother sounded like she was going to cry, and mothers didn't cry. "There's nothing to tell you," she said. "Nothing's happened." Her mother listened to Sissy's reply and got out her handkerchief. "I'm all right. I'll call another day. Jeanie's here, I've got to go." Jeanie stood up. Dot held out the phone. "Say goodbye to Sissy."

"Goodbye, Sissy," Jeanie whispered into the smelly mouthpiece, but the pips were already sounding.

As Jeanie rolls the bike up to the phone box, her shopping bags swinging from the handlebars, she can see that something inside is different and when she opens the door she discovers that the telephone is gone and the back wall where it once hung is filled with books. Fat, gaudy paperbacks with creased spines. More are piled up on the concrete floor, bulging pages where the damp has got in.

At home, she lifts Julius's mobile phone from his coat pocket when he isn't looking and takes it up to the end of the garden. It's charged, so she knows he must have been in the pub. Following the number on the card she has taken from the shop's window digit by digit, she pushes the buttons. She doesn't want to tell Julius what she's doing, not until she can say that she actually has a job.

The following day, Jeanie stands at an open five-bar gate, beyond which is an old car and an overgrown lawn with a crazy paving path snaking to the front door of a bungalow. Paint is peeling from the woodwork and last year's leaves are curled in the corner of the brown-tiled porch. The doorbell chime plays the start of "Twinkle, Twinkle, Little Star." The woman who comes to the door is wearing a flowered dress which reaches to her ankles, below which are flat sandals with leather bars over the big toes. She is younger than Jeanie expected, thirty maybe, with a jewel on the side of her nose that the sun catches, as though the woman were signalling.

"I recognize you," she says when she sees Jeanie at the edge of the porch. "You're one of the women who grow the vegetables. I work a few mornings in the deli." Her dress moves as though a draught were coming through the house, and a young child emerges from behind her skirt. With a jangle of bracelets, the woman holds out her hand to Jeanie. "I'm Saffron," she says, and Jeanie shakes it. "And this is Angel." She hoists the child onto her hip, rucking up the girl's oversize shirt, revealing chunky calves and thighs. Angel has yellow paint in her hair and on her fingers, and she smears it across Saffron's neck, which is pale against the child's hazelnut-brown skin. The woman leads Jeanie through the house, explaining how she bought the place six months ago with some money she was left by her father, who was an utter shit by the way, and how she thought she might knock it down and build something new but she's become attached to it in the couple of months she's been there. Jeanie remembers what Julius said about other people having the bank of mum and dad to fall back on. Saffron is still talking, explaining how Angel loves to run in a circle from one room to the next because each opens into another, and here's the central courtyard which she's thinking of glassing over. Without any embarrassment she says she wants to surround Angel with positive women, that's why she wants a female gardener. Jeanie isn't sure whether she should admit to not always feeling positive. They walk through the kitchen, the table cluttered with paints and paper.

Out through the french windows, Saffron puts Angel down — What names! Jeanie thinks — telling her that the garden feels like too much for her to tackle, she wouldn't know where to start. She lived in Oxford before Inkbourne and she's not yet sure about the country, but she wanted to be nearer her mother for Angel's sake. "Well, for babysitting opportunities, if I'm honest," she adds. "I'm doing a postgrad certificate in psychodynamic counselling at Oxford." Jeanie doesn't ask what this is; she's too afraid that she'll understand the explanation even less than the name of the thing. "It's a lot of work, much more than I expected, and it's hard to keep up with this one running around. It's just me and Angel. Me and her father, it was a one-off thing, you know. Never saw him again." Saffron laughs. All the information of her life spills so easily from her that Jeanie is both embarrassed and envious of her ability to be this unreserved. They stand on a patio made of concrete slabs and look down across the lawn. The grass has grown to full height, a stone birdbath in the middle has nearly disappeared, and overrun flower beds blend in on either side. The view takes Jeanie's eye past a mature tree to the far end of the garden and the fields beyond, and then upwards to a line of oaks on a low ridge in the distance. The shadows of the clouds move across the hillside and there isn't another house in sight. All is green and gold.

"It's beautiful, yeah?" Saffron says. "But what should I do? Have it mowed? It'll take for ever."

"No," Jeanie says. "Don't mow it, not all of it. Cut a winding path through the grass, plant some wildflowers, make some spaces around the trees where your daughter can play. A meadow."

"A meadow," Saffron says, and grabs Jeanie's arm with a tinkle of metal. "That's what this one was going to be called, weren't you, Angel?"

The child smiles up at them. "I had a banana," she says to Jeanie, and waits.

"Was it blue?" Jeanie says.

"Yellow, silly," Angel says, and runs off through the grass, shouting, "Banana, banana."

Saffron and Jeanie go as far as the tree, which Jeanie names as an Indian horse chestnut, and she gets the job. It's that simple, and she wonders why she has never thought to do this before. They agree on ten pounds an hour, two afternoons a week to begin with. Whichever days suit. There is a shed full of tools which were Saffron's father's, including a lawnmower and a can which they decide contains petrol when they sniff it. Jeanie asks if she can bring Maude but is too relieved to have got the job to dare to mention that she'd like to be paid in cash, and weekly. Back in the kitchen, Saffron makes tea and Jeanie sits with Angel, watching her paint a brown shape which looks like an apricot stone with lines coming off it, black splodges at one end that are too wet and run off the page when the child holds it out for her. "Is it a giant seed?" she asks. "A big brown eye with eyelashes?"

"Maur," Angel says, and shoves the painting at her.

"I think it's your dog," Saffron says, looking over.

When Jeanie gets home, she tapes Angel's painting to the kitchen wall and tells Julius that she has a job.

She is excited, amazed at what she has managed to do so easily, and although she knows that what she will be earning won't touch their debts, the idea of doing work other than looking after her own house and garden makes her feel like something inside her — as tiny as an onion seed — is splitting open, ready to send out its shoot. But Julius looks up from his plate of fried eggs and spinach, and says, "That's great." He is distracted, about the debts, the missing money, she presumes, and when he doesn't ask her any questions about what the job is or where, the seed shrivels, and Jeanie thinks that it is too late for both of them and for the cottage.

Still, the following afternoon, which is dry and windy, she cycles slowly to the bungalow with Maude running alongside. In the house, Jeanie introduces Angel to the dog and the child pats Maude so hard on her back that Saffron lifts Angel away, saying she must be more gentle, and the child cries and kicks her legs. Maude doesn't seem to mind being beaten by small hands, but Jeanie takes the dog outside where she sulks, lying on the patio with her head between her paws. Jeanie pulls the lawnmower out of the shed, careful to do it without exerting herself, and is surprised to see that it is fairly new; it starts first go. The shed is full of all the equipment she might ever need, and going through it, as well as being away from the cottage and Julius, are good distractions from her other thoughts: whether

171

Nathan was bluffing about the eviction, when Stu might ask for his money back, where her mother could have put the cash. Jeanie marks out the path with short lengths of wood which she cuts with a saw from the shed, and is excited to see the shape of it, winding down through the garden, taking the visitor on a tour of one flower bed and another, a tree, a cast-concrete urn she has found in the shrubbery.

Jeanie returns on Sunday afternoon, and when she has finished working, Saffron comes out with glasses of water, cups of tea, and a packet of chocolate biscuits. They sit on the patio — there's no table or chairs — and Angel approaches Maude again.

"Let her sniff your hand first," Saffron says. "Hold it out flat. Be gentle."

"She's a very mild-tempered dog," Jeanie says. "A bit of a coward, really." Maude licks Angel's hand, then her face, and Angel sits heavily on her backside, her chin crimping and her bottom lip rolling out. Before the wail starts, Saffron crawls on her hands and knees, bangles clinking, and nuzzles Angel's neck and then licks her face too, and Jeanie is reminded of the play fights she and Julius would have with their father, clinging on to his neck as he roared in mock anger. Angel laughs and the dog bounces off down the garden.

When they're sitting once more and Angel is focused on her chocolate biscuit, which is melting over her dimpled hands, Jeanie says, "I'll have to scythe the path first. The grass is too long to mow straight away."

"Is that a problem?"

"Just a bit more work." She thinks about the amount of physical exertion this will be and the possible consequences, and decides she no longer cares.

"Okay," Saffron says. "I guess you'd have to scythe the whole thing if I wanted it all mown."

"I thought I'd open it out a bit further down, have a circle of lawn that you can see from here so that Angel has somewhere to play."

"That would be lovely." Saffron takes Angel's wrist just before she places her hand on the ground and sucks the chocolate from each fat finger.

"Doggy," Angel says.

"I have your money." Saffron takes something from the pocket of her dress — the same dress she was wearing the day before and the day before that. "We didn't agree on how often I'd pay you, but is weekly okay? Ten hours this week, yeah? And you'll do the same next week?"

"I'm not sure which days though," Jeanie says.

"No problem. Whenever you like." She holds out the slip she's taken from her pocket — a piece of paper, not cash — and Jeanie accepts it and when she unfolds it, she sees that it is a cheque. Heat prickles the skin of her throat, and her heart begins its knocking. Perhaps it shows in her face, because Saffron says, "I can transfer the money next time. Email me your bank details and I'll send it across."

"No," Jeanie says. "Thanks, a cheque is fine."

After the wake, four days go by without Shelley Swift sending Julius a text or calling. Several times he picks up his phone and laboriously composes a message but deletes each one and puts his mobile away, feeling out of his depth, unconfident of her interest in him. There have been other women, but not for years. When Julius was in his twenties, the village hall held gigs for local bands, not his kind of music but he always went. Three summers in a row Julius slept with three different women when the gigs were over. Once in the back of an expensive car, another time on a mattress in the back of a van, and a third up against the wall behind the public toilets. He would have liked to give his number to each one of them, all interesting in different ways, but he had no number to give, and they never offered theirs. Older villagers complained about the gigs — the noise and the mess — and after the third summer there were no more bands, and no more women. Then when he was about to turn thirty-five, he met Amy. He liked her, could have fallen in love, and didn't mind when Jeanie teased him about settling down, moving out, how it was about time one of them did, and although it was banter between siblings, he knew without her saying that while she wanted him to go, she was afraid of being left with Dot, afraid she would never leave when he was gone. He didn't tell his mother about Amy, but it was Dot who casually mentioned one day that she'd seen her kissing some man outside the Plough. Julius didn't see Amy after that.

On Friday, another day without work, he goes out on his bike to Little Bedwyn, telling himself he'll knock on some doors to see if anyone he's worked for in the past needs anything doing. He hates drumming up jobs this way, the suspicion in people's faces, the thought that he must look desperate, like a beggar. He visits a farm he worked on a year ago, but the house has a *For Sale* sign outside, and instead he starts to cycle up the gravel drive of a country house where he once worked helping lay the concrete floors in the garages. They were in the middle of the work when the owner of the house appeared, an old man with a walking stick and a yellow Labrador, and said there was a telephone call for him. They all stopped — Julius and the two men he was working with. "For me?" he said, and his boss frowned, but the old man had already started hobbling back to the house and Julius followed. Someone must be dead, he thought, his mother or his sister, and he wanted the old man to walk faster. He can't remember now much about the inside of the place except that the hall was huge, with an enormous glittering chandelier. When he picked up the phone, he heard the pips and the chank of coins being pushed into the slot, and his mother was on the other end.

"It's Jeanie," she said in a shaky voice.

"Is she okay? What's happened?"

"I'm worried about her. Her heart."

"Why are you phoning me?" he shouted. "Call an ambulance, for God's sake."

"I just need you to come home."

When he got back, Jeanie was fine, of

course, or as fine as she ever was. It was his mother he worried about then.

Before he gets to the house's front door, Julius turns in a big loop and cycles back the way he's come. After that, he calls on a couple of other likely-looking farms but doesn't pick up any work. When it's five thirty he slowly rides a route which will take him past the brickworks. He hasn't much hope of bumping into Shelley Swift, and when he sees a red Nissan coming towards him, he doesn't really think it can be her. He raises his hand, unable to see clearly through the windscreen. He stops as soon as the car passes and when he looks back, the car has also stopped and reverses quickly up the road towards him with a whine. Shelley Swift lowers her window and although Julius's timing couldn't be better, he hasn't considered anything beyond seeing her and can only stare at her face and her arm resting on the door, all of which are covered in a fine film of brick dust.

"Is your boiler heating up okay?" he says at last and as soon as the words are out they sound like a joke which Jenks would make.

She laughs and says, "It's in good working order, thank you. How's yours?"

He blushes and manages some sort of reply.

"What brings you out this way?" she says and when he can't find an answer, she speaks for him. "Just getting some air? It's a lovely evening for it." She winks. "I was thinking of going for a walk. Want to join me?"

She parks her car on the verge and he locks his bike, and they walk across Two Hares Field. She is wearing unsuitable clothes for a walk: a tight skirt and a blouse, and he can tell that her heels are sinking into the damp grass. He helps her over a stile into Foxbury Wood.

"I remember you from school," she says. "You were in the year below me, always had a bloody nose from fighting. I fancied you even then."

He doesn't know what to say. He doesn't remember her at all.

This time he kisses her first, and when she presses up to him, he can feel her large breasts inside her silky blouse, soft against his chest. She puts her hands on his cheeks and kisses him back. She draws away, and holding him again with her eyes, she tugs at the silk bow at her throat — somehow part of the blouse — and unbuttons it all the way down, then lifts one of her breasts out of her bra. It is as pale as her neck, with a blue vein snaking downwards. The size and weight of it stretches the brown nipple into an oval. He puts his hand under it, excited by its warmth and its wonderful heft, and he raises it towards his mouth as he bends his head.

"Will you lie down with me here?" he says after a while, wishing he had brought a blanket or was wearing a bigger coat.

"Here?" Shelley Swift says. "In a wood?" And she laughs so much he thinks she might be sick.

When they say goodbye at the car, he is shy, but she only laughs some more. He wants to arrange to see her but doesn't know how to ask or what she might reply. It is only as he is cycling off that he remembers she hasn't paid him for the two jobs, and that it isn't ever going to be possible to ask for the money now.

14

Jeanie and Julius lock up the cottage and walk along the track in the opposite direction to the farm, and up the twisting path to the top of Rivar Down. The incline is steep and they lean into it, thighs burning. Jeanie is annoyed that Julius insists they rest every fifth step for her to catch her breath, but she complies. At the point where the hikers' route crosses, they go left along the ridge and through a stand of oak where the path is fenced with barbed wire and the grass beyond clipped by sheep. Already Jeanie can feel the sun beating on her forehead and knows they should have brought hats. How could there have been snow only two weeks ago? How could their mother be dead? The knowledge still sometimes takes her by surprise, that Dot isn't at home washing eggs in the scullery or mixing compost in the greenhouse. There are puddles on the track, and swarms of flies rise up as Maude races past. Julius doesn't have any work to go to, but both of them could — should — be spending the day in the vegetable garden. Today is the day that Nathan said he would be serving the eviction notice, and although their decision to be out of the cottage wasn't talked over, somehow they are here with Julius's rucksack packed with a bottle of water, a flask of tea, and sandwiches made from cheap sliced bread, margarine, and the previous autumn's raspberry jam. When did they last walk together without having to get somewhere in particular? Jeanie can't remember. They are behaving as though it is normal: just another stroll, just another picnic. The tea in the flask is black and unsweetened. There is no milk and no sugar.

On Ham Hill they stop to look out at the slope falling steeply below them, crisscrossed with the tracks of sheep, and further away, the land flattening to a mosaic of fields trimmed with hedges, patches of woods, and isolated houses, and between them, the dark trickle of the Ink. Berkshire to their right; Inkbourne and Wiltshire to their left. They can see Rawson's black-roofed barn and part of the farmhouse, but the cottage and the garden are hidden by trees. They walk on as far as the common, passing a couple in raincoats and walking boots, socks folded over the tops, and the man with a map in a plastic wallet hanging around his neck. They pass a group of foreign teenagers, bored and tired and being chivvied on by an exasperated leader. At the bottom of the gibbet — a twenty-five-foot post standing on the beacon — some idiot has placed a bunch of thistles, roots and soil attached, as a bouquet for the outlaws who were strung up here. Jeanie and Julius walk with their boots sideways, down the steep common, and sit below the shoulder of the hill, out of sight of any walkers.

Julius tosses a corner of his sandwich to Maude. She catches it in her mouth and it disappears with a snap of her teeth.

"You'll give her bad habits," Jeanie says. "She'll sit by your lap when you're eating at the table and then you won't be so happy to feed her." She isn't really telling him off, she likes that he feeds the dog. She pours a cupful of tea.

"Do you remember, we used to come here with Dad?" Julius says.

"We used to go to Ham Hill, not here," Jeanie says.

"No, it was definitely here. For our eighth birthday. This was where he gave me my penknife."

"It was Ham Hill. He left you alone with it and you cut your leg open."

"That was later. Not here, not on our birthday."

"God, there was so much blood." Jeanie blows on the tea and sips. "He was such an irresponsible father." She laughs. "Do you still have the scar?"

Julius lifts up the bottom of his jeans and shows his shin with a white slash across it.

"Ouch," she says, passing him the cup. "That's even worse than I remember."

Julius drinks, tugs down his jeans. "He was a good musician though."

Jeanie lies back fully on the grass and Maude runs over and sniffs her face as though to check she isn't dead, and when Jeanie opens her eyes, all she can see is sky: blue the colour of a dressing gown she had as a child, and white clouds, lacy at the edges, moving from one side of her vision to the other.

"Do you ever think about what'll happen to our music after we're gone?"

Julius takes so long to move or to answer that she thinks maybe he hasn't heard her, but he lies back too, his hands behind his head.

"No," he says.

"Mum and Dad taught us all those songs, and that's it. No one for us to pass them on to."

"I keep telling you we should do a gig at the Plough."

"I'm not doing one, so you might as well stop going on about it. Everyone will be looking, judging, gossiping. They do enough of that already, every time I go to the village."

"No one's looking at you, Jeanie. Everyone's too busy thinking about themselves. Trust me. We should do it. I bet you'd love it. We'd be paid. Holloway says he might be able to get someone to come and have a listen. Some bloke who's interested in regional folk music or something."

She interrupts him; she's never going to play at the Plough or anywhere else in public. The wake was enough. "Don't you want to pass your music on, teach it to someone?"

"What do you mean? Like give lessons?"

She isn't sure if he's being wilfully difficult. But she won't say what she means, not directly. "Not to any old child."

"Ahh," he says, long and drawn out. He understands exactly what she means. "My own kid. Nope. Never thought about it."

"You must have thought about it. Children, marriage."

"Who's to say I haven't got kids scattered all over the county already?"

There were a few times when Julius was younger that he stayed out all night, creeping home in the early morning and asking Jeanie not to tell. Once, late on a hot Sunday morning after a few hours' sleep, he put the tin bath in the yard and filled it with warm water. Jeanie was peeling vegetables for Sunday lunch and watching him from the open scullery window, sitting in the tub, his broad back and bony knees sticking out of the water. He turned and winked at her and she lobbed a piece of raw potato at him. He ducked too late and it bounced off his head. She threw the hard end of a parsnip with such unexpected anger that when it hit his shoulder he yelped. Another and another followed until he rose up out of the water, grabbed his towel, and retreated, as she yelled with a ferocity that shocked her. It wasn't that Jeanie wanted what he was having — sex or a relationship — those things left her unmoved; but she knew it would be a woman who would take him away from the cottage, from her.

On the common, Jeanie sits up. "Forget it," she says, looking out to her left, away from him. "I can't ever have a proper conversation with you."

"Sorry," he says and tugs on her shirt. "Lie down." She lies back once more, and he says, "I'm not planning on marrying anyone."

"You don't need to marry anyone to be with them, have children. With Mum gone, you can do what you want."

"I've always done what I want."

"Have you?"

"This is crazy." Now he's the one who sits up. "It's like you've been itching for a fight ever since we buried her." When she looks at him, he is a shadow blocking out the light, knees bent and arms resting on them, and for the first time that she can remember, she has no idea what he's thinking.

"I saw you took the ring," she says. She watches a red kite circling high above. He doesn't speak, although she's hoping he'll give her an explanation which doesn't involve a woman, isn't about Shelley Swift. "I remembered, you know," Jeanie continues.

"What?" He looks at her over his shoulder. "That Mum did put her wedding ring in the dish on the scullery windowsill. I remember seeing it there and it wasn't when she was gardening or making pastry. I've been trying to think why she would have

taken it off, but I can't come up with anything."

"She put it there when she went to see
Bridget in the afternoon and sometimes in
the morning."

"Bridget?" Jeanie says, sitting up again.
This isn't what she expected.

"I used to think Mum was shagging Stu."

"An affair?" Jeanie coughs out her shock.
"With Stu?"

"Or just a shag. But, I know. Not very
likely."

"There's no way she would have. She took
marriage far too seriously, hers and other
people's. Vows and all that. She definitely
wouldn't have had a thing with Stu Clements."

"Remember the second Christmas after
Dad died?" Julius says. "Not the first; that
was grim. But the second . . . she sent me
out to saw down a fir tree. The smallest you
can find, she said. But there weren't any
small ones and I had to cut the bloody thing
in half to get it in the kitchen. It was just a
stump with loads of branches sticking out,
in the end."

"And to get to bed you had to go out
through the back door and in through the
front," Jeanie says.

"That whole Christmas Mum was happy.

187

Always laughing. Dancing around the kitchen. Do you remember? That's when I first saw her wedding ring on the windowsill."

They're silent for a while.

"Sometimes though," Julius says, "don't you wish she'd had a thing with someone after Dad died?"

"Had a fling with Stu? No."

"Okay, not Stu, not a fling even, but maybe she could have done something extraordinary, for her own sake. It's always the same old path, isn't it, up the hill and down again. Worrying about money. Sometimes, I reckon, we need something to come along and trip us up when we're not expecting it. Otherwise, one day we're kids playing with the hose pipe, and the next we're laid out on an old door in the parlour."

Jeanie tries to think of something that might trip her up now, at fifty-one. It won't be eviction; she won't let that happen. Maybe, if she had been well, she could have hiked up bigger hills, mountains, she could have walked the two thousand miles of the Appalachian Trail.

"It's not going to happen." Jeanie pours more tea. Passes the cup, knowing that Julius is keeping up with her thoughts. "It's all pretence with the Rawsons. Sending

Nathan to scare us."

"I need to have that word with Stu."

"We can sort this out ourselves." She leans back on her elbows, legs straight. "It's a misunderstanding. The house is ours. It's just the Rawsons' empty threat to make us pay up."

"But we haven't paid up."

"Because we don't owe them anything."

Jeanie and Julius get home in the late afternoon. They don't talk about the eviction, each gaining confidence from the other that nothing will have happened, so that when Jeanie sees the piece of paper pinned over the front door's lock, she doesn't believe it, until Julius is pushing past her, saying, "Fuck." And even she can work out the start of the word in red letters. Then the sickness returns, the desire to go to bed and sleep to forget the debts, the worry about what they can do without, how they will manage. Only sleep takes these circling thoughts away, although that is becoming more difficult, and now even working in Saffron's garden won't stop the sweat dampening her palms or keep her heart from rocking.

"Fucking ridiculous," Julius says, reading

as he goes indoors. "A week. We've got a week."

"Is that all?" Jeanie says, although she knew it already.

"Maybe we could take it to a solicitor." Julius runs a hand through his hair, making it stick up on one side.

"Where would we get the money for a solicitor?"

He turns to her, his expression a snarl. "I don't know. Sell the piano?"

"Or Mum's wedding ring," she shouts.

"Neither of them are worth anything."

"This is crazy. We don't owe them any money." Jeanie thinks she might actually throw up. "What about the council?" She sits on a kitchen chair. Maude goes under the table. "They have to help people when they're made homeless, don't they? A council house or whatever." She can't believe it's come to this.

"I've already had a word with someone," Julius says, more quietly now.

"What?"

"That bloke who looks after the market, the one who came to the wake. He used to work in the housing department. There's not a chance in hell. We're too old, or not old enough. We need to be married or have children, or something."

■ ■ ■ ■

On Sunday morning after Jeanie hears Julius leave for a relief milking job he's managed to get for a couple of days, she goes downstairs in her nightie and dressing gown. She's barely slept for thinking about what might happen tomorrow. Every time she has tried to talk to her brother about the impending eviction, they've argued. In the early hours she decided that she would get some things together — just a couple of boxes in case they really do have to leave tomorrow. She tells herself that this isn't giving up, it's being prepared. But what do you pack when you don't know where you're going or for how long?

There had been a day in that long feverish time when she was about six and off school, that she'd woken on the sofa to see a man standing at the kitchen table, stuffing a slice of bread and butter into his mouth. The coat he wore was tied closed with a length of string and crumbs had fallen into his grey beard, which was long enough to lie on his chest. His sour odour reached her across the room and when Jeanie cried out, the man shovelled the food in faster — pieces of ham and then a whole hard-boiled egg

191

which he didn't stop to peel — his eyes darting and his cheeks bulging. Another egg went into his coat pocket, followed by an apple. At Jeanie's cry her mother hurried in from the scullery, and the tramp, perhaps used to being chased away, made a few steps towards the front door.

"Mr. Jackson," Dot said calmly. "Won't you sit down to eat?" She pulled out a chair and, cautiously, the man sat. "Mr. Jackson is our guest, Jeanette. He's come to tea." Her mother returned to the scullery for more food and Mr. Jackson relaxed, and popped the hard-boiled egg, whole, out of his mouth, shell intact. He put it in one ear and drew it out of the other before tapping it on the table and peeling it.

She remembers, dropped by the table leg, his canvas bag — his only belongings apart from the clothes he wore. What, she wonders now, did he carry with him?

In the scullery, Jeanie stands for a long time watching a beam of sunlight slide across the farmhouse sink. If they're evicted tomorrow, what will they do about their mother's body? They can't leave it and risk it being discovered, but they certainly can't take it with them. Jeanie doesn't have a solution. With a gasp and a rush of energy she goes into the old dairy, where half a dozen flattened cardboard boxes have been shoved in a corner. The cardboard is damp, and it takes her an age to find a roll of parcel tape, but she makes them up and packs them with plates and other pieces of essential crockery, wrapped in towels. She tucks in the portable radio, the torch, cutlery, two saucepans, and a frying pan, as well as whatever food she has in the cupboards. Angel's painting of Maude is secured with an elastic band and placed on top. On Tuesday, she tells herself, she will be unpacking everything and putting it back on the shelves, laughing at her own caution. She stuffs another box with two sleeping bags, spare pillows, and blankets, and puts everything in the old dairy. She is only preparing because she can't bear to be unprepared.

15

Jeanie sits in the kitchen, still in her nightie, fingerpicking the same phrase over and over on her guitar. The need to play it three times in a row at the same tempo with the same stress on the top string has kept her on the chair for an hour. She hears the back door open and Bridget call, "Jeanie? It's only me."

She stiffens, keeps the guitar on her knees, waiting for Nathan to follow on behind. But Bridget is alone and immediately talks about what a long way up the track the cottage is and how her poor car can't cope with those potholes, how warm it is in the kitchen, why for goodness' sake aren't the lights on, and what is Jeanie doing in her nightie at this time of day, and is so generally cheerful and chatty that Jeanie supposes she knows nothing about Nathan's new job or the threat of their eviction.

Bridget puts a large flat box on the table.

"There's a nice pizza for your dinner and I bought a couple of rolls for lunch." She brings out two ciabatta rolls wrapped in cling film from her handbag. "That deli is doing all sorts now," she says. "Pastries and macaroons. I sat at one of the tables outside and had a lovely cappuccino with a milky swan on top. You should go sometime, get yourself out of here." She looks around. "I don't expect you've been eating, have you?"

"I'm not hungry." Jeanie stands the guitar against the wall. It's clear that Bridget is staying.

"That's what your heart says, but the body needs sustenance. Energy." Bridget takes two plates from the dresser and wipes her hand quickly across them. If she notices that there are fewer than usual, she doesn't comment. She unwraps the food and lifts the top of each roll. "Pâté and rocket or brie and cranberries?" She sits at the table. "I thought you might need a bit of help sorting through Dot's clothes. Not a nice job, but these things have got to be done, haven't they? Mind you, I can't see Stu or Nath going through mine when I'm gone. They'll probably build a bonfire in the garden and dump everything on it. Me included."

Jeanie thinks of Dot under the ground beside the apple tree. She draws a plate towards her, suddenly starving. "Maybe Stu will go first," she says, her mouth full.

"No, it'll be me," Bridget says. "Worn out by my husband and son. I was forty when I had Nath, you know —"

"Have you seen him recently?"

"Nathan? He's living with a mate in Newbury. He comes over when he fancies a home-cooked meal or when he wants to borrow some money. God knows what he's up to. No good, I imagine." She laughs, and Jeanie is no longer hungry. She thinks about telling Bridget that Nathan came to the cottage a little over a week ago and that she might see him tomorrow, but she says nothing. If she doesn't say it, it might not happen. When Bridget has finished eating, they go up the left staircase to the bedroom. Bridget leads, clinging on to the handrail and panting, with Maude jostling between their legs to get there first, then curling up in her place on the landing when she decides nothing interesting is going to happen.

"The bulb must have gone." Bridget flicks the bedroom light switch. "In here?" she says, opening the wardrobe. Jeanie doesn't want to be doing this now. She's hoping to go to Saffron's house later, start the mowing to see if the volume of the engine will drown out her thoughts.

"Hers are on the right," Jeanie says, reaching out but not touching. When she came upstairs to look for something to dress her mother's body in, Jeanie hadn't been able to resist holding one of Dot's dresses to her face to inhale the scent of her. Mostly, though, the smell had been of the washing flakes they used. Every Monday, Dot and Jeanie used to drag out the twin-tub from the old dairy, stuffing the dirty clothes in one side and slopping them into the spinner on the other. The machine was so violent that if they went away for a few minutes, when they returned it would have limped across the room as far as the electric lead would let it as though trying to escape. Jeanie hasn't done any proper washing since Dot died, only rinsing out her and Julius's underwear in the kitchen sink and hanging it on the line in the yard. "Mum's jumpers and other things are in her chest of drawers," Jeanie says.

"There'll be clothes you'll want to keep, I'm sure." Bridget takes down a hanger with a skirt and holds it up. "Your mum wore this to the village fete last year."

"I don't remember," Jeanie says. She didn't go. She never goes to village events. Too many people, too much noise and excitement. "I don't want any of it. It can all go. The nearest charity shop." She has an urge to clear out everything. If the cottage were empty she wouldn't have to decide what to pack.

"Surely, something?"

"It has to go, today." Jeanie feels the same surge of energy she had when she got the boxes out from the dairy. With two hands she lifts off half a dozen full hangers from her mother's side of the wardrobe and chucks them on the bed. A flowered skirt falls to the floor and Bridget picks it up. "This is lovely. Isn't it from some fancy shop?" Bridget is looking inside the waistband at the label. Jeanie hasn't seen the skirt before, and it does look expensive.

"I shouldn't think so," she says. "Can you take the lot of it in your car?" Jeanie has never understood the fuss people — women — make about hair and make-up and clothes. Clothes are things to keep you warm or dry. She goes to the chest of drawers. "All this too?" She yanks at a drawer so that one side comes out first and won't come out further or go back in, and she hangs her head, pausing, gathering herself without Bridget seeing.

"What about this winter coat?" Bridget says. "This might fit you. You're a bit smaller than your mum, though."

"The coat too," Jeanie replies, without turning.

"It's good quality."

When Jeanie looks, Bridget is rubbing the wool between her fingers. Jeanie huffs and with what she knows is bad manners takes the coat from Bridget, yanks it off its hanger, and thrusts her arms into it.

"It's too big, see?" Only her fingertips show below the sleeves. "It can all go." Jeanie shoves her hands deep into the pockets of the coat. "Bridget, there's something I need to tell you — ask, really."

"It looks lovely on you," Bridget says, talking over her. "You could take up the sleeves. Putting on a bit of weight wouldn't do you any harm."

Jeanie's fingers feel a piece of folded paper at the bottom of the pocket. She pulls it out: a twenty-pound note.

"Would you look at that," Bridget says, smiling.

Jeanie laughs. Delighted and surprised, she unfolds it and holds it up to the window.

"Maybe you *should* keep it. It's a lucky coat."

Jeanie puts the money in the pocket of her dressing gown. It will be enough for another food shop. She takes the coat off and dumps it on the bed with the other clothes. "No, I can't keep any of it." She sits on the side of the bed. "I've been having a clear-out."

"A clear-out?"

"Deciding what to keep and what can go. So much clutter in this house."

"A spring clean."

"Kind of."

"But too much change all at once isn't a good thing. It takes a while to adjust after something big has happened. When I had to clear out Dad's house —"

"We don't have a choice."

"Why's that then?" Bridget takes down the remaining hangers on Dot's side of the wardrobe.

"Julius and I are probably moving out," Jeanie says fiercely, chin up, as though daring Bridget to challenge her.

"Moving?" Bridget says. Her surprise doesn't sound quite genuine. "What a shame for you and Julius to have to move out now."

"I thought you said this place wasn't fit to live in? Buckets in the corners when it rains. Freezing in the winter, damp the rest of the time."

"I'm not sure I said all that. I might have suggested that Rawson needs to pull his finger out and get the place fixed up."

"He's pulled his finger out all right."

"Your mother would be so sad. It was important to her, to keep this roof over your heads, make sure you were looked after."

"Oh, Bridget." Jeanie slumps, giving in. "Rawson's evicting us — tomorrow. Tomorrow! If it actually happens. God knows where we'll go. Julius won't talk about it. I'm not sure if he refuses to believe it'll happen or he's just ignoring it, but —"

"Well, that's terrible," Bridget interrupts, her tone odd enough for Jeanie to look up. Bridget, still facing the wardrobe and fiddling with the clothes draped over her arm, says: "We can't be having you homeless. I've known you and Julius nearly all your lives and I wouldn't want that. I tell you what, if it happens, why don't you both come and stay with me and Stu for a bit? A week or two until you sort something out."

"I don't think it would work. But thanks."

Bridget turns finally, smiling too broadly. "Of course it would. You can have Nath's old room and Julius can have the sofa. We'll manage for a while."

The moment for telling Bridget about Nathan seems to have passed. It would be like revealing to a wife that her husband is having an affair, or her child has been seen smoking pot on the village green: not your business and too close to gossip. Maybe it's

201

better to let her find out for herself, or not.
"And Stu. What will he say?"
"Stu won't mind."

In bed later, with Dot's clothes taken away
by Bridget, Jeanie lies in her nightie and
dressing gown, which she hasn't taken off
all day. She never made it to Saffron's.
Under the covers she slips her hand into
the dressing gown pocket and finds, again,
the twenty-pound note. She searched every
other pocket before Bridget took the clothes
away, in case Dot left money in another,
but she didn't find any more. Jeanie replays
their conversation and remembers Bridget's
awkwardness. She unfolds the note and
holds it in front of her. Would Dot have
folded a single note and forgotten it in a
pocket? In the dark Jeanie's face burns with
shame at her naivety as she realizes that
Bridget put the money in the coat pocket,
and this could only mean that Julius had
told her about how desperate their money
problems have become. He must have told
her about the eviction too and discussed
the idea of them moving in with her and
Stu. Did he also try to mention Nathan's
involvement? That evening, when Julius was
eating the pizza, he pretended to be surprised by Bridget's offer, maintaining that

they wouldn't need to take her up on it; they wouldn't be moving out the next day no matter what. Perhaps the suggestion for them to stay wasn't even Bridget's; maybe he went to her and begged.

16

The smell of cigarettes wakes Jeanie. It has
taken days for the smoky, beery stink to dis-
sipate after the gathering for Dot, and now
the smell sets up the same palpitations
inside her. How was it that last night, of all
nights, she was able to sleep? She hears
raised voices in the kitchen — Julius's and
several others — and she scrambles to get
dressed while Maude harasses her and
grouses, knowing something is going on.
Downstairs, Nathan is lounging in the
doorway between the scullery and the
kitchen. He appears more at ease than he
did on his last visit and he's wearing the
same suit, although it has already bagged at
the knees and the pockets have taken on the
shapes of a mobile phone and a set of keys.
Another young man is wedged into a corner
of the sofa, his eyes closed and mouth open.
He jerks awake, eyes staring crazily about
him. A third man, slighter than the others,

hollow-cheeked with eyes deep-set and red-rimmed, stands near the front door smoking while Julius rants at him about rights of entry and trespass. The man says nothing, only smiles, his teeth too small for his mouth.

Three, Jeanie thinks. Why did Rawson send three people?

"What the hell is going on?" she says, and they turn to look at her. She tries to block Maude on the stairs but the dog slips round her legs and snarls, lips retracted. The man Julius is arguing with stamps a booted foot towards her and Maude scuttles under the table.

"Jeanie," Nathan says, standing upright. "Miss Seeder. I didn't know you were home."

"Where else would I be at nine in the morning, Nathan?"

He shoves his hands in his trouser pockets and she can see the shape of his knuckles through the material.

A fourth man appears from beside the front door, carrying a toolbox. "All done, Tom," he says, handing over a set of keys.

"For God's sake," Julius says. "This is our house." He's wearing only his pyjama bottoms. His go-to uniform for emergencies, Jeanie thinks.

"Why did you let them in?" she asks.

"Didn't you hear them? They were beating the door down."

Tom slaps the workman on the back. "Cheers, mate. Settle up later, yeah?"

Through the kitchen window Jeanie sees the locksmith wandering down the path like this is just another job. The wind lifts long strands of his hair and blows them about. Tom takes a drag on his cigarette, flicks the butt into the garden, and kicks the foot of the man on the sofa, making him jump and jerk again. "Come on, Lewis. Can't fucking sleep all day. We've got work to do."

"Get out of my house," Julius says. He's at the front door with his hand on the latch.

Jeanie is standing in front of the range, its dull warmth radiating through her skirt, and she thinks that she must build up the fire — they will need hot water and the top warm for breakfast — until she realizes that they probably won't be having breakfast this morning. Perhaps the scrambled eggs she made a few days ago but didn't eat were the last she'll ever make in this house. She thinks then of the chickens — what will they do with the chickens? Nathan comes to stand beside her. "I thought you'd have moved out already," he says quietly, apologetically.

"Well, we haven't. Let's just stop this," she says. "We don't owe any money. There's no rent to pay. We'll speak to Rawson and get it sorted out."

Lewis stares about him, dazed from sleep. He stands and dozily picks up a kitchen chair, and Tom takes another. "Here," Tom calls and throws the chair to Nathan, high across the table. Nathan's reaction is slow, but he catches it.

"Wait," Julius says. "Where are you going with those?"

"Should have got rid of this shit earlier," Tom says.

"Your dad's coming to move us out today," Jeanie says to Nathan, although it hasn't been arranged. As Jeanie positions herself between him and the front door, she hears Maude fussing under the table. Nathan wavers. "We're going to be staying with him and your mum for a while." She hopes this is still possible.

"Are you running this geriatric eviction, Nath?" Tom picks up another chair. "Or am I?" He manoeuvres himself around Julius.

Nathan puts his shoulders back, hardens his face. "Rather you than me," he says to Jeanie. She wants to grab the chair from him and smash it over his head.

"Surely you can wait until he arrives with

the van?" she says.

"I don't want nothing to do with that old git, never again. I work for who I like, when I like."

"Let's put them out on the track, lads," Tom says, and the men lift the chairs above their heads and Jeanie finds herself backed against the range so that Nathan can pass.

"He did speak to you then?" Jeanie says to him. "Tell you not to do this?" He ignores her.

Julius, near the door, steps in and takes hold of Lewis's chair, trying to wrestle it from him. There's a tussle and swearing, and one of the chair's stretchers comes loose.

"Now, now," Tom says from where he stands on the doorstep. "We're just doing our job, Mr. Seeder." There's laughter in the way he speaks as if it's a joke and in a moment he might put the chair back and say, *Only pulling your leg.*

Suddenly Julius lets go of the chair and Lewis falls, pushing the parlour door open and landing heavily on his back. There's a tangle of man and chair until Julius steps across Lewis and into the parlour. Jeanie whistles for Maude and follows her brother. Just as she is closing the parlour door on the men, Tom smiles at her, his square little teeth stained, and with his index finger draws a line slowly across his neck.

"Phone Stu," Jeanie says to Julius. "Tell him to come straight away." Through the parlour window they see the men chucking the chairs over the gate and walking back up the path.

"I haven't got any sodding charge," Julius says.

"For goodness' sake, why not?"

"Because we haven't paid the electricity bill, remember?" He's shouting. "Because I couldn't charge the phone when I was milking because they've bloody got their eye on me the whole time. And I didn't go to the fucking pub after work because I knew you'd be on at me. All right?"

"All right," she says softly. "All right. I'm sorry." She's trembling and she sits in the armchair so that she can press down on her thighs. "I packed some stuff yesterday. I've just got to get our clothes together. We'll manage. It'll be okay." She's saying things for the sake of speaking, to make everything seem normal, solvable.

Julius crouches, grips her upper arms, and looks into her eyes. "I'm going to get dressed and then I'm going to find Stu and tell him he needs to come right now. Maybe he can try again to stop Nathan." Julius did speak to Bridget about Nathan, then, Jeanie thinks. She doesn't believe it will work a second time, not now she's seen Tom, but she nods. "Stay in here with Maude and you'll be fine."

While Julius is upstairs, Jeanie is drawn to the window where she sees their belongings being manhandled down the path and dumped on the track: the kitchen table, which the men have removed the legs from, the piano stool, the sofa cushions, one of the dresser drawers, and then the sofa itself. The wind is getting up, pulling at fabric and bits of paper. From beside her on the parlour chest, she takes the framed photograph of her parents and shoves it into her cardigan pocket. She takes the Toby jug too and squeezes it into a skirt pocket, splitting the seam. An unused ashtray held in the paws of a carved wooden bear with beads for eyes she puts in a third pocket, and then she stares out of the window once more.

Before he leaves, Julius holds her tightly. "I'll be as quick as I can." She watches him pass the men on the path, and there is more shouting and pushing and then he gets on his bicycle and rides off. After he's gone, she and Maude climb the right-hand stairs to Julius's bedroom. On the sloping floorboards the two single beds from Jeanie's childhood are still here. She slept in the left-hand one until their father died, when Dot said she was too old to be sharing a room with her brother and she moved into the double bed beside her mother. Jeanie knew it was because Dot was afraid to be alone. Where would Jeanie have slept if her father had lived? And why didn't Julius move to the double bed on his own? These things, like her father's murder, were never discussed. She looks out of the window, remembering the row of birds' skulls Julius used to keep here — always falling off the sill when she closed the curtains. The men have taken the armchair from the parlour, and with Tom directing, Nathan and Lewis are carrying it down the path. The cushion falls off the bottom, and Lewis staggers over it in his muddy boots.

Under the bed which used to be hers, Jeanie finds an old suitcase that she stuffs with the clothes from Julius's drawers and wardrobe: pairs of jeans and shirts pale from washing, darned socks, underpants and T-shirts, his pyjamas which he left on the floor. Tucked in amongst all the soft things she puts Julius's unloaded gun. Next, she tips in the contents of the drawer of his bedside cabinet without noticing what odds and ends it contains. Something falls out with a clink and rolls away. When Jeanie searches for it under the bed she feels only dust balls and other rubbish. On top of the things in the case she puts the photograph, the bear ashtray, and the Toby jug, and closes the lid.

When Julius returns, he again scuffles outside with Lewis, who is stupid, but younger and more agile. They each take an end of the tin bath, pushing and shoving it against each other until Julius falls backwards into the flower bed. Laughing, Lewis tosses the bath over the garden fence where it lands, the right way up, on the track. Julius scrabbles upright and Jeanie comes out of the cottage. She brushes the dirt off his clothes, and he is embarrassed by his sister, dowdy and fussing, even in front of these men who are dismantling their home. He can't remember feeling ashamed of her before, only protective, and with a mixture of guilt and humiliation, he pushes her hands off him. On the track Lewis clambers into the bath and pretends to scrub his back with a discarded broom while Nathan looks on and Tom jumps about in the wind like a monkey.

Julius tells Jeanie that Stu is coming as soon as he can and doesn't say that he was only able to leave a message with Bridget who said Stu was out on a job all day, and that she didn't believe Nathan would ever listen to his father. Julius puts his arm around his sister, red-cheeked and silent, and takes her up to the top of the garden, past the chickens still in their coop, to sit out the removal while the trees thrash about them.

"Maybe we should put it all in the old dairy," Julius says, the idea suddenly coming to him. "Most of it would fit."

"It'd still be on the Rawsons' land," Jeanie says in a dull voice. "They'll claim it's theirs."

"The track belongs to them too."

Jeanie shrugs, doesn't look at him.

Finally, when they hear the kick of engines, they stand and walk down the garden, limping and stiff as though they have been physically injured by the actions of the day.

Julius stops at the foot of his mother's grave. "I'll sort something out." He knows that the words are hollow and that Jeanie thinks he hasn't done what he is supposed to do: keep her safe.

"Fuck it," Jeanie says, and Julius, shocked at hearing her speak these words, watches as she goes to the head of the mound of earth and yanks out the poker which is stuck in the soil. He hasn't seen it since before their mother died, and he feels a prickle up the back of his neck to realize that it is here, jammed into the earth as the marker for her grave, as if Dot might have taken it and placed it there herself.

In the yard, he waits for Jeanie to feed the chickens. And then he and his sister walk around the cottage and down the front path without looking inside.

In the late afternoon Stu arrives. He lowers the van window and stares at the contents of the cottage piled across the track. Everything Nathan and the others could manage or be bothered to carry has been taken outside and heaped up: pans and bowls and mismatched plates, three mattresses with their ticking stains laid bare, the cooker ripped out from the mains, the fridge which they hadn't used for three weeks, four bedside tables, candlesticks, teapots, jugs and jars, threadbare rugs, and all the things that a house's poorly lit corners can hide the wear of. The chest from the parlour is on its side and the contents have fallen out: what remains of the linen is muddy, and the family papers and documents kept at the bottom are scattered. Many pieces of paper have been picked up by the wind and distributed across the hedges and surrounding fields. A sowing of words. Jeanie and Julius sit in their coats on kitchen chairs, the legs sinking into the mud.

"Bloody hell," Stu says. "Bridget told me it'd be two suitcases. I don't think it'll all fit in the back and it's never going to fit in the house." He gets out and stands with his hands on his hips. He's wearing his usual shorts and boots; in between, a stretch of hairy calves.

Julius picks up the suitcases which Jeanie packed — one for him and another for her. "Let's go," he says sullenly. He has no fury left, only humiliation. They load the van with the boxes of crockery and food, and another of bedding. Julius's rucksack of tools is shoved in, as well as the three instrument cases. Julius loads Dot's — now Jeanie's — bike into the van. The trailer won't fit, so he hitches it to the back of his own bike. Jeanie whistles for Maude, who has been running between the piles, sniffing excitedly.

"What about the rest?" Stu says. "You're not going to leave it here, are you?"

"Let's go," Julius repeats. Everything he does feels like an effort, as though he had aged twenty years over this one day. Jeanie sits in the front seat of the van and drags Maude into the footwell by her collar. Julius tries to catch his sister's eye to smile at her; it's a false smile, to make her think that he has some confidence in himself and a plan, but she looks straight ahead, lips stuck together, as if she spoke her last words when they were in the garden. He sees she still has the poker in her hand, and he imagines that it's him she'd like to use it on.

Fuck you too, he thinks, the effort of trying to keep positive finally failing him.

"I'll see you there," he says, and slams the passenger door.

17

Nathan's bedroom is painted blue with a repeating pattern of a white sailing boat stencilled around the walls, across the headboard of the single bed, and on the open door of the wardrobe. Some of his child-sized clothes are hanging inside, and on top are boxes of toys and half a dozen jigsaws. On the wall is a framed certificate for what Jeanie thinks says hockey, with a length of Christmas tinsel around the top. There's a desk with a computer monitor and keyboard, both with clothes heaped over them. Stacks of DVDs and CDs crowd the windowsill. A giant orange plastic ball is wedged into the corner together with what looks like a small trampoline.

Bridget hugs Jeanie, while Stu makes another journey to the van for the boxes and cases. The house, a pebble-dashed 1950s ex–council house in between two others, has been swallowed up by the new estate built on the edge of Inkbourne. Once, the view from the windows would have been of fields, but now from Nathan's bedroom window, Jeanie can see other people's neat gardens and the same modern house repeated over and over, only the colour of the doors distinguishing one from another.

"I tried to reason with him," Bridget says. Jeanie slides her eyes away. "He wouldn't bloody listen." Bridget shakes her head. "And then when Stu had a go, ranting and raving at him, Nathan just dug his heels in. Said he wasn't going to do what his dad told him to do, ever again. Why doesn't it surprise me that he's mixed up in this? Working for the Rawsons?" Jeanie looks at the carpet, which is also blue and in need of a vacuum. "He used to be such a lovely little boy."

Upstairs in Bridget's house there are two bedrooms and a green-tiled bathroom — "Be careful with the hot water," Bridget says as she shows Jeanie around. "It doesn't last long." Downstairs is a lounge with a sofa and two peach-coloured armchairs with enormous padded cushions attached to the arms, all crowding round a giant flat-screen television. Beyond this room, at the back of the house, is the kitchen and an area which Bridget calls the sunroom. It's hard to see what furniture and carpeting there is in here and the rest of the house because every surface, other than the lounge armchairs, is covered with celebrity magazines, stacks of the local paper, unopened post, jam jars with paintbrushes sticking out of them, plastic storage boxes filled with unknown things, electric fans and portable radiators, an airer collapsing under the weight of the bedding piled on it, an ironing board with a plastic washing basket on top filled with what looks like a dismantled chainsaw.

"That's us," Bridget says, lighting a cigarette when they reach the kitchen, the only room Jeanie has been in before. "Stu reckons I should retire this year, but what for? Cleaning and ironing? No thank you." They stand together at the kitchen sink; a frying pan and plates smeared with egg fill the washing-up bowl. They watch Maude outside, digging in what once might have been flower beds, now overgrown with weeds. Bridget puts her cigarette in her mouth and raps hard on the window. "Oy!" she calls, and Maude stops to look at them and then goes back to her digging. "Best keep her outside," Bridget says.

When Stu has finished unloading the van, he comes into the kitchen and says, "Fancy a cup of tea, love?" He puts his arm around

Bridget and gives one of her breasts an affectionate squeeze with a loud honking.

She laughs and pushes him off. "I could murder a cup of tea, Stu-pot," she says.

Jeanie moves out of their way and Stu fills the kettle.

By seven, Julius still hasn't arrived on his bike. Bridget and Stu have a conversation about what to eat, and Bridget takes four chicken kievs out of the freezer and puts them in the oven with a tray of chips. Jeanie brings down the food she took with her from the cottage: the remains of a jar of homemade jam, chicken Bisto, the last of the bread, eggs, vegetables from the garden, and the half-used tub of margarine.

While Bridget turns the food in the oven and puts some peas in the microwave, Jeanie loads the dishwasher with the crockery from the sink, guessing at where things go, and tries not to make a nuisance of herself. She thinks about where Julius might be — in the pub or round at Shelley Swift's. He's allowed to do what he wants, of course, just as she is. They dish up the food, saving some for Julius, put the plates on trays, and Stu and Bridget carry theirs into the lounge. Before she follows, Jeanie takes Bridget's purse out from her handbag where it hangs over a chair. In the wallet section there are too many notes for her to count. Deep in her cardigan pocket is the twenty pounds she found in Dot's coat. She takes it out, stuffs it in with the rest of Bridget's money, and puts the purse back in the handbag.

"Come on," Bridget calls from the lounge. "It's starting." Jeanie takes her own tray of food in. Bridget and Stu are each low down in an armchair with their trays on their laps. The television is on and the opening sequence of a programme is flashing on the screen. "Clear yourself a space on the end of the sofa," Bridget says, and Jeanie puts her tray on the floor, moves what looks like a set of curtains onto the back of the sofa, and then sits. They watch a police drama about two detectives in an English seaside town and a boy who was murdered on a beach. His family spend the episode not looking at each other, not touching.

"Doesn't she look like Jeanie?" Bridget says, watching the telly.

"Who?" Stu says.

"The policewoman."

"Detective," Stu corrects.

"Not so grey, of course, but a little bit toothy. Nice with it, though." Bridget turns to look at Jeanie. "And the detective's younger."

Stu leans forwards in his chair, craning

round Bridget to get a look. Jeanie stares back at them without speaking.

"Thinner," Stu says.

Blue-and-white tape encloses the crime scene, guarded by a policeman whose only job seems to be to lift it high enough for the detectives to duck under. Bridget and Stu are on episode three or four and it takes half an hour for Jeanie to work out what's going on. The detectives arrest a man, ask him to undress, and collect his belongings in a plastic bag. They swab the inside of his mouth with a giant cotton bud and take his fingerprints.

"He won't be the murderer," Stu says.

"Too early in the series for it to be him," Bridget says. "No one's ever caught that quickly."

They eat their food without taking their eyes from the screen. Periodically one of them turns to the other when something surprising happens and says, "Oh my God!" When the programme reaches the end and the music plays, Stu says, "How about another episode, Bridgey?"

She smiles. "Go on then." Bridget selects the next episode with the remote control while Stu stands in front of Jeanie and for a moment she can't work out what he wants, but then he reaches down, picks up her tray from her lap, and takes it out to the kitchen.

"Cup of tea?" he calls.

"Go on then," Bridget calls back.

Jeanie makes dinner for Maude — boiled vegetables with chicken gravy and a raw egg cracked in, the shell scrunched on top. She seems to have got used to it. Jeanie finds a trowel and collects the dog's mess, burying it in the earth behind Stu's garage. When she glances towards the house, Bridget is at the kitchen window, smoking and watching. In the disused greenhouse Jeanie makes a bed from some sacking, the dog whining as Jeanie pushes her nose to get the door closed. Back inside, when Jeanie opens the dishwasher to empty it, the cups and bowls are full of sludgy water and grit. She tips them out in the sink and washes the dirty items again by hand. Bridget sits on a high stool up against the kitchen counter and points with the lit end of her cigarette to one cupboard or another, indicating where everything goes. The bottom of the dishwasher is slimy with something Jeanie doesn't want to look at too closely. Perhaps, she thinks crazily, she could clean the house, Julius could do the garden, and they can all live here together. She would like to live in a house with a bathroom, an indoor toilet and central heating, a working fridge, maybe even a television, but already she knows she can't stay long with Bridget and Stu. Somehow, she'll get herself and her brother back to the cottage.

"I was thinking," Jeanie says, drying the drinking glasses, which for some reason have come out cloudy as though they'd been sandblasted, "about the agreement. The one we had with Rawson for the cottage." She glances at Bridget, whose cigarette indicates a corner shelf beside the window.

"I can't believe Nath was mixed up in all that stuff this morning," Bridget says. "He could have been anything, you know, when he left school. A firefighter, electrician, anything. If he'd put his mind to it."

"Was it ever in writing?" Jeanie places the glasses on the shelf. There is laughter from the lounge — the television audience's and, above it, Stu's. Jeanie thinks about the documents that were kept in the chest flying along the track and over the hedges.

"Too easily influenced by other people, that's his trouble. Who did you say was there with him?"

"Someone called Lewis and another lad."

"Shaved head? Thin?" Bridget sucks in her cheeks.

Jeanie nods. "Tom, that was his name."

"They live together, Nath and Tom. Tom's

always been trouble, ever since he was little. A terror he was at school, and worse since he's grown up. His mum died when he was five, you know — breast cancer. So quick, it was." Bridget snaps her fingers. "Here and gone, just like that." Jeanie wonders if Bridget clicks her fingers when she tells people the story of Frank's death. "Poor little mite. His dad was bloody useless, let the kid go feral. Apparently, when he was about ten, someone found him picking up roadkill and taking it home to eat. But I'm sorry it's come to this. Your mum will be turning in her grave."

Jeanie looks quickly away and picks up a fork.

"You don't have to take them one at a time, you know. You can lift out the whole cutlery basket." Bridget grinds out her cigarette in a full ashtray.

"So was there ever anything in writing?" Jeanie tries again.

"Oh, I shouldn't think so. Not your mum's style, was it? Doing things officially."

They hear Stu laughing.

"I've got a job." Jeanie empties the cutlery from the basket into a drawer where nothing appears to be in any order and crumbs clog up the corners.

"Really?" Bridget says it like she didn't

think Jeanie could have managed this.

"For a woman who lives on Cutter Hill. She wanted a female gardener. Just mowing the lawn, things like that."

"Cutter Hill?" Bridget says. "Near the old phone box that's been turned into a library?"

"Saffron did that."

"Saffron? That's her name?" Bridget sounds incredulous, and Jeanie wants to defend her new employer, her friend. Jeanie still has the cheque Saffron gave her, folded in half and tucked into her coat pocket. There's nowhere to cash it in the village and she's not sure she would be able to even if she caught the bus to Devizes or Hungerford.

"And her daughter's called Angel."

"Saffron and Angel!" Bridget puffs a dismissive breath.

Stu shouts from the lounge and Bridget seems glad of the distraction. "What?" she calls back.

He laughs. "Brilliant!"

Bridget heaves herself off the stool and goes to see. As Jeanie closes the dishwasher, she hears Bridget laughing too.

Bedtime comes and still no Julius. Bridget gives Jeanie a sheet, pillow, and duvet to make up the sofa for him, and when she's done that she sits on the edge of Nathan's single bed and waits until she hears Bridget and then Stu finish in the bathroom. She moves from anger at Julius for leaving her here on her own to terror that something has happened to him on his ride from the cottage to the house, imagining him in a ditch with his bicycle buckled. Perhaps he won't ever come back, and what would she do then? How would she manage? Finally, after an hour of staring up at the wall, she hears a noise downstairs — something smashing — and she jumps up and runs to see. Julius is in the kitchen, holding on to the counter and swaying in the dark. The hall light goes on behind her and Stu is there.

"How did you bloody get in?" Stu says, putting on the kitchen light, dazzling them. He's wearing a T-shirt and checked cotton shorts. Jeanie realises she must have left the back door unlocked. She doesn't say anything. "Turning up in the middle of the night?" Stu continues. "Drunk, the man's drunk." Bridget is there too now, in her nightie, tying the belt of her dressing gown. Jeanie sees them all reflected in the kitchen window, lit up like the family on the telly.

"Sorry, sorry," Julius slurs.

Around his feet are broken pieces of a china fruit bowl. Three old apples are lined up against the skirting board. Jeanie edges past Bridget and Stu and begins picking up the larger pieces of china.

"You're only here because Dot was Bridget's friend," Stu says to Julius. "And you'd better start remembering that. If you can afford to get drunk, you can afford to find your own place."

"Stu," Bridget says, tugging on his T-shirt sleeve. "Their mother just died, and our son had a hand in all this, don't forget."

"Coming in drunk in the middle of the night, wrecking the kitchen. Waking people. It's time you took a bit more care with the place you call home."

On her hands and knees, Jeanie feels a wave of homesickness for the cottage, for her own bed, her own things. She stands and puts the pieces of china in the bin.

"Mind your feet," Bridget says.

"I'll get him to bed and then I'll sweep the floor." Jeanie takes Julius around the waist. "You go," she says to Bridget and Stu. "I'll sort this out."

She makes Julius drink a pint of water, puts him to bed in Nathan's room, and then gets under the duvet she's laid out for her brother on the sofa. She tries to sleep —

the first time in her life she has slept somewhere other than the cottage — but she lies with her eyes open, the clutter of the lounge around her, wondering what she and Julius are going to do now.

In the morning, Jeanie is up with the bedding folded away before Bridget and Stu stir. She has formulated the angry speech she will give Julius when she goes in to wake him, but he comes into the lounge first, dressed in yesterday's clothes and smelling of old cigarette smoke and stale beer. His eyes are bloodshot and his skin sallow. She'd like to ask him whether he's spent the money he earned from the milking job, but she doesn't want to sound like Stu. Julius puts his arms around her and she is rigid for a moment, but then relaxes with the relief that he is here.

"I'm sorting out somewhere for us to live," he says.

"I can't stay here," Jeanie says. "I can't do it. I'll camp out in the woods if I have to."

He squeezes her tighter. "I know, I know. Another night or two, that's all."

18

Avoiding the middle of Inkbourne will add an extra mile or two on to the cycle ride from Bridget's to the cottage, but for Jeanie it's preferable to bumping into someone who might have heard about the eviction. How would she explain why she and Julius are homeless? What would she say if anyone asked where they're going to live now? She moves the trailer from Julius's bike to hers and gets Maude to climb into it so that she can practise going slowly up and down the road outside Bridget's house before she sets off. After they get going, when Jeanie glances behind, Maude is facing into the wind with her mouth open, jowls flapping.

Jeanie cycles past the farmyard and up the track, shocked again to see their possessions flung out along the verge. Items and objects she'd taken for granted when they were indoors — the blue cupboard which always stood on the right-hand landing, a china washbowl with a chip in its rim, the embarrassment of a chamber pot tipped on its side, a box of assorted woolly hats and gloves — all lie in odd juxtapositions, as though a huge hand had picked up the cottage and shaken it for fun, letting the contents tumble out, before setting the building back on its foundations. It hasn't rained overnight but the morning's dew has left beads of moisture on the polished furniture and soaked into the fabrics. Maude jumps out of the trailer and capers around it all, racing down the track, happy to be home.

Although only a night and a morning have passed since she and Julius left, Jeanie expects something to be different; without them here surely something should have altered — new people moved in or workmen started on renovating the place. But there are no vehicles on the track, and when she peers through the front windows the disarray in the parlour is as it was before, while in the kitchen, the dresser remains against the wall and the piano halfway across the room, where Nathan, Lewis, and Tom gave it up as too heavy. She rattles the front door, although she knows it will be locked, and when she goes around the cottage, the back door is of course bolted from the inside. She lets the chickens out and gives them food and fresh water. They are disgruntled that it is so late, and the small brown one has fewer feathers on its back, but there are eggs to collect which she can take with her and give to Bridget. She walks up the garden, avoiding the grave, and considers gathering everything that will burn and building a bonfire so that Rawson, or whoever lives in the cottage next, won't get the benefit of it. But there have been too many years of double digging, too much back-breaking flint picking and plant tending to destroy the garden, and besides, what is there that would burn? The rough fencing, the compost bins? Jeanie fills the watering can from the outside tap and waters the tomato plants, which are drooping in the greenhouse.

When she's finished the urgent jobs, the cottage draws her back. She cups her hands around her eyes and stares in through the scullery window and sees a similar untidiness as in the front rooms. In the old dairy she lifts down a wooden ladder which hangs from brackets on the wall, and with some difficulty manoeuvres it outside and around to the front. Julius wouldn't like her doing it, but he isn't here. She props the ladder against her bedroom window, jabbing the feet into the earth to secure it, and climbs. Maude, at the bottom, yaps at her. Jeanie's bedroom window has never closed securely and in winter she and Dot would stuff the crannies with rags and balls of newspaper. Now she gets her finger in the gap, pulls the window open, and clambers inside.

Even after only one uninhabited night, the cottage smells abandoned. The wardrobe and the metal frame of the double bed she shared with Dot are still in the room — it seems the men were unable to find a spanner of the right size to take the bed apart — but the base, the mattress, and the bedding are outside. With fresh eyes she sees the things that were inconsequential when it was her bedroom: the spot around the window where the plaster is blown, the blooming stains on the walls like great circles of ringworm, and the hole in the corner of the ceiling which mice would drop out of, and where they used to catch the water in a bucket when it rained. Downstairs, Jeanie's footsteps echo, and the house seems cavernous. After a week or a fortnight, a month, without anyone living in it, she knows the cottage will slip further into decay. The flagstones in the kitchen will lift higher, soot will blow down the chimneys, rats will come to gnaw and scratch, until, in time, the house will regress into its constituent parts, becoming earth, grass, stone, and wood.

She stands in front of the iron range, which radiates its coldness against the backs of her legs. The fire hasn't ever been allowed to go out completely before. Often when the flames leaped up again, Dot would say it was the same fire she'd lit aged eighteen, the day Frank carried her across the threshold. She wonders where her mother's wedding ring is; has Julius kept it safe? A collection of oil lamps lie on the floor with their glass shades smashed, and she steps over them, unbolts the back door, and whistles for Maude, who is still barking at the front. Back in the kitchen, she eases the full log basket across the room and, perching on its lip, opens the piano lid and plays a minor chord. She learned the piano by copying her father, although she has always preferred the guitar. The piano is even more out of tune than before, but she plays an introduction and sings:

"It was on one fine March morning when I
    bid my home adieu
And took the road to London town my
    fortune to renew

234

I cursed all foreign money, no credit could
  I gain
Which filled my heart with longing for the
  trees of Hadlington."

The piano jangles loudly, its out-of-tune-ness amplified. She hums along while she tries to get the piano part correct. It's a song she has only played on the guitar.

She sings another verse, hesitantly, but enjoying the reverberation of the piano bouncing around the empty room. She closes her eyes to see the fire lit again behind her, Julius eating at the table, Maude twitching in her sleep on the sofa.

"If it weren't for the wolves and the bears, I'd sleep out in the woods . . ."

Another voice joins hers, and she jumps off the log basket, the falling piano lid closely missing her fingers. Julius is leaning on the doorjamb, a smile on his face.

"I knew you'd be here," he says.

"Aren't you meant to be putting up a fence somewhere?" She sits again.

"It doesn't feel like ours any more, does it?" He looks around. "It's already stopped being a home, somehow. Just a horrible, mouldy little house."

His description offends her. "Go back to work, Julius. We need to give Bridget some

235

money for food. We need to pay Stu back." She doesn't say *and Rawson*.

"Turns out the work was twenty miles away. I would have had to go in the van."

"Oh, Julius." She half rises to go to him, but he shifts his shoulders, rejecting her sympathy.

Perhaps he realizes it and tries to compensate by sounding concerned. "I'm not sure you should have lifted that ladder on your own."

"It was fine. I managed."

"I phoned Richard Letford earlier. The kitchen fitter?"

"Another job?"

"Not exactly." He smiles. "I needed to check on something he mentioned at Mum's do." Julius comes to the log basket, nudges her along with his hip, and she moves over. He opens the piano and plays a few chirpy notes with his left hand.

"I have some news," he says over the piano, his right hand joining in to make the music swing.

"What news?" She's impatient, she doesn't have time for his teasing, the way he likes to make her wait.

He carries on playing the jingly tune and sings:

"When I was a little girl, I wished I was a
    boy
I tagged along behind the gang and wore
    my corduroys
Everybody said I only did it to annoy
But I was gonna be an engineer."

"Julius." She gives him a shove with her
body, and he sways sideways to almost
horizontal and comes back upright, still
playing and singing.

"Julius, what news?" she says, laughing
now. She's heard him play this song before.

"Mamma said, 'Why can't you be a lady?
Your duty is to make me the mother of a
    pearl
Wait until you're older, dear
And maybe you'll be glad that you're a
    girl.' "

"Tell me." She closes the piano over his
fingers and he has to stop.

"I think I've found us somewhere to live."

"Really?" She wants so badly to believe
that he has.

"I haven't seen it yet, but I think it'll be
fine. We'll make it fine. Better than living
with Bridget and Stu." He stands.

"Anything will be better than that. Where

237

is it? What is it? Another cottage?"

"Richard's giving me a lift there this afternoon. Let me go and see it first, and then I'll take you."

"A lift? Will you be okay?"

"It's not far. Ten minutes in a car."

"Why don't I come too? If we can move in today, we could get the things off the track before it rains."

"I'd better go." He lights up his phone to check the time. "Richard's picking me up from the village." He goes into the scullery, Maude and Jeanie following.

"But you haven't told me anything."

"And I meant to say, I bumped into Dr. Holloway too. He's got us a gig."

"A gig? No, Julius."

"At the Plough. He said he put in a good word with Chris, the landlord."

"No. I can't play in front of people."

"You played in front of everyone after we buried Mum."

"That was different."

"Then you can play with your back to the audience. Anyway, we might not have an audience." He gives her a quick hug and is through the door. He pokes his head back in. "I'll put the ladder away."

Julius cycles to the village with his fiddle in

its case strapped to the back of his bike. He's hungry and hot but he can't go to Bridget and Stu's because they haven't given him a key, and what would he do there? A pint of bitter would slip down easily now, and one of the Plough's steak and ale pies. He doesn't have enough cash for that, although tomorrow he has another relief milking job starting for a week. He wonders if Chris would let him order a pie and pint, and pay later, but in the end he buys a bottle of Coke, a sandwich, and a bag of crisps from the shop and eats them standing on the pavement, reading the adverts in the window. Someone's advertising an upright piano, free to anyone who can collect it — Frank's old one left in the cottage isn't going to be worth anything either.

Julius waits for Richard opposite the fish and chip shop, looking up at Shelley Swift's windows. She'll be at work now, but he has a date with her later, and he thinks he might play her something on the fiddle. He's not going to tell her about the gig in the pub; he hardly acknowledges the thought, but he doesn't want her to see him with his sister again — her clothes, her funny hair and lack of make-up. Holloway has told some bloke about their music — a journalist or collector of regional folk songs, Julius didn't quite follow — and this man is hoping to come along. Waiting for Richard, Julius decides that he won't play the usual folky stuff for Shelley Swift, but something else. Something classical.

On Sundays when he was young, his mother and sister would be in the cottage cooking a roast, and he and his father would sit side by side in the old dairy with all the little jobs Frank was supposed to catch up on piled in front of them on the workbench: a basket with a broken handle, the sole of a shoe which was flapping loose from the leather upper, old tools that needed sharpening. A tiny radio the colour of English mustard and small enough to fit in a pocket stood on the windowsill, tuned to Radio 3. The *Third Programme,* his father called it. Frank liked Beethoven, Chopin, and Bach — Mozart was dismissed as too sweet, music for the ladies. His father spoke over the pieces he knew well, saying, "Listen to this bit, listen to this," and waving a shoe or a chisel in the air. Sometimes he would sing along — sounds, not words — so that although Julius couldn't really hear the music over his father's commentary, he was swept up in Frank's enthusiasm. When Dot and Jeanie were out of the house, he and

240

his father would attempt to play some of the pieces they'd heard — his father on the piano and Julius on the fiddle, although he learned to call it a violin when they played classical music. "That's it," Frank would say encouragingly. "You've got it." A month or so before his father died, Julius overheard him talking to one of his pals from his social club. "Plays like a dream," Frank said. "A bloody dream." Julius listened harder. "She gets it from her mother, of course, both of them are naturals."

Jeanie rounds up the chickens early and sits beside Dot's grave to eat a sandwich she made at Bridget's. Already the earth mound is green with a forest of seedling weeds and the area is visible only if you know to look for it. She feels as though she should apologize to Dot for making a mess of things in such a short space of time, when her mother managed to keep them all together in the cottage for more than fifty years. Undone in a couple of weeks. Although perhaps her mother should share some of the blame, except Jeanie can't unravel it yet; doesn't have the energy for it until she and Julius are settled. She's excited that he has found somewhere, hopeful — as always — and she tries not to remember the schemes and plans that have gone wrong in the past. Instead she picks some spinach, garlic, and the last winter cabbage and cycles with Maude in the trailer to Cutter Hill, to work on Saffron's garden. Saffron and Angel are not at home, but an envelope has been taped to the handles of the lawnmower and inside is another cheque. Jeanie wonders how easy it is to tell that a cheque hasn't been paid into an account — she has heard about online banking, but she can't imagine how it works. She puts the envelope in her pocket, knowing that, just like Julius with Shelley Swift, she is working without being paid.

To get to Bridget's from Saffron's house, Jeanie has no choice but to cycle through the village. Across the green is the fish and chip shop, already open, with a woman at the counter being served by Doug, and five children climbing on the bench inside, pressing their hands and faces against the glass. Jeanie would have cycled past but she is tired, and she slows and comes to a stop, wondering if she has enough money for some chips. One child, seeing her looking, puts his open mouth on the window and puffs out his cheeks like some peculiar sea creature, his mouth a pink hole. Above the fish and chip shop, the grubby windows on the first floor seem to be positioned too close together, giving the front a shady cross-eyed look. Ignoring the boy at the glass, who is pulled away by a sibling, she hears the notes of a violin coming from the windows above and the thing inside her chest shifts and kicks. She gets off the bike and, holding Maude on the lead, loiters outside the village hall next door and pretends to read the leaflets on the notice-board. The violinist makes a couple of false starts, and when they do get going it isn't any music she's played with her brother, but she knows it is Julius and she knows this is where Shelley Swift lives. The piece is classical, something he played with their father accompanying him on the piano. Bach perhaps. Their mother scorned the classical stuff: rich people's music, she called it, and Jeanie hasn't heard this piece played in years, maybe not since their father died. The music flows out of the windows one wavering note at a time, achingly sweet, a pear drop caught in her throat. When the playing is finished, she hears Shelley Swift and Julius laughing, and she knows that she's lost him.

19

In Nathan's old bedroom, Jeanie searches through the things that Stu brought from the cottage. It isn't that she needs confirmation that Julius's fiddle is gone, but that she wants to see if he has taken anything else, something that might mean he's gone too. She comes first to her mother's banjo case behind the stack of boxes. No one has opened it since Dot died. She sits on the bed and takes it onto her lap. The smell of the interior is the same as she remembers. Dust in the crevices of the green velvet insides, the comforting odour of an old bus: worn upholstery mixed with engine oil.

She removes the banjo from the case and plucks at the five strings, out of tune, of course. She sets it beside her and opens the case's top compartment: a yellow duster and a thumb pick which Dot never used. The second compartment, below where the neck of the banjo would sit, is smaller, and wedged in tightly is a brown envelope, thick with whatever it contains. When Jeanie takes it out, she sees a single word on the front in her mother's poor handwriting and, trying to work it out, can't get past what might be the letter *S*. But inside are sixteen fifty-pound notes.

Once again, in the early evening, Jeanie and Bridget stand at the kitchen sink looking out at the unkempt garden and ignoring the noise Maude is making. The only way Jeanie was able to persuade the dog to go into the greenhouse this time was to tempt her with gravy and a raw egg, although Maude had already been fed tonight. When the food disappeared, in less than a minute, Maude, realizing she was locked in, began to bark.

Bridget fries pieces of frozen diced chicken and adds a jar of white sauce to the pan which she says is Chicken Tonight. She does a funny dance around the kitchen, waggling her elbows, bending her knees, and singing about the sauce, but Jeanie doesn't know what the hell Bridget is doing, and shaking her head and laughing, Bridget goes back to the pan on the stove. Jeanie suggests they add some of the spinach and fresh garlic she brought with her, but Bridget says Stu can't stand garlic, and when she reads the ingredients on the back of the jar she says it has carrots in it already, so they don't need more vegetables.

"Sorry about last night," Jeanie says. "Julius coming in drunk."

Bridget makes a grunt that isn't quite acceptance or forgiveness.

"And the broken bowl. I'll get you another."

"Well." Bridget leans in, confidentially, "I have to admit that Stu does have a bit of a temper when something annoys him."

"Easily riled," Jeanie says, and Bridget stiffens as though she's allowed to say that her husband gets angry, but Jeanie isn't supposed to agree.

"Will Julius be eating with us this evening?" Bridget's tone is pointed. She pours white rice into a saucepan and puts the kettle on. Jeanie is irritated that Bridget doesn't rinse the rice first; it will be full of starch and stodgy when it's cooked.

"I saw him earlier, but he didn't say." She isn't going to tell Bridget about him finding them somewhere to live. Bridget will ask her about it, and when Jeanie admits she knows nothing more, Bridget will roll her eyes and dismiss it as one of Julius's fantasies. She can almost hear the *fuh* which Bridget likes to make and see the wave of her hand. A long tale about the many things Julius has begun and not completed will follow and Jeanie will feel the conflict of needing to defend him and wanting to agree. And besides, now she's found the money, perhaps they can sort things out with Rawson and move back into the cottage.

"Probably with Shelley Swift," Bridget says in a voice designed to hurt. "I've heard he's sniffing around the fish and chip shop." She laughs as though this were a brilliant joke. If she and Bridget are to remain any sort of friends, Jeanie thinks, she will have to leave this house very soon. Bridget moves on to the story of how she met Stu when he and Ed came to clear the contents of a house belonging to some dead relative. It was love at first sight and Stu kissed her within an hour of them meeting. Jeanie has heard it before and can't understand the attraction, not just between Stu and Bridget but between anyone. She has never felt any longing, any desire, and notices that this is something others feel only when she can't avoid it. While Bridget is talking, she thinks of a time in the cottage's kitchen when she was thirteen and Bridget was visiting. It must have been late May, nine months after her father died, because the tomato plants were ready to be moved outside. Jeanie was at the table cutting pictures from a magazine. Bridget and Dot were sitting on the sofa talking about a local farmer.

"Apparently, he died on the job," Bridget said. Dot's head jerked sideways, and Jeanie started to pay attention to the women's conversation. Bridget didn't notice Dot's warning and continued with her story.

"You remember what a big man he was, stomach out to here, heavy with it." Her voice dropped but not so low that Jeanie couldn't hear. "Died with it inside, and her trapped underneath for three hours before anyone heard her shouting."

"Poor woman," Dot said quietly. It was one of her unhappy times.

"Poor man more like. His heart stopped just like that!" Bridget snapped her fingers and Dot lunged for her friend's hand, pulling it down and shushing her.

Later, Jeanie was in the greenhouse, cramming potted-up tomato plants into the wheelbarrow so she could take them out to the cold frames. Dot, sitting on an upturned crate, started speaking in a rush as though to get the words done with. "You know when a woman and a man fall in love, they might go to bed together?"

Jeanie, who couldn't believe her mother was talking about this now, kept her head down. "They sleep together, they make love," Dot said. She hesitated and Jeanie hoped her mother wasn't thinking of the times she must have done it with Jeanie's father.

"I know all this," Jeanie said, hoping to shut her mother up. Jeanie had missed the sex education lessons at school and had tried to piece together the bits of information she heard from other girls, who talked about having to roll rubber johnnies over bananas after the boys left the room and being made to watch a horrific film about having a baby. But there were gaps in her knowledge of how it worked and terms that meant nothing.

"It can get quite strenuous," Dot said.

Jeanie thought of the stallion she'd once seen mounting a donkey, all bared teeth and hooves. "They did this at school, Mum, last year."

"Yes, but listen. If the man or the woman has a bad heart like that farmer had, it can be dangerous. And if his sperm reaches her egg, they might make a baby." Even Jeanie knew Dot was skating over the details. Jeanie mixed up the birthing film she'd been told about with what little she knew, and imagined a tiny hinny — the product of a stallion and a jenny — sloshing out from between a woman's legs. "And if they do — make a baby, I mean — it's always hard for the woman, hard for her heart, carrying a baby around inside for nine months. And you know, Jeanie, that you have a very special heart." Here her mother paused, her hand on her own heart, tears maybe in her eyes. Jeanie looked away, embarrassed. "It would be dangerous for you to have a baby. Not good for your heart, Jeanie. Do you understand?" Jeanie quite liked the idea of having a hinny, but the sex stuff and the boyfriends she couldn't care less about.

"I understand," she said to her mother.

Jeanie, Bridget, and Stu watch another two episodes of the police drama with their dinners on their laps again, and then the two women go into the kitchen — Bridget to smoke and Jeanie to empty and reload the dishwasher; she needs to feel she's earning her keep. Bridget talks about her day at the doctors' surgery and who came in with what, a long flow of information about illnesses and prognoses. Jeanie interrupts to say, "Stu told me that Mum borrowed some money from him."

Bridget stops talking and blows smoke up to the ceiling. "You shouldn't worry about that now. You can sort it out when you're settled somewhere."

"The Rawsons say we owe them rent. They say Mum got behind. Did Julius tell you?" Jeanie turns off the tap where she's been rinsing the dirty plates.

Bridget stubs out her cigarette and puts a Polo mint in her mouth. "I tell you what, how about a nice cup of hot chocolate?" She gets up, opens the fridge, and takes out the milk. The interior light makes her face look sick.

"Stu said she borrowed eight hundred pounds."

"I expect it was about that. I leave the lending to him."

"Was it to give to Rawson?"

"I think she did get a bit behind."

"So, she was paying for the cottage all these years?"

"There was some sort of arrangement, you know that." Bridget speaks in a way which makes her sound desperate not to have to answer fully. She spoons chocolate powder from a jar into three mugs, adds milk, and opens the microwave.

"When did Stu lend her the money?" Jeanie feels like she's wading through deep water and Bridget isn't going to help pull her out.

The microwave's interior is splattered with old food. Bridget presses buttons. "Why does this matter now?"

"Please."

Bridget sighs. "I suppose it might have been a month ago, or a bit more." Jeanie slaps the counter with her palms and Bridget startles. "Don't upset yourself," she says. "You know it isn't good for you."

With her fingers on her ribs, over her heart, Jeanie closes her eyes. "I'm trying to understand. The agreement is that we can stay in the cottage. That the cottage is ours until we die. And free. There was no rent to pay, ever. And now we find out that all this time Mum's been paying the Rawsons. She borrows money but doesn't use it to pay off the debt, which isn't due in the first place. It doesn't make sense."

"Maybe she mislaid it," Bridget says hopefully.

Jeanie shakes her head. "It was in her banjo case. I found it today. She wouldn't have forgotten it there." Jeanie waits to see if Bridget will suggest she return the money to Stu.

The microwave pings, and Bridget opens the door, stirs the hot chocolate, and resets the buttons. "Just let it go. Maybe it's best you're out of the cottage, the place is damp and falling down. Keep the money, use it as a deposit for somewhere else. I won't tell

Stu you've found it. You can pay him back whenever."

"What I don't understand is why she didn't tell us any of this. The rent, getting behind, borrowing from Stu. Being ill, even. We're adults. We could have helped."

"You and Julius need to move on, and you'll be fine. Buy yourself something nice. You deserve it." The microwave pings a second time. Bridget puts a mug in front of Jeanie. "Bring it into the lounge," she says, heading out of the kitchen with the other two mugs. But Jeanie doesn't follow; she stays at the counter, remembering how her mother used to make hot chocolate with powdered cocoa and sugar, heating the milk in a saucepan with a glass disc in the bottom so she would know from its rattle when the milk was boiling. Where is that glass disc now? Probably cracked and ground into the mud outside the cottage.

Later, when Bridget is in the bath and Stu is still watching television, Jeanie counts out five hundred pounds of the cash, leaving three hundred in the envelope, and goes into the lounge.

"Here," she says to Stu. He takes a moment to draw his eyes away from the television — another crime drama.

"What's that?" he says.

253

"Five hundred quid. Some of the money Mum borrowed."

Stu mutes the television and stands.

"So that means, just to be clear," Jeanie says, "that we owe you another five hundred — three for the rest of the debt and another two hundred for the coffin. Plus whatever for the beer at the wake." She still feels sick about the coffin, all that money, chopped up by Julius's axe and stored in the old dairy ready to go on the fire — the fire they won't be having again in the cottage. "Here." She thrusts the cash at him, and he takes it.

"Are you sure? You can pay it back later, when you're more sorted."

"I'm sure," Jeanie says.

He puts the cash into a baggy pocket in the side of his shorts. As she's leaving the room he says, "I hear you and Julius are going to be playing at the Plough."

She comes back towards him. "Who told you that?" she says.

"They've put a poster up. A week tomorrow."

"Well, they should take it down. We're not going to play."

She's about to turn to go when Stu picks up the remote control and says, "I remember my mum playing the piano. Classical stuff, you know, but without the boring bits. She died when I was four, and that's all I ever remembered about her. Not even her, really, just the music and her shoes. Brown lace-ups on brass pedals."

"That's a lovely memory, though," Jeanie says, itching to leave.

"Yeah," Stu says, sitting down again, staring at the telly. "Except I saw my aunt a few months ago. Another bloody funeral. Hadn't seen her for years. Told her about Mum playing, you know, and the shoes. She said Mum never played the piano. We never actually had one. It was my aunt I'd remembered."

20

Pepperwood farmhouse stands face-on to the lane with a grand front garden full of clipped laurel and box kept tidy by a gardener who visits once a week. The house is symmetrical with a central footpath up to the door. Jeanie ties Maude to the wrought-iron gate, walks up the path, and lets the door knocker fall. The thud reverberates deep inside the house.

The previous evening Stu mentioned that the Rawsons had returned from wherever they'd been. Stu had gone with Ed to the Plough, where it seemed to Jeanie that all sorts of information was exchanged and overheard. She wanted to ask Stu if Julius had been in there — her brother had arrived quiet and sober at Bridget and Stu's after they'd gone to bed — but she didn't want to rouse Stu's anger, and she also didn't want to know the answer.

Jeanie expects a housekeeper to open the

Rawsons' door, had planned on introducing herself and asking for Mr. Rawson. If the nature of her visit was enquired about, she'd practised saying it was a personal matter. Now she stands on the doorstep, heart chafing, the creature thrashing about in its tiny cage. But it is Caroline Rawson who answers the door in her tight white jeans and a leather jacket which wouldn't save much skin if she fell off a motorbike. Under it, her shirt is tucked in only at the front. She must be a couple of years younger than Bridget, but she has the complexion of a forty-year-old.

"Oh," Mrs. Rawson says, caught in the moment of poking around in her oversize handbag hanging off one arm. "Jeanie."

Jeanie is suddenly aware of the cardigan she's been wearing for at least two weeks, the long thick skirt, tatty coat, and wellingtons. She finds her voice. "I'd like to speak to your husband."

Mrs. Rawson discovers her phone in her bag and presses a button. "He's not in, I'm afraid." She sounds formal, businesslike, but perhaps not as hard and unfeeling as she had been when she came to the cottage. She looks out, down the lane, over Jeanie's shoulder.

"Well, can I speak to you?"

"Actually, I'm going out. My sister should be arriving any minute."

"It won't take long."

Mrs. Rawson looks out at the lane again, then perhaps good manners take over and she lets Jeanie in. She leads her towards the back of the hall and into a kitchen so light and bright it hurts her eyes. A see-through dining table and eight see-through chairs dazzle under a glass roof and in front of a wall of windows which overlooks a patio and a swimming pool. None of it is like it was when Jeanie was a child. The white kitchen cupboards reach up to the ceiling and have no handles, and in front of them is a long central island made of white granite, with two sinks, each with arcing silver taps. Mrs. Rawson puts her handbag on the island and stands beside it. "If this is about the cottage, that's my husband's business. It's nothing to do with me."

"But you came to see me," Jeanie says. "To tell me we owed two thousand pounds." She almost laughs at how ridiculous that sounds.

Mrs. Rawson drops her mobile phone into her bag in a gesture of resignation. "Well, yes, I did," she says, and for a moment Jeanie thinks that the woman is going to say it was a mistake, all of it — the money, the eviction — but then she seems to gather herself inwards, stand straighter. "But like I said, what Dot owed is for my husband to sort out. I'm very sorry that you lost your mother and so suddenly, but —"

"You know we've been evicted? Turned out of our own home?"

"I had heard that, yes." When Mrs. Rawson blinks, her eyes stay closed for a second too long.

"Nathan gave you and your husband a full report, I suppose? Paid that young man well to do your dirty work, did you?" Jeanie shakes her head in disgust, thinking now that her mother's silence in return for the cottage was not worth it. Dot should have gone to the police and told them that Rawson was responsible for Frank's death. Shown them the bolt that Julius found in Priest's Field. Let Rawson go to prison. They might have lost the cottage back then, but what's the difference — they've lost it now.

"Nathan Clements is being paid for doing a job," Mrs. Rawson says carefully. "It's his choice about whether to take the work or not."

"Jesus, you people."

Mrs. Rawson's smile is hard. "Well, I'll tell my husband you called round. I'm sure he'll be interested to know what you had to say."

Jeanie doesn't move. She lets her anger sink. She didn't come here to have a fight with Caroline Rawson or anyone else. "Two thousand pounds, you said? Yes?"

Mrs. Rawson holds out her arm to shepherd Jeanie towards the door.

Jeanie stays beside the kitchen counter. "I have it here. Some of the money. Not all of it, but something." She takes the envelope with her mother's handwriting on the front from one of the deep pockets of her coat. She hasn't been able to find her handbag, not that there was anything much in it. It's not in any of the boxes in Nathan's old room and she can't find it amongst the stuff still on the track. "Perhaps you could give the money to your husband, have a word with him, and then my brother and I can move back in. To the cottage." Mrs. Rawson is staring at her. "My brother and I are staying with some friends, well, a friend of my mother's, but it's not — it's not — great. And that cottage, you know, is our home." Jeanie is mortified to hear her voice wobble, but she presses on. "Julius and I were born in that cottage, it's where we've lived all our lives, it's where our mother died, and where . . ." Jeanie stops herself before she admits that it's also where she's buried. Her hand is outstretched, with the envelope trembling over the polished work surface.

Caroline Rawson clasps her hands together.

"Please," Jeanie says.

Mrs. Rawson continues to look at her. There is no softening in her face. "No," she says.

"No? No, what?" Jeanie withdraws her hand and the envelope with it.

"No, I can't take it."

"Why not?"

"Because apparently your mother already tried to give my husband the money. She came here like you with an envelope of cash and he wouldn't take it." She gives a weird laugh that Jeanie doesn't understand.

"Why not?"

A car horn sounds from outside. "I'm sorry, but that'll be my sister."

"Why wouldn't he take it if you think there's some rent owing?"

Mrs. Rawson gives up on waiting for Jeanie to move and scoops up her bag. "It's my husband you need to speak to about this, not me." She walks towards the hall. "Alexa, kitchen lights off," she says, and the room darkens. Before Jeanie can work out how that happened, she hears the front door open and hurries after Mrs. Rawson. As soon as they are both outside, Maude stands where she's been tied up, expectant. On the doorstep, as Mrs. Rawson locks the door, she says, "Look, just keep the money, okay? Use it as a deposit on somewhere else. I'm sorry." She flaps her free hand in front of her face and hurries to the waiting car, a green sports car, low, with a long bonnet, and she gets in the passenger seat. Through the windscreen Jeanie watches Mrs. Rawson and her sister embrace, holding each other tight for a full two minutes. Her sister does a three-point turn and they drive away.

21

"Man flu," Bridget says quietly, wrinkling her nose. She and Jeanie are standing on the landing outside Bridget's bedroom where Stu lies in bed with a box of tissues and a mug of Lemsip on his bedside table. "But you don't need to worry — Stu's already phoned Ed and he's on his way now." She looks at her watch. "And I have to get to work."

Not Ed, Jeanie thinks. Anyone but Ed. "Maybe we should put it off until Julius has a free day or wait until Stu's better," she says. Julius is still doing his milking job but says the place is too far for him to cycle home between shifts, and he has no choice but to hang around the dairy for hours in the middle of the day. He said he'd tell them he couldn't take the job, but Jeanie said she couldn't stay at Bridget and Stu's even one more night, and she'd insisted they needed his earnings.

"God, that could be days, a week or more." Bridget is already at the bottom of the stairs putting on her coat, and Jeanie follows her down. "Ed owes Stu a favour for something or other. Just don't let him pull a fast one; that man will do anything for money."

Ed grabs the boxes and suitcases from Nathan's room at a run, up and down the stairs to his pickup, while Jeanie manages two trips and four bags. He's strong for such a small man.

"More than double what Stu told me it'd be," Ed says.

All the time that Jeanie has been at Bridget and Stu's — three days and four nights — she has walked to the cottage in the morning to see to the chickens, collect the eggs, tend the garden, and talk to her mother. The place calls her back. It began to rain heavily one afternoon when she was due to cycle to Saffron's, and she did her best to cover up the things outside on the track using the remaining linen from the chest and a tarpaulin she dragged out from the old dairy. But the day after she went to see Mrs. Rawson, Jeanie noticed that a chest of drawers and a bedside table had gone, as well as the tin bath. She thought about asking

Bridget if the stuff could be stored in Stu's garage, but what would he do with the crap that it was already full of? Each time Jeanie left the cottage she stuffed a couple of carrier bags with small things: a tin of plasters, cotton reels and needles, an alarm clock which might or might not be working, some offcuts of material. As she sorted through it all she hoped to find Dot's wedding ring, but never came across it. Jeanie stashed the bags in Nathan's old bedroom.

"What have you got in here, bricks?" Ed shoulders another box into the back of his pickup.

"Just bits and pieces." Jeanie forces a smile.

"You do know where we've got to take this clobber?"

She hates the word *clobber*. She clenches her jaw, breathes. "To a little place in the woods," she says. That's all Julius would tell her.

"Yeah, right," Ed says, laughing and shaking his head as he lifts up her bike.

When they're sitting in the cab with Maude — the footwells and the gap between the windscreen and the dashboard are stuffed with disposable coffee cups, cans, burger cartons, and bits of paper — as Ed is about to turn the key in the ignition,

Jeanie says, "When you've dropped this lot off, I'd like you to collect some things from outside the cottage too. Things that were put outside when we were evicted." And before he can say no, she adds, "I'll pay you." She still hasn't told Julius that she found the money or that she visited Mrs. Rawson. Julius will have other ideas on how to spend what's left of it: some idiotic business plan to open a cocktail bar in the village or divert the Ink and grow watercress, but if she can't have the cottage, Jeanie wants her things around her.

Ed pulls the key out and leans back but doesn't say anything. In the moment where neither of them speaks she worries he is going to say no, that he's too busy. "I have the money," she blurts out. "It'll be three trips, I think."

"Outside the cottage, is it?"

"On the track. The rest of our things."

"What sort of things?"

"Kitchen things, clothes, some furniture."

"Furniture, is it?"

"A sofa and a few chairs, not much."

"But I'll need someone to help me, see. With the lifting, if there's a sofa." He smiles and she sees that he's missing some of his back teeth. His voice is gummy, she can hear his tongue filling his mouth.

266

"A hundred, I was thinking," Jeanie says, and Ed seems to mull it over.

"Stu won't be able to help me, not with him laid up in bed, like. I'll have to find someone else who's free today and they'll want paying, of course."

"A hundred and fifty then." She wants to save some of the three hundred she has left for emergencies, for food, for the electricity and gas and council tax for the new place. Talking about money makes her palms sweat, her heart tick too fast. She needs him to say yes.

He eyes her.

"Two hundred," she says. "And I want you to bring our piano from inside the cottage," she adds quickly, as though dropping it in at the last moment will make the task insignificant, a simple extra. If Dot's banjo is coming, she wants Frank's piano. "The back door should be unbolted."

"Collect a piano for two hundred quid?" Ed scoffs. "Do you know how heavy those things are? I don't reckon I'll have time to get any of it. I'm only doing this one trip because Stu did a favour for me a while back. I'm supposed to be on another job after this and I'll have to rent a dolly to move a piano."

"Two hundred and fifty," Jeanie says, and

suddenly worried that he won't do any of it, she adds rashly, "Plus the chickens. Ten hens, the coop, and the run." She hates the thought of her chickens living with this man but taking care of Maude and worrying about Julius already feels too much.

He weighs up her offer. "I s'pose whoever I get to help might take them in part payment but they'll still want some cash. It'll have to be three hundred."

"Done," Jeanie says. It's all the rest of the money.

"Done," Ed says with a smile, and she knows she's made a bad deal. "I'll need the money now," he adds.

She takes the envelope out from her coat pocket and turns away from him to count the cash. She knows the remaining three hundred is all there, but she counts it to make sure. She takes it out, the envelope empty, and hands it over. As she puts the envelope back in her pocket, she feels like weeping. Julius can't ever know about it now. Ed counts the money, puts the folded notes in the top pocket of his shirt, and starts the pickup.

Maude rests her head on Jeanie's knee as they drive out of the estate and through Inkbourne, past the village green. They go north on the main road for four miles and turn onto a lane Jeanie has never been along before.

"This is it," Ed says.

He pulls into a lay-by and she stares out of the passenger window. The cracked concrete of the small parking area is studded with common plantains and the perimeter is overrun with nettles and thistles. Scrambling through it is old man's beard.

"Here?" Jeanie says. There's no house.

Ed reverses the pickup a short way down a rutted track between straggly alders and past scattered heaps of rubbish. Jeanie can see the faded colours of a paddling pool, a broken plastic bread crate, decaying sheets of what might be plasterboard piled on top of a disembowelled armchair. Further in, sticking out of the ground elder, is a wheelbarrow with a flat tyre, and the handlebars of a child's bike.

"It can't be here," she says, thinking that Ed must be dropping something off, flytipping, except that all the things in the back are hers. He gets out and lets down the tailgate while she stays in the front, waiting. A cushion is propped against the back of the driver's seat so that Ed can reach the pedals and the steering wheel. When she looks behind, he's scooping several bags into his arms and walking into the scrubby woodland.

She lets Maude out and the dog runs off, nose lowered, and then she gets out herself. The narrow path of trampled weeds that Ed went down leads further into the thicket, dense with holly and more alders and nettles. There is birdsong: blackbird and robin, and the football rattle of a magpie. In the distance Jeanie can hear the intermittent drone of wheels on tarmac from the main road. She passes a scorched circle with a couple of logs for seats and a few blackened cans. People come here, she thinks. Drinkers, down-and-outs, druggies, the homeless.

Above the top of more scrubby bushes she sees a greenish-white roof.

"That's it," Ed shouts from a little way ahead.

When she sees it fully, she thinks again that there must be some mistake. This can't be the place. Ed puts down the bags and smirks, as though waiting for her reaction so he can tell the story in the pub later. How he took that oddball, Jeanie Seeder, to live on some dirty no-man's-land. She won't give anything away; she won't cry out. She waits until he walks off for another load to do that.

The caravan must have once been white

but is now more of a mottled green, darker on the roof where leaves have fallen and decayed to slime. About ten feet long, it has one window — also green — on the side facing Jeanie, beside the open door. Both ends are propped up on bricks and there is another small stack in front of the door, for a step. Beside it are the remains of an awning over a wooden structure half-destroyed by creeper. She remembers Nick's mother's caravan: white and clean. She can't bring herself to step forwards, and she looks through the trees in case Ed might have got it wrong and there is a cottage further on.

"Stu said your brother gave it a clean," she hears Ed call. She goes to the step and looks in. The smell assaults her: fungal, damp wood, and the urine stink of animal, maybe even human. Through the murky underwater light, she sees dirty plywood, a curved ceiling, lino curling at the edges of the floor, green mould in the corners. This can't be the place. She goes to step up, and before she can stop her, Maude jumps inside, running the few feet between a table with bench seats at one end and a single fitted couch at the other. When Jeanie steps in after her, the caravan rocks. The bench seats have fitted cushions, stained and torn —

showing their foam insides — and on the table is the dented metal dustpan and balding brush from the cottage. Above the fitted couch is another window the width of the room, also with a greenish tinge. Maude jumps on the couch, sniffing and pawing at the cushion, her claws ripping the already decayed fabric, and it is clear from the smell and the crumbs of stuffing that something has been nesting here. "Off! Off!" Jeanie clicks her fingers at Maude and the dog jumps down but stuffs her nose in the cushion. Jeanie leans past her and the foul smell to pull back the curtain — the fabric is yellowed but its repeating 1970s pattern of a boy on a tractor is just discernible — and she is left with a ragged corner of material between her fingers. She flicks it off in disgust. Through the window a mossy-coloured Ed is already on his third journey.

She looks behind her. They can't live here. Along the side opposite the door is a laminated countertop, and she lifts half of it to find a filthy two-ring stove. Cautiously, she lifts the adjacent flap and screams. Inside, lying in a plastic sink, is a burnt hand, cut off at the wrist and curled in on itself. She drops the flap, stumbles backwards into Maude, who yelps and dances around her, and then Jeanie bends, hands on knees, slowing her breathing. She makes herself lift the sink lid again and, looking closer, sees a workman's glove, stained and empty.

Ed is back and she stays in the caravan to avoid him. Can she tell him now that she doesn't want him to collect the rest of their belongings from outside the cottage, and that of course she doesn't want him to fetch the piano? She remembers his grin and the long drawn-out way he said *done.* She will not tell him she's changed her mind; she'll have him collect everything and the piano too.

But how will she and Julius stay here even for a few days? Most of their belongings, certainly the furniture, won't fit, and there's only one bed. What will they do for water, for the toilet? When Ed has gone for what must be the final box, Jeanie goes outside and turns away from the caravan, following a track which might be used by badgers, ducking under branches, pushing through bushes until she comes up against a wire fence. On the other side is a back garden with a shed, a new wheelbarrow propped against it. There is a compost heap with perhaps the first grass cuttings of the year dumped on top, and beyond this is a lawn and, at the end, a brick house. A woman enters a downstairs room, holding a cat over her shoulder. Jeanie puts her fingers through the wire, gripping tight enough to feel it digging into her skin. The woman dances with the cat, turning one way and then the other to some unheard music, until together they dance out of the room.

22

For an hour or more Jeanie sits on a broken wall which must once have been part of a small building — an electricity substation or an outhouse. Maude runs about, nose down, following smells and rustles in the undergrowth, returning every few minutes to check Jeanie hasn't moved. There is the almost constant undertone of cars on the main road, and when Jeanie closes her eyes the sound might be waves on shingle. She went to the seaside once on a day trip organized by the social club her father had belonged to. An act of charity she supposes now, since Frank had died the previous year. It seemed to take all day to drive there in the coach, and although she was disappointed that the beach was made of pebbles rather than the golden sand she'd imagined, she and Julius huddled under towels to change out of their clothes in the raw wind. While her brother hobbled as fast as he could to the water and charged straight in, Dot insisted that Jeanie stay close and only paddle in the shallows.

When finally Jeanie hears men's voices — Ed and his mate with the rest of the stuff, she presumes — she dusts off her skirt and returns to the caravan, Maude bouncing along ahead. Inside, she hums a tune, loud enough for the men to hear, while she sweeps thoroughly. She opens the sink and flings the glove out of the door, and then takes hold of the fitted cushion on the couch to brush behind it. As she pulls, it splits open and four tiny pink creatures tumble out. Maude eats them in an instant and Jeanie shrieks at the shock of it, kicking the cushion outside.

Ed is there, next to the step. "Problem, love?" he says.

"No." Jeanie hugs herself. "Just doing some clearing up."

"That damn piano's gone as far as it's going. Even with the dolly and some planks, it's not gonna budge now."

"Where is it?"

Ed points towards the lane. " 'Bout halfway. Near where some kids have had a fire."

What does it matter, halfway or all the way to the caravan, it was never going inside.

"You'll go back for everything else?"

276

"There is nothing else."

"The things outside the cottage, on the track, like we agreed."

"That's what I'm telling you, ain't nothing there."

"Where is it, then?"

"How should I know?" Ed says. "It was your stuff to look out for."

"There's nothing there? Are you sure?"

"A few bits of paper, box of old shoes. Didn't think you'd want them."

"But the furniture? The table and chairs?"

"Someone must have took it."

"Who? Who would have taken it?" With a rising panic Jeanie sees their possessions: the bucket her father mended, the binoculars for when they watched birds together, the rag rug her mother made from old clothes. These are people and memories, not just objects.

Ed shrugs, gives her a look that suggests she's stupid to think it would still be there. "We'll be off then," he says. "Let you get settled in." There's that smirk again and Jeanie thinks about punching him, asking for her money back, but there's something about him that makes her afraid, and she lets him go.

She sits on the step and puts her head in her hands, and Maude, disturbed, comes and paws at her leg. She puts her arms around the dog. "All of it gone," she says. Maybe she should call Ed back to double-check that he's correct — that he went to the right place, that he looked hard enough.

Julius pushes his bicycle with the loaded trailer past the bushes at the opening to the little area of wasteland. Everything glows with a green freshness and a clarity he's not noticed before. The outlines of the new leaves on a magnificent beech, the feathery seed heads lifting from clumps of coltsfoot in the slight breeze. The thought that his mother is dead and the cottage gone continues to jolt him at odd moments, but he can't keep down this feeling of joy. And then, amongst the lanky grass near a clearing where someone has had a fire and where the light falls to the ground in yellow puddles, there is a piano. An upright piano. He leaves the bike and comes round the front and sees that it is their piano from the cottage with its ornate front panel and candle sconces. Here, cockeyed, with two wheels sunk into soft earth, it seems fantastical, part of a fairy story, and he laughs. He lifts the key lid and, bending, plays the beginning of the Bach prelude he played for Shelley Swift on his fiddle. The notes go up and away like his music never did in the cottage or her flat, echoing off the trees and expanding skywards. He has half a mind to get his fiddle and see how that sounds too. He's been humming the music for three days and now here he is, in a wood, playing it on their own piano.

When he played the Bach for Shelley Swift she said it was the most romantic thing anyone had ever done for her. He kissed her while they sat on the sofa and then, in a quick move, she straddled his lap to face him, her legs either side of his thighs. She pressed herself against his chest, against his erection inside his jeans, and she took both his hands and put them on her breasts. When they stopped kissing, he said, "I found somewhere else to live today."

"What?"

"A caravan in a little bit of woodland. Off the main road. You should come out sometime for a visit. Reckon you'd like it."

"A caravan?"

She moved off him and adjusted her skirt. "Me and camping don't mix. Insects, moths. Squatting in the bushes." She laughed.

"It's not camping, not exactly."

She had a hand in her bra, adjusting herself. "For your sister too, is it? The caravan?" And Shelley Swift's laugh had rolled out again.

Now in the spinney, Jeanie says from behind him, "I wanted it," and Julius stops playing the piano as though he'd been caught doing something he shouldn't, something pleasurable that is his alone. But he can't take his fingers off the keys, he can't let go of his laughter yet. "Ed brought it over. Stu's ill in bed."

He plays quietly and the prelude becomes something syncopated, his fingers running across the keys in unexpected ways.

"We can't live here, Julius," his sister says, and he knows he should stop and listen to her, but it's an effort to drag himself away from the music. After a few more notes he stands straight and faces her.

"It's small, but we'll make it cosy." He does believe what he says: Jeanie is a good homemaker, and he will look after her. "Did the move go okay?"

"It's all gone," Jeanie says. She knows she's being deliberately obtuse as though to make him realize it's his fault. She needs someone to blame.

"What's gone?"

"All of it." She speaks petulantly, like a child, and then is angry. "Someone's taken everything." And she sees that a delicate joy

280

which was in her brother's face while he was playing has gone. "I asked Ed to fetch it, but it isn't there."

"I don't understand. The things at Bridget's?"

"The things from the track, outside the cottage." She snaps at him to make him feel stupid for not understanding quickly enough, or guilty for having been happy.

"All the things? Who the hell would have taken them?" He closes the key lid.

"I don't know, Julius. Who do you think? Nathan or one of his mates? Rawson or maybe even Ed? You tell me. Who do you think?"

Julius runs his hand through his hair, the lines in his face deepening, and then suddenly gone. "It's just stuff. Things." He puts out an arm and at first she resists, leans away from him, but not so far that he can't get her, and she lets herself be tucked into him, and her body relaxes.

"It's nearly everything we own." She's almost crying.

"Come on, come on," he says. "I brought some water and a bottle of gas. Let's make a cup of tea. I'm knackered."

She pulls away as she sees that the trailer fixed to the back of his bike is loaded with a large water container and an orange gas cylinder, both strapped on with bungee cord.

"I was paid today," he says.

She knows he wants her to say thank you, but she can't do it. "There was a mouse nest in a cushion and there's only a single bed, and no loo. We can't live in this place, Julius. It's not possible." Her pulse beats in her throat.

"It's just temporary until I sort something else out. It's better than Bridget and Stu's, isn't it?" His voice is cajoling, working on her.

"You'll always bloody sort something out and now see where we are."

"I'm trying. For God's sake, I'm doing my best."

The thumping anger of her heart makes her bend over, palms on knees again, her breath coming fast.

"I'm sorry." He rubs her back. "Breathe, just breathe. Slowly."

When she can stand upright, he says, "Come on, I'll show you." And he pushes the bike and trailer towards the caravan and there is nothing else for her to do except follow on behind. She stands in the door-way, trying not to inhale the terrible smell, while Julius manipulates the table and the bench seats. "See," he says when he's finished. "Another bed. We'll have to do something about the cushions, re-cover them. And here's the sink." He lifts the counter to show her the sink she's already found. "I'll attach the water in a moment." He's like a child allowed to camp out overnight and excited by the equipment: the billycans which fit one inside the other, the sporks, and the tin opener you have to lever up and down by hand. But he hasn't thought about how much more laborious these things are to use for longer than a weekend, and how in the middle of the night he'll be frightened and want to go back to his proper bed.

"I'll fix up the gas and we'll have a cup of tea. And I have another surprise for you — a treat."

"What happens when the owner of this crappy piece of land finds us living here and chucks us off?" Jeanie says, from outside. "What then?"

"No one owns it."

"Everywhere is owned by someone."

"It's been forgotten, cut off. Why else do you think this beauty is still here?" He slaps the side of a cupboard. "It's just until we get back on our feet. Save up some money so we can rent somewhere decent. It'll be fun, living in the woods. Look at Maude, she loves it." Behind Jeanie the dog is running, stopping to dig through last year's leaves and running again. Julius comes out and goes to the trailer and lifts up a carrier bag. "Get some water boiling for the tea because here's your surprise." He opens the bag and wafts it under Jeanie's nose. "Fish and chips," he says in a sing-song. She thinks about Shelley Swift living above the fish and chip shop and wonders whether he bought some for her too, but Jeanie's empty stomach rumbles and her mouth waters at the smell of fish and vinegar. And once more, she forgives him.

23

Jeanie tucks her knees in tight where she lies on the bed which Julius made from the table and bench seats. She is freezing in her sleeping bag even with a blanket on top. From the other end of the caravan, her brother's slow, sleepy breaths both reassure and irritate. Under her head the cushions are damp and the stink of them is in her nose. Tomorrow she will find somewhere else to live. Tomorrow she will heat a pot of water on the stove and clean the caravan thoroughly. Tomorrow she will take the cushions outside and air them in a patch of sunshine. The previous evening, before it became too dark to see, they brought the instruments indoors and as many of the boxes and bags as they could fit; the rest they tucked under the caravan. The piano remains where Ed and his mate left it.

She turns on her back and traces the outlines of grimy stains which blotch the ceiling. It is ten past five on her wristwatch when she hears the first drops of rain tapping on the caravan roof. A steady patter and, within a minute, a downpour.

24

In a corner of the lounge bar of the Plough, Jeanie and Julius tune their instruments. They are watched without curiosity by two elderly women sitting under the front window with their coats on. Jeanie can imagine what they're thinking; what they will whisper to each other later. Two sherry schooners, almost empty, are on the table in front of the women. Behind Jeanie is chatter and the chink of glasses and cutlery from the few people eating in the conservatory, while to her right the counter curves out of sight into the public bar, where conversation and laughter outdo each other in volume. The red swirled carpet, the beaten copper over the fireplace, and the lights reflecting off the bottles and mirrors all press up against Jeanie's eyes, and the thought that there are only two people in the audience makes her hot with embarrassment, even while the idea that anyone else may come and listen — or worse, watch — makes her queasy with nerves. She doesn't understand how her brother talked her into this.

Jeanie and Julius haven't discussed what song they will begin with. When they play at home, either of them will start with a note and the song is begun. But here, self-consciously, they dither, starting and stopping and beginning again, until Jeanie, in exasperation, begins definitively with "As I Walked Out One April Morning." One of the two women at the far end picks up both glasses, takes them to the bar, and passes the musicians on her way to the ladies. Jeanie doesn't catch her eye. The slow song is about a French girl who has been convicted of killing her lover and who asks her executioner to make her death under the guillotine quick and sharp, and Jeanie hasn't realized how interminable and dreary the song is until she sings it to the silent and mostly empty lounge bar. She cuts out the penultimate verse, and Julius, not noticing that now the girl seems to live, plays three more notes after Jeanie has finished, then stops abruptly and frowns at her. The barmaid appears and fills two new schooners with sherry. The woman returns from the ladies.

"We should go," Jeanie says from the corner of her mouth.

"We won't ever get another booking."

"I don't ever want another booking."

The public bar is quiet and then suddenly loud with laughter. The women at the far end continue to sit and stare.

Julius raises his fiddle, strikes a note, and starts very fast.

Jeanie shakes her head, she can't do this, she won't do it, but Julius carries on, one foot stamping out a beat. He sings, *Hoi, hoi, a pretty little maid.* Shouting it above the hooting coming from the other room.

"A pretty little maid," Jeanie repeats, half-heartedly.

"Had a demon lover."
"Had a demon lover."

The women in front of the window sit up straighter. After the next verse the barmaid comes back through to the lounge and rests her forearms on the bar to watch. When someone shouts that they need serving she shouts back that they'll have to come through to the lounge if they want a drink — she's listening to the band. Julius winks at Jeanie. There are three men and a woman in the pub's lounge when that song finishes,

289

and two more when they play the jig "Bryan O'Lynn." The newly arrived women, middle-aged and drunk enough to be slightly unsteady on their feet, hold each other around their waists and join in with the chorus:

" 'It'll do, do, do, do'
Says Bryan O'Lynn, 'it'll do.' "

A few people call out song names, most of which Jeanie hasn't heard of, but they play a version of "Scarborough Fair" which the crowd sways to. The people in the conservatory finish eating and join the others in the lounge bar, and more come through from the public. Jeanie sees a smiling Dr. Holloway, and Bridget taking a photo on her phone. Behind her is Stu, pint in hand, which he raises to Jeanie. She grins back, she can't help herself, and then looks down. At the table beside her and Julius, the drinks line up.

Each song is the same as the version they have always played and yet different, recomposed by a change in emphasis, an alternative word, a minuscule modification, which has always made Jeanie wonder at what point in its mutation it can be said to be a different song. When people join in with the chorus she strains to hear their own music and voices, but she is always aware of Julius — an indication that he is passing her the lead, that he is slowing when the lyrics are sad, and his pause before the final phrase so that they end together, to applause and whistling. They finish the evening in harmony, with "Polly Vaughn":

"He ran up beside her and found it was she
He turned away his head for he could not bear to see
He lifted her up and found she was dead
A fountain of tears for his true love he shed
She'd her apron wrapped about her and he took her for a swan
And it's so and alas, it was she, Polly Vaughn."

As they walk back to the caravan, Jeanie thinks she might be drunk, although she doesn't know what being drunk feels like and she only had a couple of the drinks that were bought for them. She has a giddy, giggly excitement which makes her want to talk and laugh. She and Julius debate each song they played and the audience's reaction, singing snippets loudly and shoving each other about. There is a full moon and by its light the wasteland is transformed into a charming spinney. The rubbish is invisible and only the trees and bushes, in black and white, remain. They stop by the piano. Rain has crazed and flaked the varnish, water has penetrated the top and the key lid; some notes don't play and those that do have a hard quality, without resonance. But Julius puts his fingers on the keyboard and they sing nonsense songs together — "There Was a Frog Living in a Well" and "The Herring's Head" — songs they sang as children with their parents. They belt out the words, making up those they've forgotten, unconcerned about the missing notes, and stopping only when Maude's excited barking from inside the caravan becomes too frenzied to ignore.

25

In the week that follows, Julius's exhilaration from the pub gig keeps him going, even though he learns from Holloway that the man who wanted to come and hear them play didn't make it. Next time, Julius thinks. The job in the dairy continues but now he cycles home between milkings and works on sealing the caravan skylight and the places where the rain gets in, mending the awning and digging a pit latrine a little way off in the woods. He feels an unlimited energy buzzing through him which won't let him sit still. While he works, he thinks up band names and wonders whether a third player would be helpful or a disruption. He imagines them playing in a bigger venue, touring or headlining a folk festival, and when he looks out at the crowd there's a woman in the front row with freckled skin, and they can't take their eyes off each other. A couple of evenings, he cycles to the pub after work and has a few pints, spending his milking money, and on another he visits Shelley Swift in her flat.

Julius returns to the caravan with plank offcuts and a sheet of corrugated iron that he has come across and stashes them away, together with the old wheelbarrow which he drags out of the nettles, thinking that he'll buy a new tyre for it, patch up the rusting bottom. One evening he uses Jenks's smartphone to find out about the law on *adverse possession,* and imagines living in the spinney for twelve years and claiming it as their own. He decides not to mention this to Jeanie yet, but thinks he must get around to painting the word *Private* on a board and nailing it to a tree near to the lay-by. Jeanie no longer talks about looking for somewhere else to live and he thinks she's getting used to their place in the woods. Although she often goes to the cottage to work in the garden, she also scrubs the caravan, sweeps the little clearing they've made in front, and cooks on the two-ring stove. One lunchtime when they have a moment to stop, they sit outside on two plastic garden chairs he's salvaged from a skip, and as though he hasn't looked at his sister for a long time, he is surprised at how content she appears. He remembers the same expression on his mother's face at intervals which sometimes seemed to last years. There had been periods though when Dot had clearly been unhappy, and he'd never thought to ask her about it. What went on in people's heads was a mystery to him. He remembered his parents speaking to each other through him and Jeanie: "Ask your mother to pass the butter." "Tell your father to take his boots off in the house." And another time his mother had sent him to the field where his father was working, with a note folded in half. Julius shoved it in his pocket and dawdled. He was looking for a burst of feathers in the long grass that would show where a bird had been caught by a predator. If he was lucky, the head would have been left and he'd take it home to boil up and add to his collection. When he finally reached the field where his father was supposed to be working, he wasn't there. Julius took out the note and read his mother's message: *If you don't get back here now and mend the yard gate like you promised, I'm going to leave you.* Julius felt sick. He ran all the way home, ready to explain to his mother that it was his own fault for taking so long. In the kitchen, Jeanie was playing the piano and his parents were dancing together around the table and laughing. Later, after his father died, Julius took his collection of bird skulls, all thirty-three of them, each neatly labelled with the species and where it had been found, and threw them away.

Jeanie keeps the radio on while she works, listening to a dramatization of *Vanity Fair,* a piece about the evolution of the earliest language, an interview about the impact of Brexit on organic milk prices. She makes new curtains and seat covers, sewing them by hand from a patchwork of fabric scraps. She listens and she sews and tries not to think about what winter will be like in the caravan with no heating, the outside latrine, the mud and the wet. By then she will have found a way to get them home, she's sure of it. She doesn't mention her thoughts to Julius. Only during the nights when she can't sleep does her anger towards him return. Then she refuses to use the latrine and instead clumps out of bed and pees hard and furiously into a bucket behind the curtain she's hung across the middle of the caravan, knowing the noise will wake him.

Most days she goes with Maude to the cottage. Nothing really is changed since Ed took the chickens, except that someone — Rawson, she assumes — must have been inside because the back door is bolted again. She can't stop herself from peering through the windows and remembering her life as it once was.

The garden demands her attention, everything ripening together: thumb-sized radishes, the white clouds of early summer cauliflowers, hairy gooseberries, beetroots strangely chilly with their damp, tapered bottoms. If she can find a few glass jars from somewhere, she will boil the beetroots and pickle them with some eggs. Digging up the first early potatoes is her greatest joy every year. Pushing the fork into the soft soil around the yellowing potato plant and unearthing a hoard of pale treasure. She sits on the warmed ground with a dozen in her hands remembering how her mother would have nudged her playfully with the fork and said there was plenty more work to be done and she should stop dreaming over a few new potatoes. She starts taking vegetables to Max again; there are too many for her and Julius to eat, and at some point she will have paid off the debt her mother accrued.

She goes to Saffron's house two afternoons as agreed, and although Jeanie stops to have a cup of tea with her and her daughter, she doesn't tell Saffron about where she's living. Saffron continues to write Jeanie cheques which she takes home in her plastic bag that she uses instead of the handbag she's never found.

Jeanie learns the topography of the spinney and walks its triangular boundary in fifteen minutes. The caravan is about in the middle, the lay-by and the entrance are on the shortest side, and the backs of a few gardens adjoin the narrowest corner at the wire fence. No one sees her. No one is looking. She is invisible; to Julius too, she often thinks. Sometimes he is home later than she might have expected but she doesn't ask where he's been or who with. He attaches a bolt to the inside of the caravan door and another with a padlock, for the outside, and gradually she comes to feel safe, sitting in the evenings next to the small firepit they've made, on one of the plastic chairs. Jeanie waits for Bridget to visit, and at first when she doesn't Jeanie is offended, but then she thinks that perhaps they have spent enough time in each other's company for a while.

The steps outside the caravan are new. Julius made them from plank offcuts and by laying bricks in the ground as a foundation to keep them stable. Jeanie sits on them in a patch of sunlight with a bowl on her lap, peeling the last of the old potatoes and watching a butterfly hovering over the pink-

and-white flowers of a dog rose. The radio is on in the caravan, tuned to a programme that repeats the best of the week, and she listens to a snippet about a Japanese garden designer's favourite songs. Julius didn't come home in between milkings today, and now she has a pan of water on the boil for the potatoes and for him to wash with when he returns. There was a day when she was in the village shop and smelled a sour odour; perhaps, she thought, some fruit had rolled under the display and lay rotting and undiscovered. She passed a man along one of the narrow aisles and saw him turn away with his face screwed up in disgust, and she realized that the smell came from her, from her clothes. Now she washes a few items every day in the tiny sink, using hot water from the kettle, hanging the clothes on a line outside if it's dry or draped around the caravan if not.

She stops peeling when she hears the throat-clearing cough of a couple of dirt bikes. The noise isn't coming from the main road, whose whoosh of traffic she no longer notices unless she listens for it, but from the entrance to the spinney. The bikes don't go past the lay-by; instead the whining becomes louder, closer, among the trees, and with it, whoops and shouting. She puts down the bowl and stands, clicking her fingers to call Maude to her. There is laughing, more shouting and the engines ticking over, and after a pause, a run of notes on the piano and then a thump which she feels through her feet, at the same time as she hears the jangle of piano strings. Her hand goes to her chest. Perhaps they, whoever they are — and she has a good idea — will stay near the piano and the old fire patch.

But the engines come closer and she sees two yellow-and-black dirt bikes race past — each with a central section like a wasp's thorax. Mud and shredded plants fly from the tyres as they turn, skidding into the clearing in front of the caravan. Maude barks, hackles and tail raised. The riders are laughing, calling out to each other as they get off and remove their helmets: Tom on one bike, Nathan on another with Lewis riding pillion. Jeanie moves closer to the caravan, and Maude scurries behind her legs.

"We heard you was out here," Lewis says. "What a dump."

He kicks at the washing-up bowl Jeanie has been using and it turns over, water, peelings, and potatoes spilling out. Lewis laughs. Jeanie steps towards the men and lets her anger rise, but Maude is still barking in the corner formed by the caravan and the steps. Jeanie clicks her fingers at her to stop. Now Lewis goes to the washing line where her and Julius's underwear is pegged out, and he stands behind a pair of tights, sticking his head under the crotch, holding the legs around his chin so that he seems to be wearing a bizarre tan-coloured bonnet.

"Looks like you brought most of your shit with you though," Tom says, strutting about. Jeanie tries to keep in mind what Bridget said about his mother.

"Or what was left of it," Lewis says. He smiles as he speaks, and Jeanie knows for certain who has taken what remained outside the cottage.

Nathan stands in the clearing, looking around him, taking it in. He's wearing leather trousers and a motorbike jacket. His hair is roughed up from where he removed the helmet and there is blond stubble along his jaw.

"I'd like you to leave now," she says, low and steady.

"She'd like us to leave now." Lewis's poor impersonation of Jeanie has him doubled over with laughter.

"But we only just got here," Tom says. His nose and eyes are too big for his face, as though he has some growing to do. "We

301

want a tour of your beautiful mansion. Don't we, Nath?" He puts a foot on the bottom step. Maude growls but it is only for effect.

Beside the plastic chairs, Nathan hesitates, and chooses to sit on a log as though he needs an invitation to take a proper seat. "Yeah," he says, although he doesn't sound enthusiastic. He draws his packet of tobacco from a pocket and starts to roll a cigarette.

"Just get back on your bikes and go, and we'll say no more about it," Jeanie says. Tom takes another step up. "You can't go in there." She snatches at the sleeve of his hoodie.

"Hey, lady!" Tom pulls his arm away. "What have you got in here that you're so bothered about?" Then he's inside and Jeanie can't stop him. She looks from one to the other of the two men outside, trying to assess what they could do without her watching, then she follows Tom indoors.

"Like a TARDIS, innit?" He strides the two steps from Julius's bed to the table and back, all the time looking around. She turns off the gas under the boiling water and he takes the photograph of her parents from the wall where Jeanie has hung it next to Angel's painting, looks at it, and puts it back, tipping a corner so that it dangles crookedly. There are still voices coming from the radio, and Tom moves the dial until the conversation between the garden designer and presenter changes to a static hiss. He flicks up the long cushion on a bench seat as though they might be in the habit of keeping things tucked underneath. Below is a finger hole to access the storage space. He pulls the lid up, revealing their spare saucepans, plastic bags, wellington boots, and he lets the lid fall with a clatter. Moving around the space, he slides open a cupboard above the cooker, lifts the lid to the sink with one finger and lets it drop. "I heard you got more than cups and plates in this shithole." Beside the cooker, he squats and opens the cupboard to look inside and, when he stands, kicks it shut. China rattles.

Jeanie turns off the radio. "My brother will be back soon, and he won't be happy to find you here." She doesn't know when Julius will be home, whether he'll come straight from work or go somewhere first.

"I wouldn't want to make that batshit brother of yours unhappy. I see him now and then, you know, making a couple of pints last all day in the Plough."

She will not rise to his needling. Tom takes a step towards the door and she exhales, but his move is a feint and he stops to lean against the jamb, blocking her exit.

"I used to come to these woods years ago," he says. "Before they chopped down the trees and built them new houses. Shooting rabbits, pigeons, whatever I could find. I might come out here again one of these days with my gun. Still some things worth shooting, I reckon." He straightens his right arm and points it at her, forming his hand into the shape of a gun — two fingers out, two curled in, thumb cocked — and then he turns and aims out of the door at Maude. He jerks his arm. *"Pkwoo, pkwoo,"* he says, firing. Jeanie flinches and Tom puts his arm down and casually looks around. "So, you can tell me where it is and we can bugger off."

"Where what is?"

He yanks at a drawer and it comes all the way out, the contents — cutlery, potato masher, spoons, and the poker — crashing to the floor. "Whoops," he says. "What a mess."

"Get out!" Jeanie grabs the drawer from him and holds it up in front of her like a shield.

"I've heard you've got a big wad of money stashed away somewhere in here. A brown envelope full of cash."

She thinks about when she gave the money

to Ed in the pickup, how she'd turned away. Perhaps not far enough. Or when she waved the envelope at Mrs. Rawson across her kitchen island. "We haven't got any money, you idiot. Do you think we'd be living here if we did?"

"Takes all sorts. I thought maybe you get a kick out of shitting in the woods."

From outside she hears a beat, a regular hollow rhythm, and she pushes past him to the door, pressing the drawer to her chest. Lewis is sitting on a plastic chair with the upturned washing-up bowl between his knees. With straight fingers he is beating out a steady tempo. "Where's the money? Where's the money? Where's the money?" he chants. Nathan is still sitting on the log smoking his cigarette and looking at the ground.

"Stop that," Jeanie says to Lewis. "Stop it! There isn't any money." She goes up to him and pulls the bowl away so that she's holding it in one hand and the drawer in the other, as though these are the only things she's managed to save from a burning house or a sinking ship. Tom comes down the steps and Maude backs herself into the space under the caravan.

"Jeanie? Hello, Jeanie?" a woman's voice calls, and a second later, Bridget, shiny-faced and with her handbag over her shoulder, arrives in front of the caravan. "So, this is where you've been hiding for the past two weeks," she says as though she's been practising what to say, uneasy with the fact that she hasn't visited before. In the next instant she takes in everything else: the shabby caravan, the bikes, the two young men, and, lastly, her son. Her expression moves through surprise, to confusion, to something that Jeanie struggles to read, suspicion perhaps.

"Mum," Nathan says. He throws down his cigarette and squashes it under a boot.

"What are you doing here?" she says. "And Lewis? And you too, Tom." She turns her head one way and then the other. Nathan's friends nod to her, mumble their greetings. Only then does Bridget notice that Jeanie is holding a washing-up bowl and a drawer. "What's going on?"

Tom moves to his bike, puts on his helmet which he left on the seat, swings a leg over, and starts it up. "I've got to get off, Mrs. Clements," he says above the noise of the engine.

"Wait a minute," Bridget says.

Tom turns to Jeanie and smiles. "Very kind of you to let us come and see your new place, Miss Seeder. I'll definitely be back soon."

Jeanie clutches the bowl and the drawer closer. They watch him leave.

"Jeanie?" Bridget says. "Are you okay?" She goes towards her, but on the ground in front of the caravan's steps the six peeled potatoes make her stop. Their pale exposed insides are smeared with dirt and two of them have been crushed into the earth by a heel. She looks from Jeanie to the mess, to Nathan.

"I'd better be off too," Lewis says, and when he's beside the bike seems surprised that he needs Nathan in order to leave.

Nathan stands and walks around Jeanie and Bridget, leaving a wide gap, as though he thinks his mother might reach out and grab him.

"Nathan," Bridget says. "What's going on here? Why have you come to see Jeanie?"

"Let him go," Jeanie says. She wants it over with.

"See you, Mum." Nathan tugs his helmet on, climbs on the bike, and starts it up.

"What have you and Tom been up to? You get off that thing and tell me right now." Her voice rises.

Nathan revs the engine but Lewis, perhaps thinking it's impolite to leave while she —

Nathan's mother — is speaking, lingers. "We were just having a bit of a laugh," he says.

"I can't see Jeanie laughing."

"Nice to see you, Mrs. Clements," Lewis says, sitting behind Nathan and putting his own helmet on.

Bridget stands beside the bike's high front wheel. "I hope you're not still working for those Rawsons," she says fiercely. "Is that what you're doing here?"

Nathan doesn't look at her, doesn't reply. Lewis puts his hands on Nathan's waist, the bike roars, and Bridget jumps back.

It occurs to Jeanie as they watch Nathan and Lewis leave that while Tom did come looking for the money, Bridget is right, Nathan didn't join in with the search or the chanting and must have come on some other business, the Rawsons' business, and she isn't sure what that could be.

"Did you pass a piano?" Jeanie says to Bridget. She puts down the bowl and the drawer and crouches in front of the caravan, clicking her tongue. Jeanie thinks she can hear Maude panting under there, little whines at the top of every breath.

"I saw what I thought was a piano," Bridget says.

Jeanie slaps her thigh, but the dog doesn't come.

"It was on its back. Ed told Stu that you'd got him to bring it. What were you thinking? And why did you invite that Tom out here?"

"Damn them. I loved that piano." Now the men have left she's shaking with anger as much as with fear. "I didn't bloody invite them. They just turned up and started pulling the place apart and threatening me and Maude."

"Oh, Jeanie. I'll send Stu round again to see Nath. He'll have to listen this time."

"And the bloody potatoes are ruined."

"Come on. Don't worry about the potatoes. Sit down. They've gone." Bridget squeezes Jeanie's arm. "I came to see how you're getting on. How about I make us a nice cup of tea?" She looks around, unsure whether that's possible.

Jeanie doesn't want to sit, the anger is surging through her and she wants more than ever to let it take hold, creep along her veins, into her jaw, her gums, sparking the roots of her teeth, down into her heart. She could be anything — a boxer, a fighter, a murderer. She breathes in deep through her nose, puts her finger to her neck, and blows out slowly. "I'm okay, Bridget. Don't fuss.

But there is something I want to show you, something I want you to do for me." Jeanie goes to the caravan and Bridget follows, stepping over the potatoes and, once inside, over the cutlery strewn across the floor.

"Did those boys do this?"

From under the lining paper in the kitchen cupboard which Tom slid open, Jeanie pulls out the empty brown envelope.

"Let me pick up this mess." Bridget bends towards the floor.

"Leave it. Just sit down," Jeanie says. "Please," she adds more gently. Bridget sits on Julius's couch. "This is the envelope that had the money in it. The one I found in Mum's banjo case. I gave a bit of it to Stu to pay back some of what Mum borrowed, and the rest to Ed for moving us out here." She isn't going to admit to the mistake of paying Ed too much.

Bridget puts her handbag down beside her. "I know Stu'll wait for the rest. But you weren't supposed to pay Ed for moving you, that was meant to be a fav—"

"Bridget." Jeanie catches her before she can go on and holds out the envelope. "I want you to tell me what's written on the front."

Bridget takes the envelope warily but doesn't look at it.

"I know it's Mum's handwriting but I can't work out the word."

"Why don't you read it? Although, come to think of it, your mum had terrible handwriting — I was always saying that it was illegible."

"Because I can't."

"You can't read it?" Bridget hasn't looked at the envelope and she seems embarrassed on Jeanie's behalf.

"I can't read or write, not properly. I know that you know." She always thought it would be a monumental effort to admit this lack out loud, this failing, this stupidity, but the words slip out easily and she doesn't feel any shame.

Bridget's mouth opens a little and then she closes it. "Well, I had an idea but —"

"What does it say?" Jeanie nods at the envelope.

Bridget hesitates, sighs, looks down, and smooths the paper across her large thighs. Finally, she speaks. "Spencer." She is unsurprised.

"Spencer?" Jeanie says. "What, as in Spencer Rawson?"

"Spencer Rawson, that's right."

"Mum wrote that man's first name?" She and Julius and their mother had never used Rawson's first name on the rare occasions

311

they spoke about him. They didn't even use *Mr.* Somehow, it seems impossible that Rawson has a first name because it must mean he had parents and was once a baby.

"He's not that bad, Jeanie. If you just gave him a chance."

"He killed my father."

Bridget looks down, the envelope held out, and when Jeanie, still standing, doesn't take it, she puts it beside her on the seat and with a groan kneels on the floor and begins to gather up the cutlery and the poker.

"Don't worry about that," Jeanie says, but she waits until Bridget has collected them all. Bridget stands with an effort and looks around for the drawer and, perhaps remembering that it is outside, puts the things on the counter where they spread out with a clatter.

"What was going on between Mum and Rawson?" Jeanie says.

"It's best left," Bridget says. "Your mum's gone. It's finished."

26

After Bridget leaves, Jeanie picks up the potatoes. Two are pressed so deeply into the ground that she has to dig them out with a knife. She lobs them into the bushes, angry with herself for not standing up to Tom more, for not pushing him out of the caravan. The remaining potatoes go in a pot to boil, and in a frying pan on the second ring she cooks six sausages until they are brown, and then adds to the potato water a few handfuls of broad beans which she picked that morning.

When the sausages and vegetables are ready, she puts them on plates with saucepan lids on top to keep the food warm, and she sits in a plastic chair with a blanket across her shoulders, waiting for Julius. At nine when the bushes and trees turn shadowy, she puts Julius's plate on the ground and whistles for Maude. She sits with her own plate on her lap and eats savagely, using her fingers to hold the sausages. She knows where Julius is. He'll be with Shelley Swift, sitting on her sofa, nice and warm, watching television, snuggled up close, her feet in his lap. Jeanie throws the rest of her food on the ground, but the dog hasn't come. She whistles repeatedly. She's sure Julius will be home later. He's got to be up early to get to Stockland's Farm again, the other side of Froxfield, for the milking. She sits and watches the bats, quick black shadows flitting amongst the trees. If Julius isn't back soon, she'll bolt the caravan door and he'll have to hammer on it to be let in, and then she'll take her time getting out of bed. She calls for Maude and goes inside, leaving the door open. First, she'll make cocoa — the milk won't last another day. When the pan is on the stove she goes to the door and calls once more but still the dog doesn't come. She turns off the gas and whistles from the bottom step. She has a sudden idea that they're gone together, Maude and Julius, exploring what's out there in the dusk, without her. Julius hasn't spent a night away from home for years, and surely he wouldn't do that without telling her, and Maude always comes back eventually. But when did she last see her? When Bridget left or after that? Maybe before that. It occurs to Jeanie that Julius might be injured, perhaps he's been kicked by a cow, had his jaw broken and is in hospital with no way of telling her. The idiot.

But she doesn't need Julius; she's perfectly capable of taking care of herself and the dog. The bloody dog. She calls and then fetches the torch, silver and heavy as a club, and listens: for dog noises, for the sound of Julius stumbling home, for the rev of a dirt bike. She remembers Tom forming his arm and his hand into the shape of a gun and shooting at Maude. There are only the normal rustlings and scuttlings in the undergrowth, the hoot of an owl, the occasional car on the road. She is less fearful of the spinney than when they first arrived and she has never been afraid of the dark, but it feels different now. She knows the location of every bush and tree, where the paths connect, and how to avoid the remains of the brick structures. A crescent moon shines, making the shadows blacker, but the places where the light falls are bright enough to see without the torch.

"Maude!" she calls. In front of the caravan she whistles, turns around, whistles once more. Her lips are dry and the whistle seems to travel only a yard or two.

She walks to the latrine first. Julius is going to dig a new hole next week and move the rickety shed-like structure he's built around it. Four short planks surround the hole to keep the edges secure. There's another plank to hide the hole, but it's cumbersome to manoeuvre and most times they don't bother. When she gets to the latrine, she calls, disliking her voice away from the caravan, as if there might be people out there listening. The smell is of damp earth, nothing bad. Should she have locked the caravan door? Perhaps Maude has been lured away so that she — Jeanie — can be lured away too. Quickly, she shines the torch into the hole — it's dark but not so deep that if Maude had fallen in, she would have disappeared. There is no dog down there. Perhaps she's already back at the caravan, but when Jeanie returns there's no sign of her, and the sausages and the other food remain on the ground, uneaten.

Jeanie padlocks the door and walks the rest of the spinney, calling and whistling. As she comes full circle she can't help running to the caravan, sure she will see Maude resting on the ground with her front legs out, or Julius tapping his foot impatiently on a tree stump, although of course they would both have heard her calling. Again, no one is there. No dog. Inside, she sits at the table for a while but can't settle. With every noise she unbolts the door, expecting Maude, damp and muddy. She whistles from the doorway. It is midnight and she's livid with Julius. If they weren't living out here on a disgusting piece of wasteland, then the men wouldn't have come, and Maude wouldn't have run off. The wood is silent. Perhaps the dog has gone as far as the main road following the scent of a rabbit and is this moment lying hurt on the verge.

Her wellingtons on, Jeanie jogs through the spinney, hand clamped to chest as if to keep the egg of her heart safe inside. On the main road it's pitch-black until a car rushes past and she almost falls in the hedge, and a couple of the drivers, seeing her at the last second, blast out their horns and flash their lights. She trudges back to the caravan and lies on Julius's bed, fully clothed, with her boots on and the heavy torch beside her. She sees three o'clock come and go on her wristwatch and falls asleep.

Just a quick pint, Julius thinks as he cycles through the village on the way back from his day at the dairy. There is more relief milking coming up and he reflects that apart from the stink of the shit and the early mornings, he likes the cows and he's probably pretty good at this job. Maybe he could do it full-time, perhaps he'd be able to save enough for a deposit so he and Jeanie can rent somewhere decent, buy his own herd of cows, lease a field. How hard can it be? When he comes out of the pub, he can't resist wheeling his bicycle past the fish and chip shop. He props it against the window and writes Shelley Swift a text: *What you up to?* He imagines he can hear the ping of her phone above his head. *Reading,* comes back immediately. *You home?* he asks. *Why?* she texts. *Look out your window,* he writes just before his phone's battery dies.

He always means to go back to the caravan; Jeanie will have cooked for him, and she isn't used to being there on her own after dark. But she has Maude, he thinks, she's fine. Shelley Swift invites him in for a drink, and then to stay for supper — which turns out to be fish and chips from downstairs which he pays for — and supper leads to her bed. Even when he wakes in the middle of the night he has the intention of leaving, but rests in the dim light thinking about the effort of finding his clothes, which lie in a trail from the sitting room to the bedroom, like a seduction scene in a romance novel, except that Shelley Swift was the one doing the seducing. He strokes her back and they make love again. In the morning when he wakes fully, he reaches out to touch her once more, but she laughs and elbows him away, saying she has to get to work. He hears the shower, then the kettle boiling in the kitchen, and the smell of toast reaches him. He's still in bed when she comes back in to shed her dressing gown and choose underwear from a drawer. She balances half a slice of toast and Marmite on a pile of paperbacks. As she passes the bed, he makes a grab for her and she falls backwards, laughing. He kisses her and the taste of Marmite is awful, but he wants her.

"Don't you have a job to go to?" she says, escaping. She picks up his underpants and flings them at him. He was meant to be at Stockland's Farm three hours ago but he doesn't care. "Come on, lazy bum, time to get up and out."

He raises himself on his elbows and watches her get dressed. "Can I see you tonight?" he asks.

"Tonight?" She folds the rest of the toast into her mouth and lights up her phone. He remembers that his is dead and his charger in the caravan. "I'm not sure," she says, her mouth full. "I'll probably be catching up on the sleep I missed." She winks at him and then stares at something on the screen, types fast with both thumbs, and only when she's finished does she give him her attention. "I've got to go. Make sure the front door is locked when you leave." She blows him a kiss from the bedroom doorway.

Just after six, the morning sun hits Jeanie's eyelids and wakes her. Outside, everything is as it had been before she fell asleep: the firepit, the plastic chairs, the washing line. Last night's dinner has been disturbed by a fox or some other creature, but it can't have been Maude because she would have eaten the lot. The air is fresh and cool, and the weak sun warming as she turns her face up towards it. She whistles for Maude and listens: only birdsong and the early traffic on the road. For no reason, except that she didn't think of it the night before, she crouches to look below the caravan. At one end are planks and corrugated iron that Julius has salvaged, but in the middle the grass is long and yellow, tangled with bramble. A brownish lump lies amongst the plants, unmoving. Jeanie's breath catches and she is down on her stomach, scrabbling forwards, saying, "No, no." She pulls herself towards it — dog-shaped now, she's sure —

unaware of the thorns tearing her skin and clothes. It is a cardboard box, one they left out in the rain when they first arrived and must have emptied and shoved under there out of the way. Jeanie lies flat, her feet in wellingtons sticking out beside the steps, her head resting on the rotting cardboard, and cries.

27

All day, as Julius shovels cow shit — the job he's been given because he arrived so late for his shift — details of the previous night with Shelley Swift return in flashes to jolt him. The coffee-coloured mole at the top of one thigh, the pinkness of her unpainted toenails, the hollow where the back of her head meets her neck, hair dark with sweat. She, in return, seemed to enjoy his attention and was a much more enthusiastic and vocal lover than any of the three women he slept with when he was younger. When he cycles home from the dairy to the caravan there is a Shelley Swift buzz running through his veins.

In the early evening, Jeanie sits on the top step with another bowl of water on her lap, carrots in the bottom this time, swirling them with her hand, trying to remember what she's supposed to be doing. Her head feels too large for the rest of her body and dizzy after her walk to the cottage and around the fields looking for Maude. There's nothing for dinner apart from these carrots. No milk, no bread for the morning or for Julius's sandwiches, no eggs, and she doesn't care. She waits and she washes carrots.

She hears Julius coming, recognizes the *siss* of his bicycle as he wheels it through the spinney. The way his feet snap twigs.

"Hello," he says.

"Hello." The word is barely there and she won't look at him.

"Okay, let's just get the apologies over and done with. I'm sorry." He props his bike against the caravan and squats beside her with a quiet groan of tiredness. "I'm sorry I stayed away all night. I'm sorry I didn't let you know."

She can hear the smile in his voice. The carrots are clean, but she swills them and watches the dirt settle. She can smell the sweat on him and the fetid, shitty stink of cows. There's no water on for his wash. "You can do what you like, Julius," she says finally, her words seething. "I'm not your mother and you're fifty-one." She is the pot of water on the stove, bubbles forming on the bottom, coming to the boil.

"What's for tea?" Julius says, still trying to mend it. He stands, stretches.

"I don't know, what is for tea?"

"Don't be like that. I've been at work all day. I'm starving. I want to wash, eat, and go to bed."

"You didn't get enough to eat last night? Enough sleep?" She speaks under her breath.

"What's that?"

"Either you live here or you don't."

"*We* live here."

"While you are *living here,* Nathan and his two bullies came around on their dirt bikes, making threats and tearing the place up. They thought we had some money hidden away. Money!"

"Oh, Jeanie." He takes the bowl from her, sets it down, and gently lifting her hands, makes her stand. If she lets him put his arms around her she knows that all her anger will seep away. She isn't going to cry.

She feels with her foot for the step up behind her and withdraws her hands from his. "No more 'Oh, Jeanie'! You also wouldn't know that Maude has gone. I think she must have been run over or else they've poisoned her. Shot her, maybe. I thought those bloody men were going to kill me too!" She didn't know she thought this, but now, in the way her hands are shaking, she sees it's true.

"You should have come and got me."

"Where from? Shelley Swift's?"

"You know I was at Stockland's."

"And what good would that have done?" She grips the sides of the doorway, her heart's excited little punches goading her on.

"Well, either you think I can help or you think I can't."

"I don't care any more. I really don't care. I thought we were in this together, but we're not."

From the bottom of the steps he reaches up for her, a moment of contrition or guilt. "We are, we are. We'll always look out for each other."

"Not if you're not here! How will we look out for each other if you're not here?"

"Jeanie, please."

Suddenly her energy for anger is spent. "Go back to Shelley Swift. Really. I think you should go now. I'm fine here. I managed without you last night and I'll manage again." She reaches to grab the door. Its side scrapes against him as she pulls it closed, and he wrenches back on it, but she slams the door and for a second his fingers are jammed, and he swears as he yanks them out. She bolts the door quickly and stands with her back to it, head up.

"Jesus! Jeanie, don't be stupid. Open the door."

She presses against her heart while he hammers, the same beat Lewis made on the washing-up bowl.

"Go away, Julius. I don't need you."

She sees him at an angle, peering through the window beside the door. Before he can move to the window at the far end, she draws the curtains closed and sits on the couch. She puts her head in her hands, dizzy, hoping she isn't going to faint. Julius comes back to the door and she jumps at his thumping.

"You know what?" he shouts. "You're just like your mother. Why shouldn't I spend some time with a woman? One that isn't my mother or my sister? What's wrong with that? It's completely normal. She always had something to say about anyone I liked, listing all the things she thought was wrong with them, putting me off. It was just a way of keeping me at home. Like she kept you at home too, Jeanie! Well, now she's gone and there is no bloody home any more, so why shouldn't I have a life? Find someone to love? You said it yourself, we're fifty-one. Fifty-one! Bloody hell. You should get out,

Jeanie, leave home, finally. You might find you enjoy yourself."

When she doesn't reply or open the door, she hears him go. There is a pain in her throat, a constriction which travels down her chest. She stands, one hand on the counter for balance, and calls her brother's name, but he has already gone.

Julius cycles recklessly to the village in the dusk and arrives hot and sweaty. He sits for an hour next to Jenks at the bar in the Plough. He buys the last bag of pork scratchings hanging from a cardboard display and a packet of salted peanuts, washing them down with a second pint of bitter. Working on the farm always makes him hungry and thirsty. He's angry with Jeanie for locking him out, even if she has good reason. And then, feeling guilty, he thinks that tomorrow he will phone the police or the RSPCA about the dog, although he still needs to get his damn charger from the caravan. Tomorrow he will go and see Stu about Nathan and the others, in fact he will bloody go round to wherever it is Nathan lives and have a word.

Jenks talks to Julius about how great the music session was, how amazing Jeanie's playing and singing are, as though Julius wasn't one of the musicians, wasn't even there. Julius makes noises of agreement while thinking of Shelley Swift and wondering whether in a few months' time they will be retelling each other the story of how they met and became lovers, girlfriend and boyfriend, partners, whatever the word is when you're fifty-one: the stuck window, the pilot light, their first kiss on the landing, the time in the woods, and the fiddle playing. By nine thirty, Julius has had enough of Jenks's endless chatter of football matches and dated jokes about knockers and priests. He stands in the doorway of the pub. It's raining, and he wonders whether Jeanie will have calmed down enough to let him in. It's a long way to cycle to the caravan in the rain just to find out that she hasn't. He unlocks his bike and pushes it quickly up through the village.

The pain in Jeanie's chest grows into a burning that she can't ignore. She takes a couple of painkillers with a swig of water, holding a fist hard to the middle of her chest, and wonders if this is it. All the rests she took, all the things her mother wouldn't let her do, all the places she didn't go, have come to this moment. It could be hours before Julius returns, if he ever does. She imagines being found in the caravan in a day or a week. Dying or dead. She lies on the bed, crying with the pain and for Maude, and for herself. Rain patters on the caravan roof. For the first time she wishes that she had a mobile phone. After an hour when no position, standing or lying, relieves the pain and it is dark outside, she takes the torch, locks the caravan, and walks. Her coat isn't properly waterproof, she didn't think to pack an umbrella when they left the cottage, and the rain runs down her face and the back of her neck. Every few steps she has to rest, doubled over and groaning, the torchlight illuminating the muddy toes of her wellingtons. In the village she heads for the telephone box next to the bus stop. She will phone the police about Maude, she will phone Julius's mobile — although she isn't sure she can remember the number — she will phone for an ambulance. But when she opens the red door, the telephone is gone, replaced with a circular yellow box printed with an image of a heart with a lightning bolt through it, and a figure kneeling beside the body of another, hands on chest. She is reminded of Julius kneeling beside the body of their mother on the kitchen floor, only six weeks ago. Perhaps Julius will be in the Plough, sitting with a pint in the public bar, and not at Shelley Swift's. Please, she thinks, do not make me have to knock on Shelley Swift's door and ask for my brother; she doesn't look up when she passes the fish and chip shop. It's just before ten and the yellow lights from the pub shine out through the windows. It looks inviting, warm, dry. She goes into the public bar where a few tables are occupied, a slot machine jingles to itself, and the only man in there turns to look at her.

"It's Jeanie, isn't it?" the man says. "Jenks." He nods a hello. "Why've you been walking in the rain? Let me get you a drink. You look in need of a hot toddy."

"Is my brother here?" she says.

"You've just missed him. He's gone up the road." Jenks tilts his head, a knowing smile on his face. "You know. Up the road. What are you having?"

Jeanie holds on to the bar as another spasm grips her. She inhales and exhales slowly. "No drink, thank you. Can you phone him or text him?"

Jenks picks up his phone from beside his pint. "No problemo. Text might be best. You never know what he could be in the middle of." He raises his eyebrows. "Run out of credit, have you? Are you all right?"

Jeanie tries to smile. "Ask him to come

330

home, would you? To the caravan."

"You don't want him to come over here?" Jenks says.

"As soon as possible. It's an emergency. To the caravan," she repeats. Jeanie can't wait for him in the pub, talking to Jenks, pretending everything is okay.

"Asap," Jenks says.

"And tell him — tell him I'm sorry."

"Right," Jenks says, typing with an index finger into his phone.

The lights are on in the sitting room above the fish and chip shop. Julius pushes his bike into the alleyway and locks it. He knocks on Shelley Swift's door and hears her clumping down the stairs.

"Julius," she says, surprised. "What're you doing here?"

"I was thinking about you," he says.

"Really?" She laughs. A happy laugh, he thinks; a pleased-to-see-you laugh. But she stays in the doorway and doesn't invite him upstairs and he notices that she has a book in her hand — *Death in the Afternoon* — closed on her index finger to mark her place. "And what were you thinking?" she says.

"This and that."

"Yes, but what exactly?" Her smile is coy,

as though there's a secret word he needs to say before she'll let him in.

"About how I can't get enough of you."

She seems pleased with this. "You'd better come in then."

He follows her upstairs. She's wearing a shapeless jumper and a pair of grey jogging bottoms with the word JUICY up one leg. He wants nothing more than to put his hands on her large behind and take her back to bed, but as soon as he's in her sitting room he becomes blundering and tongue-tied, and although he didn't notice it in the pub, he's suddenly aware of the ripe smell of the farmyard and his own sweat coming off him. He feels a surge of anger that Jeanie didn't let him into the caravan at least to have a wash after work. No wonder she's alone, even the dog has deserted her. He is immediately ashamed of the thought. While Shelley Swift makes coffee, he uses the bathroom, dampening the corner of a hand towel and scrubbing at his neck. He tries to sniff his armpits and washes these too.

Julius sits on the sofa next to Shelley Swift's giant cat. Paperback novels are piled on the coffee table. "Did you know," she says as she brings in two cups of coffee and a glass of water on a little tray, "there's one of those old phone boxes on Cutter Hill full

332

of books? Loads of thrillers. Not as easy as reading on my Kindle, but they're free."

"I like real books too," Julius says because he wants to agree with her.

"Yeah?" she says. "What are you reading at the moment?" She nudges the cat off the sofa and sits beside Julius. He leans over to kiss her without answering because he has no answer, but she shoves him gently away.

"I'm too hot for all that stuff," she says, and picks up a folded newspaper from the floor and flaps it in front of her. Her laughter creases her eyes into slits and makes him want to kiss her even more. She takes off her jumper and her scent wafts out, lemon soap and brick dust. Underneath, she's wearing the silky blouse she had on that afternoon in the woods. She plucks at its front. "I think I must be having a hot flush." Her throat and cheeks are red, and he can't stop looking at her. Women's bodies are complicated, they do things Julius doesn't want to understand although he's lived with two of them for fifty-one years. But everything Shelley Swift's body does intrigues and delights him. She puts the newspaper down, picks up the glass of water, and holds it to her neck, tilting it against one side and then the other. "Is it warm in here or is it just me?"

"I love you, Shelley Swift," he says, and he can feel it in his body like an ache.

She laughs again. "Don't be silly, Julius Seeder."

He puts an arm around her, making her tip her glass, spilling some water on the sofa.

"Watch it," she says, pulling away and standing. She puts the glass down, and in between the coffee table and the gas fire, she twirls in front of him, arms raised.

"Will you marry me?" The words are out before he even thinks them. He has a fleeting image of Jeanie in the caravan, alone, and then it's gone.

"Marry you!" Shelley Swift continues to turn and laugh. "You are joking, aren't you?"

He can imagine her shrieking the words down her phone to one of her friends or typing them into her mobile in capital letters. "What's so funny?" he says. "I've got a wedding ring."

She comes to a stop. "You've got what?"

"A ring. Not on me, but I've got one." He can't exactly remember where he put his mother's wedding ring. Perhaps in the bedside drawer before they had to leave the cottage. What happened to it after that? The bedside table was out on the lane with everything else, and then it was taken.

Shelley Swift flops back beside him onto the sofa. "Oh, Julius," she says softly. There are dark stains under her arms, and he loves these too. "You're serious, aren't you? You're such a sweet man. So old-fashioned, with your funny fiddle music. But I can't marry you. I've known you all of five minutes."

"Give it ten, then." He smiles.

"I don't want to marry anyone."

For an instant he thinks it's another joke, that in a second she'll start laughing and say yes, but she only stares at him and then seems to decide that he needs an explanation. "I've got this place and my job," she says. "I can take early retirement in a few years. Why would I want to get married?"

For love, he wants to say, *so that we can be together,* but he lets her carry on. She is almost talking to herself.

"I'm fifty-two. Too old for all that settling-down stuff. I'm not the marrying sort. You know me." She looks at him sadly. He thinks that he doesn't know her. But he would like to.

"We can live together, then." He knows he sounds desperate.

She puts a hand on his knee. "I'm not that sort either. I have Pixie, she's enough. You must be able to see it wouldn't work. You're a lovely man, Julius. A good man."

335

Good. It's the word everyone used about his mother. The horror of it must show on his face because she gives his knee a squeeze and says, "We can still have a bit of fun though, can't we?" She moves her hand higher up his leg.

He stands. He wants to be out of there, he wants never to have asked her. "I should go." He picks up his damp coat and gets one arm in while the other flails around for the corresponding hole.

"Don't be like that. Come on." She pats the sofa. "Sit down."

His arm finds the place it's supposed to go.

"Last night was wonderful," she says. "We don't need to make any plans for the future to do that again, do we?"

Pixie, who is under the coffee table, comes out and, with ease, jumps up to the seat Julius has vacated, settling herself there in a circular motion. He doesn't know how to tell Shelley Swift that he won't be able to see her again, can't ever come back after this. Still sitting on the sofa, she reaches up and takes his hand, and he looks at her freckled fingers, feels her soft skin. And then he pulls his hand out from hers.

28

Back in the caravan, Jeanie strips off her wet clothes and puts on dry ones. The pain in her chest has gone so completely it might never have existed, and she thinks perhaps it was only indigestion — isn't that meant to feel like a heart attack? — and she will have made Julius come home for no reason. She doesn't like this feeling of being in the wrong, of having to apologize for a false alarm. Not bothering to fold the table down into her bed, she lies on Julius's couch again, trying to listen for the tick of his bicycle through the hammering of the rain on the roof. She wakes an hour later, cold and with aching joints, to knocking on the caravan door. It's dark outside and in, and although she expects it to be Julius worrying about her, she unbolts the door cautiously. A different man stands on the ground in front of the bottom step and it's a second before she recognizes Rawson in a three-piece suit with a yellow tie.

"Miss Seeder," he says. "I hope you don't mind me calling round so late. I couldn't sleep."

She hesitates. He is the last person she wants to see.

"Could I come in? Just for a moment. It's getting heavier." His hair is wet and his shoulders hunched.

Perhaps he has something to tell her about the cottage. Maybe he has tried to let the place and has finally realized that no one else is going to live in it in that state. She stands back. While she lights a few candles, he looks around and wipes his face — his startlingly black eyebrows and that white moustache — with a folded handkerchief he takes from his pocket. The top of his head almost reaches the caravan ceiling. She sees him notice the piles of bedding, the clothes, the food which there isn't enough cupboard space for, the homemade curtains and still-curling lino, and then he says, "What a nice place you've made for yourself here."

Jeanie folds her arms. She misses the security of Maude at her heels, although that soft dog never provided any real protection.

"Mr. Rawson," she says warily.

"Quite a little home." He is not very good

338

at hiding what he really thinks, she can see the shock in his face, no matter what he says. "Though not so easy an approach as to the cottage." They look at his polished brogues, what might be a leaf stuck to one toe.

"Maybe I should phone the council and ask them to come and lay a footpath from the lane to our door so that visitors don't get their shoes dirty."

He tries a smile, and she sees not only horror but pity. "Talking of the cottage, how are you getting on with the garden? There must be a lot to keep up with at this time of year."

She tilts her head, trying to work out the reason for his visit, what this small talk is leading to. He certainly hasn't come to ask how her broad beans are doing.

"So what if I've been going back? No one else is looking after it." She thinks she hears the throaty noise of an engine somewhere outside, closer than the main road, on the lane perhaps.

"Quite right. It would be a waste to let everything rot." His tone is gentle, she might say sincere if she weren't suspicious of his motives.

"The vegetables are ours — mine — anyway. We grew them. My mother and I put years of work into that garden."

"Dot, yes." He pauses. "But it's not just the garden you've been visiting, is it? I know you've been going inside. You left the back door unbolted and the ladder wasn't put away properly." She feels an unwelcome blush rising at being found out. "Could we sit?" he says. "Discuss this in a civilized fashion?"

She nods to the couch, Julius's bed. Rawson looks behind him and stays standing; she had no intention of sitting with him.

"Caroline, my wife, would probably say that although you've grown those vegetables, they're on our land and you're selling them at the end of the lane and elsewhere."

"And you want a cut? Is that it?" She laughs sourly. "The amount I earn from the vegetables barely pays for the rest of our food."

"No, no." He holds his hands out, palms up. "That's her view, not mine. This is nothing to do with money as far as I'm concerned. It's your attachment to the place, to the land, that I'm talking about. I'm a farmer too. The earth is in our blood, isn't it? Caroline doesn't really get it, never has. But it was the same for your mother, she loved that cottage, that garden."

Jeanie thinks she can see what he's trying

to do: align them, attempt to find common ground, shared desires, although she can't work out why. But she isn't going to have any of it.

The whine of an engine is definitely in the spinney and knowing it sets her heart ticking. "But you still had us evicted." She spits the last word and he flinches.

"That wasn't my doing. Caroline insisted we go —"

She cuts him off. "And anyway, what do you know about my mother?" She takes a step forwards, ready to throw him out.

"More than you think. You're a lot like her."

"You don't know anything. And I don't know why you've come here, but now you're going to leave."

He doesn't move. "Dot wanted a place she could call home," he says. "To have her family around her, a bit of land, feel the sun on her skin. What many of us want when it comes down to it."

"Is that why you're here? To tell me things about my mother that I already know?"

Rawson rubs his hands together awkwardly as though he's gearing himself up for something. "I'd like to offer you the cottage back."

He is dangling a hook hidden by a twisting worm, she thinks, but the animal in her heart jumps to swallow the bait. "In return for what? Rent? Rent we've never had to pay, and you know exactly why. And your wife has the cheek to come round saying we owe two thousand pounds. Two thousand pounds! It's crazy. Then she won't take any money anyway!" Jeanie goes to the cupboard, pulls out the envelope from under the lining, and waves it at him. "So tell me, what is it you want this time? You wouldn't take the money Mum borrowed, so why would I believe your bloody offer now?"

Rawson runs his hand over his eyes. "Your mother never owed me money," he says. "She never owed me anything. You're right — I never asked for any rent, not since your father died."

Jeanie puffs out air. She doesn't want to hear it; she just wants him to leave.

"And I can't tell you how sorry I am about the eviction. That was down to Caroline. She insisted we go away, to try and patch things up, she said, but she arranged the eviction while I wasn't here. I should have come to see you as soon as I got back, to explain, but — well, there has been a lot to try and sort out between us. Caroline was so angry. More angry than I'd ever seen her.

I promised her . . . I promised her so many times."

Jeanie doesn't want to hear what he promised his wife. Won't hear. But he doesn't stop.

"Caroline found out, you see. About me and Dot." His voice breaks when he says her name and for a moment Jeanie sees the unhappy man under the person she has always hated. "It started a year or so after your father died —"

"Was killed by you," Jeanie says.

"Well," he says. "We can get into all that if you like, but it's not as straightforward as you were led to believe. One of your mother's conditions."

"What does that mean?" she asks aggressively.

Rawson looks away, doesn't answer, and Jeanie screws the envelope into a ball. The sound outside is the engine of a dirt bike.

"You've brought your friends with you?"

Rawson listens. "That's nothing to do with me."

Jeanie goes to the door and bolts it. She'd rather be inside with Rawson than take her chances with whoever is out there.

"We knew it was wrong," he says. "I was married. We ended it so many times, and I promised Caroline. I promised her it wouldn't start up again. Dot felt bad about it too. But we couldn't stop. I loved her," he says, and his voice softens and slows. "Whenever your mother could get away, we'd meet. If Caroline was off somewhere, Dot would come to the house. Often, we'd just talk, play the piano. Sometimes we only managed once a month."

Jeanie wants to clamp her hands over her ears like a child. Her mother and this man. It can't be true, even while she knows it is, has always known in some way. She turns her head, can't look at him, but lets him go on.

"I loved her," he says again. "And she loved me too. I know it. Perhaps it was only escaping the daily grind of making a living, looking after you two without a husband to help her, running a home, but I like to think it was more than that. We talked about the farm, the garden, the state of the world, the cottage. I wanted to do it up, put in decent plumbing, rethatch the place, but she thought you and your brother would be suspicious.

"She had strong opinions, your mother. Interesting ideas. And she liked to tell me about you and Julius. She loved you both very much."

Jeanie can't bear the tremble in Rawson's

voice, the tenderness, the grief.

"We often talked about whether we could be together properly, but there are . . . well, there are things that happened a long time ago to Caroline and me, and in the end, I couldn't do that to her — leave her. And your mother said her job was to look after you, and Julius of course. It was a promise she'd made to herself; she wouldn't ever tell me why. But she loved you being at home with her."

"None of this is possible," Jeanie says angrily. "I don't believe you." An image flashes into her head of her mother's wedding ring on the scullery windowsill, and even as she speaks she understands that she and Julius were the last to know.

"As I think Caroline said when she unfortunately came to see you, there's a receipt book at home. It was a joke between me and Dot — signing her initials by each date. When she got ill it became harder for us to meet. I was so worried about her, but she wouldn't let me help. I suppose she felt guilty that she wasn't giving anything in return for the cottage, and so she offered money. I didn't want her money. I only wanted her."

There's a prickle in Jeanie's nose and the thump of blood in her ears.

"I always told her the cottage was hers, and yours of course, for as long as you and Julius needed it. I said I would sign it over to her, but she wouldn't have it. She was a bloody stubborn woman when she wanted to be, wouldn't take anything from anyone unless she was giving something in return. But I didn't tell Caroline that Dot wasn't paying any rent; I let her see the receipt book and she believed what she wanted to believe. And then, after Dot died, it all came out, that no rent was ever paid and that we were still in love." He finishes on a kind of sob.

Jeanie puts her fingers against her heart, but she can no longer keep her voice regulated. "And so just like that, out of guilt or whatever bloody thing it is you think you're suffering from, you've come to offer me the cottage back. Is that it?"

"I want to make amends. Sort things out between us. You and Julius can move back into the cottage, and I — well, I would like to invite both of you round to the house sometimes if you wanted to come. Caroline isn't there — we're having a trial separation, just to see what happens. Dot talked about you and your brother so often." His hands find each other and his fingers twist. "I'm afraid I haven't expressed this well."

346

He looks at Jeanie suddenly, directly, and they stare at each other in the candlelight. "What do you think?"

"What do I think?" Jeanie is shouting. "I think you want a ready-made family. A bit lonely are you, now your wife's gone and your mistress is dead?"

Rawson pulls back. "I want to help you. You're Dot's children — and Frank's, of course — and I just want some connection to her. Only that."

"Get out."

He doesn't move.

"Get out!" She throws the screwed-up envelope, but it doesn't even touch him, only falls at his feet.

Rawson remains motionless while Jeanie, keeping her eyes on him, edges towards the kitchen drawer. She yanks it open and delves inside with her hand. Her movement rocks him from his rooted state as though a great wind had come towards him and abruptly he is released, and he pushes on the caravan door, fumbling with the bolt, as Jeanie turns towards the drawer and finds the poker. She pulls it out and spins round, the point raised and forwards. Rawson is gone into the dark spinney, leaving the door swinging open. The rain has stopped but all about there is the pattering of drops falling

347

from the leaves and, again, the bike's engine. She steps back inside, bolts the door once more, and rests her forehead against it, holding the poker with both hands.

Thirty-eight years, she thinks. The man who killed her father. She doesn't believe it. She can't. She won't.

For several minutes the dirt bike circles the spinney and with each lap it seems to draw closer to the caravan. And then the engine is switched off and she hears men's voices shouting. She kneels by the door, straining to listen, the poker still with her. She can't make out the words, but she understands the tone. Rawson, she thinks, and one other — Nathan? There is silence for one, two, three breaths, and a yell which might be a name. Then a single gunshot. So loud and close that she jumps, knocking against the table leg and ending curled on the floor with her arms wrapped around her head. She is all heart and pumping blood. From outside comes the kick of the bike's engine, a rev, and it is away, growing quieter until she thinks she hears it on the lane, and then it's gone. Still she lies curled on the caravan floor, waiting.

Nothing else comes, except drops of water plunking on the caravan roof. She gets to her hands and knees and, finally, stands.

Listens again. Silence. With the poker in one hand she unlocks and pushes the door open: the firepit, the lean-to shelter with the tarpaulin, leaves shifting in the blackness, the smell of damp earth. In the dark, nothing seems changed.

29

As she stands in the doorway, Jeanie thinks of Tom and how he raised his arm to shoot at her dog, and then she sees a vision of Maude lying out there somewhere, like a heap of wet cardboard. Tom can turn the caravan upside down looking for the non-existent money, he can take every belonging she has left, she doesn't care, as long as she doesn't find Maude injured or dead in the undergrowth. If it is Rawson, well, it will bloody serve him right. Jamming on her wellingtons, she is quickly down the steps, poker brandished, and standing in front of the caravan, listening. She goes around the side, creeping out into the spinney, placing each foot carefully so as not to rustle a leaf, snap a twig. The dirt bike may have gone, but has the man with the gun? The layout of the spinney is clear in her head even in the dark, and as each shape looms she knows it: the trunk of the single beech, the holly — higher and wider than the caravan — the fallen tree, the stumps and mounds of hidden rubble. She holds the poker aloft as though she might have to use it to hack her way through a jungle. Whistling for Maude and hoping that anyone out there will think the sound is an animal, she stays off the main path, inching her way through the ivy.

Near the tipped-over piano an indistinct form lies in the ground elder: she feels instant relief that it's not dog-shaped. Instead it is long, stretched out on its back, legs splayed. A man. She moves closer, head low, wary that it might be a trap and he could suddenly rise up, gun in hand. With the poker ready, she approaches him from the feet, seeing the soles of his boots, jeans, coat flapped open, arms down. For another moment in the gloom she can't identify the body, the features, isn't able to arrange them. Then she covers her mouth with her hand, drops the poker, and kneels beside her brother. She can smell his odour of soap, tobacco, and sweat, mixed with scuffed humus and leaf mould. Her shadow covers him and she shifts to see him better. His right cheek and forehead are peppered with holes: the face of a mediaeval church carving, singular and stately, punctured by woodworm. There is very little blood.

"What have I done?" she whispers, thinking of the text she made Jenks send. "Julius!" She shakes his shoulder and presses her fingertips to his neck but in her anxiety can't work out where his pulse is meant to be — she who feels for her own every day. She presses his wrist — nothing — remembers the picture of the figure on the yellow defibrillator where the public telephone used to be, leaning over the person on the ground. Something to do with pushing on their chest but in what way and for how long? Her thoughts fumble from one idea to the next. She rummages in Julius's coat and jeans pockets for his mobile and pulls the phone out along with a scattering of coins. The phone remains dark even when she jabs at the numbers and pushes the button on the side, holding it down like she's seen Julius do. In a panic of indecision, she stands quickly, drops the phone, and immediately kneels again, shaking him hard this time. "Julius!" His head jiggles loosely.

Then she runs through the spinney, galumphing past the fallen piano, not caring about the racket she's making, the way her heart is leaping and the pain in her lungs. She follows the tyre track of a single bike to the lay-by where Rawson's car, if that's where he parked it, is now gone. Here she hesitates — left to the village over the fields and whichever house she comes to first? She turns right. On the main road cars roar past every few minutes in both directions, headlights glaring. As one comes towards her, she puts a boot onto the tarmac, waving her arms and yelling, but the car is faster and closer than she anticipates and it swerves, sending her stumbling back into the ditch. Its horn blares and fades as the car disappears. After three or four minutes, as another comes towards her, she waves again and this one stops a little further on. Its hazard lights flash, and she runs to it. The driver has lowered the passenger window and she can hear him shouting.

"You flipping idiot. You can't hitch-hike here. Do you want to get yourself killed?" He is leaning across the empty passenger seat and he quietens when she looks in, perhaps having expected a teenage boy, not an older woman. Jeanie grips the edges of the door with both hands. The man is old, maybe in his eighties, bald, long-faced. "Get in." He stretches to open the door. "Quick. I can't stop here. It's too dangerous." Jeanie gets in, closes the door. Her seat is low, cradling. "Put your seat belt on. I nearly didn't see you, really, you'll cause a crash hitch-hiking at night like that. Where is it you're trying to get to?" The man indicates and pulls out.

Jeanie is oddly calm and polite when she says, "My brother's been shot. I think he's dead. Do you have a mobile phone?"

"What?" The man looks at her as though she might have her own gun shoved into a pocket or tucked into a belt.

"In the spinney." Jeanie flaps a hand behind her. "In the spinney," she shouts like he might know the place. The car accelerates too fast and they lurch forwards, and when the man overcompensates with the brake, they bounce back against their seats. His glasses slide to the end of his nose, but he doesn't push them back up, only hunches over the wheel nervously.

"I'll find somewhere safe to stop," he says, although they go past one turning and then another, and she wonders if he's driving her to a police station to report her and hand her over as a carjacking maniac. Finally, he pulls into a floodlit industrial unit where forklift trucks are loading crates into the back of an articulated lorry. It's the man who makes the emergency call in the end. Jeanie's hands won't hold the phone steady, her index finger doesn't seem to have the strength to press nine three times. The person on the other end wants a location for the emergency and Jeanie gives the man who has driven her here the name of the lane, and she tries to describe the lay-by with the track that leads into the spinney, while the man repeats the information into his phone. Jeanie clamps her hands between her knees and clenches her jaw to stop herself from shaking and stares out at the illuminated forecourt and the people who work all night doing jobs she has never imagined. They have to reverse into a corner of the yard so that the lorry has enough space to turn and leave. A man in a high-vis jacket comes over, the foreman, and raps on the driver's window.

"No private vehicles," he says loudly.

"Sorry, sorry," the driver of the car says, waving, smiling, but not putting down the window. He pulls out after the lorry, heading in the opposite direction to the spinney.

"I have to go back," Jeanie says. "Will you take me back?"

"That's where we're going, isn't it?"

"It's the other way." She turns in her seat, looks over her shoulder, wonders if this man is too old to be driving.

They have to find another place where he can turn the car, and he drives slowly, prudently, like Bridget, and cars overtake them, even in the dark. He twitches and shuffles in his seat as though he feels they should be making conversation, and casts sidelong glances at her. At last, he says, "I've got a brother. He lives in Australia. He was a bloody pain in the backside when we were young, but I miss him." She doesn't have anything to say to that.

They overshoot the turning to the lane and only realize when they pass an ambulance with its blue light flashing, going in the opposite direction. Again, like some awful comedy radio play, they have to find yet another place for the man to turn the car round.

When they reach the lay-by, two police cars are already there, along with the ambulance. Jeanie has the car door open before the man has turned off the ignition, and she runs towards the spinney, but a couple of police officers steer her away, and in the headlights of the man's car they ask her who she is, who Julius is, their relationship. There are lights in the woods, voices, orders being given.

She pushes at the police officers. "He's my brother for God's sake. Let me through."

They tell her to calm herself down, that the paramedics are with him. They make her sit in the back of a police car and carry on asking her questions, but she sees two people bumping a stretcher up the track and she tugs on the door handle, which won't open, and twists in her seat.

"Is he alive?" she says. "Is he alive?"

She sits waiting at a table in a small room with only a clock and a few posters on the walls with warnings she tries to read but can't focus on. A man puts his head around the door and says they'll be with her as soon as possible.

"How's my brother?" she asks. "Do you know?"

"I'll find out," the man says, but he doesn't return.

She shouldn't have agreed to go with the police, she thinks. Should have insisted that she travel in the back of the ambulance with Julius. "You're not under arrest," they said. "We'd just like to ask you a few more questions and it might be more comfortable in the station. We'll keep you updated about your brother as soon as we know anything. You can leave at any time."

The clock says it's just after twelve, but her body can't work out whether that's midnight or noon. She leans over the table, pulling her cardigan around her; she didn't stop to put a coat on when she left the caravan. She wants to go, but she doesn't know where they have taken Julius or how she might get there. So, she waits. There's no window in the room. There is a pain behind her eyes and all her limbs and muscles ache, and her internal organs are heavy; she needs to sleep but thinks sleep will never come again. Finally, the door opens a second time and she stands. A woman and man introduce themselves, and the word *detective* is all she can remember. They put a mug of tea in front of her and apologize for keeping her waiting.

"How's my brother?" she asks, and the woman says, "That's just what we were trying to ascertain. I've asked someone to come in and tell us as soon as there's any news. Have a seat."

The man puts a notepad and pen on the table as though he expects Jeanie to write. There was a time when these objects would have sent her into a panic but they don't scare her now. The detectives sit opposite her and ask about what happened, and the man writes things in the notebook.

Jeanie's story is jumbled at first, out of sequence and complicated. She tells them about Shelley Swift who lives above the fish and chip shop, and about Nathan, and Lewis, and Tom; she tells them about the cutlery and the eviction. She says that her dog is missing and she cries, and the woman passes a box of tissues from her end of the table. "Has a stray dog been handed in?" she asks. The male detective says that the police don't deal with stray dogs, she'll have to contact the dog warden at the council. She explains that she's been visiting the cottage to tend the garden and that Rawson came to the caravan to talk about it. She tells them she thought she was having a heart attack and she got Jenks to send a message for her brother to come home. The female detective asks her if she needs a doctor, but it's too late for that. She has to explain who Jenks is. She says that Bridget Clements came to the caravan yesterday and picked up the cutlery from the floor. She says she spilled some potatoes which got trampled and she had to wash them again. They tell her to stick to the important information. She wants to say that potatoes are important, but instead she tells them about the sound of the dirt bike and the two men's voices, arguing, and Tom's pretend shooting of Maude. They ask if she knows his full name and where he lives, and for a while they both leave the room. When they return, she tells them about the poker, that she lay on the floor of the caravan, and about the awful noise of the shot in the dark.

She tells them everything except what Rawson told her about his relationship with her mother.

The woman explains that they need Jeanie to write a statement in chronological order about everything she's just told them. The man pushes a form and the pen across the table. Jeanie pushes them back. "I find it difficult to read or write," she says, chin up, expecting them to argue. A glance passes between them and then laboriously they go through the sequence of events once more with the man writing Jeanie's words, and then reading them out to her.

"Sign here," he says.

"A cross will do," the woman says.

Jeanie sniffs, picks up the pen, and signs her name, using the same scrawl she used at the register office.

They ask if they can take her fingerprints and she wonders whether they will want to swab the inside of her mouth with a long cotton bud, and if they will ask her to undress so they can take her clothes away in a plastic bag. Julius would have been shouting about his rights and his liberty by now, but she lets them roll her fingers in the ink and across the paper. When they say she is free to leave, she remains in her chair and they have to say it again.

In the reception area the lights are painfully bright. A policeman comes out from behind the desk and sits next to her on the moulded plastic seats. "We've heard from an officer who's been waiting at the hospital," he says gently. She imagines a cold tiled floor, the folding back of a sheet. She remembers her mother's body on the door in the parlour, and then suddenly, ridiculously, feels a pang of concern about what underwear Julius is wearing. "Your brother's having surgery at the John Radcliffe in Oxford," the policeman says. "There's no more information at the moment, but your friend telephoned. Mrs. Clements? She's on her way, she says she'll take you."

Bridget arrives twenty minutes later, bursting into the reception area. She opens her arms and this time Jeanie clings to her. "Oh, my love," Bridget says. "What happened?"

Jeanie shakes her head against Bridget's shoulder.

"Come on," Bridget says. "I've got the car outside." She grips the tops of Jeanie's arms, holding her up. She looks hard into Jeanie's eyes. "Just remember, he's alive."

The sun is rising as they drive, a deep yellow spreading above the tree-line like a distant city burning.

"I rang the hospital," Bridget says. "They wouldn't tell me anything. I knew they'd only speak to close relatives, but Jesus. I think you should prepare yourself. A gun." She shakes her head.

Jeanie rests her temple against the window and closes her eyes, drifting off to the rhythm of the engine, while Bridget smokes and talks some more.

"I'm surprised the police didn't ask for my statement at the station, maybe they'll come to the house later. We only found out because Nath called first thing. I had that terrible feeling when I heard Stu's phone ring. You know? How your stomach turns over when the telephone goes in the middle of the night?" Jeanie doesn't know, but Bridget keeps on. "You always think the worst. *Nath,* that's what I thought. And not *Something's happened to him,* but *What's he done now?* Isn't that awful?" Bridget lowers her window a little way and flicks her cigarette ash towards the gap.

"Anyway, Stu was on the phone and making all these noises so I knew something terrible had happened, and I was about ready to pull the bloody mobile from his ear to

362

find out what was going on, but then he covered the mouthpiece and said, 'Julius Seeder's been shot and Jeanie's being questioned at the police station.' And he carried on talking to Nath. 'Jeanie!' I said. 'Jeanie's shot Julius!' And he said, 'Don't be silly, Bridgey. She's there to give a statement.'

"Christ, I was out of that bed and getting dressed to come and find you, or Julius, or someone. I don't know. Putting my tights on back to front, in a right state. Then Stu said, 'They've already got the lad who did it.' And it was that Tom, the one who was round at the caravan the day I visited, the one who lives with Nath."

Jeanie lifts her head. "Tom?" She isn't surprised.

Bridget shakes her head again, drags on her cigarette. "I couldn't believe it. Tom, with a shotgun. We drove straight over and Nath was just sitting on the sofa in his boxers. Just sitting there. Stunned, white as a ghost and shaking. In shock, I think. I wanted to call 111 but Stu said I was making a fuss. The police had hauled Tom off by then. Apparently, he came back from your place with the gun and woke Nath up. Crying his eyes out, Nath said. Nath called the police, and they came and took Tom away. Christ. Nath has to go in later to make a proper statement." Bridget stubs out her cigarette and begins negotiating another out of the packet; she's stopped bothering with the Polos. "Can you believe it? Poor Julius. What was that lad doing out there in the middle of the night with a shotgun, that's what I'd like to know."

"Rob us, I suppose. He didn't believe me when I told him we didn't have any money." Jeanie closes her eyes. She tucks her hands under her thighs — her fingers are freezing, all the heat of her body is contained in her core, her heart is expanding and crushing her lungs, squeezing her stomach. "It was my fault, Bridget. I got this bloke — Jenks — in the pub to text Julius and tell him to come home. I thought I was having a heart attack."

"A heart attack! Why didn't you phone for an ambulance?"

Jeanie shakes her head. "I don't know. I just didn't. The pain went away. But Julius came home. He was there in the spinney because of me."

"Oh, love." Bridget sucks on her cigarette. "You mustn't think that. Maybe he was on his way home anyhow. Maybe he never saw the message."

Jeanie keeps her eyes closed, hoping

Bridget will think she's asleep. She wants her to drive faster. What if Julius dies while they are in the car because Bridget is pootling along the dual carriageway like she's on a Sunday afternoon outing? When Jeanie opens her eyes, the sky is white and morning has come and cars are overtaking them one after another, their drivers on their way to early shifts or home from late ones. Jeanie looks at Bridget, mascara caught in the lines at the corner of her eye, her body tilted forwards, concentrating on the road, driving Jeanie to the hospital when she could be comforting her own shaking son.

"Did Mum visit you sometimes without her wedding ring on?" Jeanie asks.

"What do you mean?" Bridget changes down a gear for no reason, the engine squeals, and she changes back up.

"That's what she used to tell Julius — that she was going to see you. You were her excuse, her alibi. Except she always left her ring on the scullery windowsill, that's what Julius remembers. Me too, maybe."

Bridget glances at Jeanie as though to assess something, the extent of her knowledge perhaps.

"Rawson came to the caravan," Jeanie continues. "He told me about him and Mum."

"He told you?" Bridget looks at Jeanie again and the car swerves towards the side of the road and back out.

"Thirty-eight years. How could we have not known? All that time."

Bridget sighs, a long, drawn-out sigh, and her body relaxes.

"You knew, didn't you?" Jeanie says. "Everyone knew."

"She made me promise not to tell." Bridget shrugs her shoulders. "She said she was never going to tell you and Julius, even though I told her she should. I kept saying you'd understand."

"Understand? What is there to understand? Rawson is an awful man who took advantage of a woman when her husband had just died —"

"Oh, Jeanie, no, it wasn't like that. It was nothing like that." Bridget reaches out her hand and then seems to think better of it and returns it to the wheel. "There was something between them even before your dad died. Dot said they never did anything about it and I believe her. And the thing with Spencer didn't start until at least a year after Frank had gone. When she was with him, Spencer, I mean, I think those might have been the only times she felt like something more than a mother. She liked his

366

company, and probably, yes, the sex too. I know you don't want to hear it. But why shouldn't she have had some fun? Your dad was dead a long time."

Jeanie can't reconcile this woman Bridget is talking about with her mother. She turns her face to the window.

"It's the eviction I can't understand," Bridget says. "Why Spencer Rawson would chuck you out of the cottage. Your mum said he always had a soft spot for you and Julius."

"That was his wife's doing," Jeanie says. "I suppose that's who Nathan is — was — working for."

Bridget sighs again. "But it belongs to Rawson, doesn't it? The farm, the cottage?"

"She didn't tell him she'd had us evicted. She must have thought she could do what she wanted if he wasn't there to stop it. He told me we could move back in," Jeanie says.

"To the cottage?" Bridget sounds excited, hopeful for her.

"He suddenly wants to play happy families. Pretend everything's all right. Have me and Julius over for tea or something. Like he can replace Dad." Jeanie can feel the bump of her heart, insistent. Her breath steams the window and she sits upright.

Bridget glances at her and the car weaves.

"Would that be so bad? Not a replacement, but he did love her, you know, and she loved him."

Jeanie makes a dismissive *pfff.*

"What did you say?"

"What did I say? You have to ask? I told him to get out."

They are in the city now and Bridget slows the car to a crawl until someone hoots behind them. "Bugger off!" she shouts, and then, "Wait, I have to concentrate, I have to see where to go." She peers to look up at the road signs. Aloud, she reads, "Hospital, A&E."

30

Jeanie lies on the stained orange sofa and closes her eyes. They are dry and itchy, all of her is dry, as though the fabric beneath her is drawing the moisture out from her body, and if she lies here for long enough she will become a hollow husk, some kind of giant chrysalis from which no butterfly will ever emerge. She knows she won't be able to sleep, and she knows that Bridget will make a fuss if she doesn't appear to be trying. There's a single long window in the Relatives' Room which overlooks a car park. Bridget is out there having a cigarette and putting a permit in the car, which the Neuro Intensive Therapy Unit receptionist has given her. Already Jeanie is learning the terminology. She wants to open the window for some air but there is not even a locked catch. The sky is a light cloudless blue, and she thinks about the things that need doing: the plants in the greenhouse and polytunnel that should be watered, the fence behind the compost heaps where rabbits are getting in which must be mended, and in Saffron's garden the newly planted lavender will be demanding attention. She has to phone the council about Maude; where is Julius's phone, and his clothes? There was a policeman here earlier, but he's gone now. Julius was wearing a good shirt and he'll want it back. Jeanie's thoughts run on. She and Bridget have been waiting for hours. Someone, they were told, will come and speak to them when the operation is over.

When Bridget returns, she brings sandwiches and two teas in disposable cups, and asks Jeanie if she's slept, though Bridget must have been gone for less than fifteen minutes. The smell of her recently smoked cigarette hangs around her. Jeanie worries about the cost of the sandwiches and the tea, calculating prices in her head and wondering whether Bridget will expect her to buy the next round. She takes a bite of her sandwich but can barely swallow. She doesn't want to eat, and she doesn't want to talk. Just as she lies down again, two men come into the room and she sits up. One, in blue scrubs and a matching cloth hat, introduces himself as Mr. McKenzie, the surgeon who has operated on Julius. The other man, Mr. Jones, says he's an intensivist, and when he doesn't explain further, Bridget leans towards Jeanie and says in a confidential tone, "That's a doctor who specializes in the care of very poorly patients." They all sit.

"Your brother has made it through the surgery," Mr. McKenzie says to Jeanie. "But he did come to us pretty poorly." She wonders if there are similar coverings to his hat but for beards, or whether they simply wear the hats upside down. "Three shotgun pellets went into his brain and unfortunately I wasn't able to remove any of them." The surgeon's shoes have rounded toes like clogs or those Crocs that everyone was wearing a few years ago. His are splashed with brownish marks. Jeanie has been given a pair of paper slippers to replace her muddy boots. Mr. McKenzie is still speaking, something about a piece of Julius's skull being stitched into his abdomen. Surely she has misheard? She feels Bridget's hand touch hers and clasp it. She tries to focus.

"I wasn't able to save his left eye, but there's no damage to his right."

"He'll be able to see, then," Jeanie says. "One eye is enough, isn't it?"

Bridget squeezes Jeanie's hand.

"Well," Mr. McKenzie says. "It's not his

sight I'm worried about." He leans, bare elbows on blue knees, hands clasped. "We're keeping him asleep and we'll just have to see what happens over the next few hours and days."

"A medically induced coma?" Bridget says.

Jeanie sees a glance shared between the two men.

Mr. Jones speaks: "Julius will be under my care while he's in the unit."

Bridget wags her head and says, "Intensive Therapy Unit, ITU."

The man feigns a smile. Bridget doesn't notice. "He's being monitored and he's having help with his breathing, but we'll hopefully be able to remove his breathing tube soon and have a go at waking him up, and we'll keep an eye on how well he responds."

"Can I see him?" Jeanie says.

There are four beds in the Neuro ITU, and more women and men in blue clothes checking monitors and charts, writing things. Julius is furthest from the door, and when Jeanie walks past the other beds with Bridget, she doesn't look in them, but she sees the weak smiles that each visitor beside each bed gives her. Julius is in a hospital gown with a sheet pulled up to his chest.

Most of his head is bandaged and a wodge of dressing covers his left eye, a yellow stain showing around the edge. A man in a similar blue uniform as the rest introduces himself as Julius's nurse, and explains what each of the tubes, wires, and monitors is for. Jeanie doesn't take any of it in. The room is hot, airless. The person in the bed doesn't look like Julius and she wonders if she's been brought to the correct bed, or perhaps it wasn't Julius in the spinney after all, and they have picked up and operated on someone else. Perhaps her brother is in the caravan now, waiting for his dinner and complaining about where the hell she is.

"I should have brought his pyjamas," she says. Bridget shushes her and puts an arm around her shoulders. The nurse is speaking but his voice is distant. When she looks down, she sees that she's holding an information leaflet with a picture of the hospital on the front. When was she given that? She's cold but her forehead is sweating. She presses her fingers to her chest, and the egg inside her cracks.

"Oh!" she says.

When she comes around, she is lying on the floor in the corridor, a pillow under her head and her feet on a chair. Bridget and nurses surround her. Shouldn't they be looking after Julius? "She's got a heart condition." Jeanie can hear Bridget's voice. "Rheumatic heart disease. She had rheumatic fever when she was a child."

I'm alive, Jeanie thinks, and touches her chest above her heart. There is no blood, nothing has burst out of her.

They want her to go to A&E, and a wheelchair is brought. She sits in it but refuses to go, although she knows that Bridget is disappointed at missing the opportunity to push her through the hospital. Instead Bridget sits beside her and tells her how it's now thought best to elevate the legs rather than lower the head to the knees when someone faints. The nurse who helped her up isn't happy that Jeanie won't go to A&E and has her promise that she will make an appointment with her GP as soon as possible. Bridget wheels her back to Julius.

In the car on the way home, Jeanie rests her head against the window and tries to sleep but still sleep won't come although she's never been so tired. She watches silhouettes of the drivers who overtake them on the A34, their headlights sweeping the verges. She looks for a bulky shape motionless by the side of the road, and then squeezes her eyes closed against the thought. She misses

Maude with a physical pain which aches in time with the beat of her heart. That dog could listen without talking back. She thinks of the things that Rawson told her about her mother and how he has turned everything she knows on its head.

"Rawson said something about Dad too," Jeanie says.

"I thought you were asleep," Bridget says, reaching for her cigarettes.

"It was about how Dad died," Jeanie continues. "Something else that Mum insisted we shouldn't be told. I've been trying to work out what it could be."

Jeanie tries to get her thoughts in order, make herself wake up. "Julius and I have always thought that Rawson made the tractor's hitch pins, that he was the one who insisted on making new ones out of nuts and bolts. When they broke, Julius was thrown into the hedge and Dad died."

Bridget fumbles for a lighter in the storage compartment in front of the gear stick and drops it.

"And to stop Mum telling the police or the health and safety people about Rawson and what he did, we were allowed to stay in the cottage, rent-free. That's what we assumed, that's what she let us believe. But I'm not sure that's right." Jeanie scrabbles for the lighter amongst the rubbish in her footwell and lights the cigarette. Bridget's face glows orange.

"The reason we were able to stay in the cottage wasn't because Mum agreed to keep quiet about Rawson making the hitch pins. We were able to stay in the cottage because they were" — Jeanie falters, searching for the words — "having an affair. So that must mean she had nothing to keep quiet about, there wasn't anything she was keeping from the police or the health and safety people. Or not about Rawson, anyway."

A speck of red ash falls on Bridget's skirt and goes out.

Jeanie is following her thoughts now, one after the next, each making a path in front of her: a line of stepping stones she has never walked across before. "If there was nothing for her to keep from the police about Rawson, that means he didn't make the hitch pins. He didn't kill Dad.

"It was just a story to make it seem believable that we could stay in the cottage. Mum insisted on that lie, so that we wouldn't find out about them, about their affair. It must have been one of her conditions. That's the word Rawson used in the caravan: *conditions.* Julius and I have hated Rawson for years because we thought he killed our father, and it wasn't true. Dad made the hitch pins, didn't he?"

"Yes," Bridget says, her eyes on the road. "He did."

Jeanie sighs. "None of them are the people we thought they were. Not Mum, not Dad, and not Rawson."

When Bridget turns the car west along the A4, Jeanie says, "The police told me there's a warden at the council who deals with stray dogs. I was thinking they might have found Maude. Can I call them tomorrow morning on your mobile? I think the police must have Julius's. Or your home phone if that's easier."

Bridget pitches the end of her cigarette out of the window and closes it. Jeanie sees, in the car's poorly lit interior, that Bridget has become suddenly rigid, embarrassed. "Of course you can. But I've been thinking about you staying with me and Stu tonight. I know you can't go back to the caravan, but you'll have to sleep on the sofa, if that's all right. It's just that Nath's come home. We brought him back with us when we went to see him. He's in his old room. I think it'll be good for him to be with us, spend some time with Stu. Sort himself out."

Jeanie feels unexpectedly unmoored,

shaken with the realization that Julius isn't here to fix things and there is no plan to get them out of trouble, however crazy. "No problem," she says, knowing that Bridget doesn't really want her on the sofa even if she feels she must offer it. "That's great — that Nathan's home. It must be a relief. Actually, I was thinking I could stay with Saffron. The woman I'm gardening for. I'm sure she won't mind."

"No," Bridget says. "You should stay with us."

"Really, Saffron won't mind."

"Without any warning?"

"She's very relaxed. She has a nose piercing. It'll be fine." They are being so polite with each other. "Could you drop me there? She lives on Cutter Hill. Near the old phone box. She's the one who keeps it stocked with books."

"Are you sure she won't mind? I'm not working tomorrow, so I can pick you up in the morning and take you back to the hospital."

"I can get the bus," Jeanie says, although she has no idea if she can afford a ticket.

"Don't be silly. I'll take you. A bus to Oxford would probably be about three changes and you'll be on it for hours. All round the houses. You know what they're like. I'll pick you up outside Saffron's at eight thirty. How does that sound. Where is it exactly?" They are already on Cutter Hill.

"Up here, on the left," Jeanie says.

Bridget pulls the car up to the driveway entrance and lets the engine idle.

"Will she be able to give you something to eat? I can call her now. Is she even in?" They peer through the windscreen. Jeanie hasn't thought about food since the biscuit she was made to eat after she fainted. "Perhaps you should come back with me. Nath can sleep on the sofa."

"Look, there are lights on," Jeanie says. "It'll be fine." She pulls on the car door handle. "If you're sure you can take me tomorrow? Can you pick me up from the village? I've got to see Max, have a word with him about deliveries. Eight thirty, then." Jeanie has one foot out of the car.

"If you're sure," Bridget says.

"Of course," Jeanie says, and she's out, the door closed. As the car pulls away, Jeanie puts a hand on the gate and with the other, she waves.

Police tape is strung from orange cones placed at intervals across the lay-by. But there is no police car parked there, no officer standing in the night, guarding the spinney and ready to stop her entering, or to lift the tape for her to duck under. She takes the path that the paramedics and police took before her — grass flattened, the moonlight showing white residue in tyre and boot prints. The place doesn't scare her, its familiar shapes and sounds are a comfort, like coming home, but it feels as though she has been away for months. Only the out-of-place shadow near the scorched circle brings her hand to her mouth until she recognizes its boxy shape and sharp angles as the toppled piano.

The caravan door is closed but police tape has also been attached here, and ripped off, and when Jeanie opens the door, nothing inside is as she left it. The cupboard doors are open, the contents strewn across the floor, trampled clothing, Julius's phone charger, their sleeping bags and pillows. Immediately she thinks of Tom, but he has been taken in by the police, and Nathan is at Bridget's. It must have been Lewis, although he won't have done this on his own; or perhaps it was Ed. Maybe one of them told someone about the place: probably unlocked and vacant apart from a non-existent stash of money. She steps inside. The plastic bag she's been using to carry her things and her little bit of cash around is in the sink, and when she lifts it up, she sees that it has been emptied. The photograph of her parents is on the floor, the glass smashed, the handle is broken off the Toby jug, and Angel's painting of Maude is torn. She wonders if the police have Julius's wallet as well as his phone and clothes, and how much money is in it. The lids of the bench seats either side of the table are open and what was inside is topsy-turvy, and when she checks, Julius's gun has gone — most likely taken by the police — but also the fiddle and banjo cases. It's then that finally she shouts and kicks at the stuff on the floor — the dog's water dish, the washing-up bowl, a frying pan — and slams her palms against the caravan walls, making all of it shake, making something else fall from a cupboard. Yelling incoherently, she sweeps the detritus off from Julius's couch, raises the lid, and there, unexpectedly, is her guitar case, heavy when she lifts it out. She takes the guitar from the case, cradles it, and weeps, her tears falling onto the wood. After a while she begins to play.

"Then home he did run with his dog and
    his gun,
Crying, 'Mother, dear Mother, have you
    heard what I have done?

I met my own true love, I mistook her for
    a swan,
And I shot her and killed her by the
    setting of the sun.'
She'd her apron wrapped about her and
    he took her for a swan,
And it's so and alas, it was she, Polly
    Vaughn."

After she's finished, she gets up and bolts the door, finds her coat and puts it on, and lies down on Julius's bed. Her limbs ache as though she is coming down with flu, and her head pounds. She puts her hand against her heart, but its rhythm is regular.

When she opens her eyes again, a greenish light is flowing over her from the window. There are birds singing in the holly bush and the whoosh of cars on the main road. Her teeth are woolly when she runs her tongue across them, and she gets herself up with a groan. It's just after six. She finds a mug and holds it under the tap, pumping the water pedal with her foot. When the mug is half-filled, the water splutters and gives out. Julius was the one who brought the water and changed the gas bottle. She brushes her teeth and drinks; she would like to wash but that isn't possible. She'll need to get water and maybe gas on her bicycle using the trailer, but she knows before she even steps outside to look that they will have been taken. Julius's bike, which he must have pushed through the spinney, isn't anywhere either — did she see it when she found him in the woods? There is a tin of baked beans in a cupboard and a saucepan on the floor, and she heats the food on the gas and gobbles the beans straight from the pan with a spoon which she wipes first on the bottom of her cardigan. The beans make her thirsty. She changes her clothes and underwear, and into her plastic bag she puts her toothbrush, toothpaste, a bar of soap, another tin of beans, and some soup. The soup doesn't have a ring pull, so she searches until she finds the tin opener, and at the same time she comes across a pair of Julius's pyjamas and a flannel. She shoves in as well the ashtray with the wooden bear with bead eyes. The plastic bag is full now, so she looks for Julius's rucksack of tools but it is gone too. She finds a large carrier bag with others shoved inside, and in the biggest she crams a sleeping bag and a jumper, some clean underwear, her hair-brush, the spoon. With the bread knife she cuts open the rest of the plastic bags and wraps them around the guitar case — with the guitar inside — as best she can. Before she leaves, she pushes it below the caravan, hiding it under the disintegrating cardboard which is there.

Carrying her two plastic bags, she walks to the village and goes to the public WCs that abut one end of the village hall. The brown concrete block is covered with a filigree of ivy strands, white and dead after the council put weedkiller on the roots. In the ladies, there is a hand dryer, two sinks, and two cubicles with blue wooden doors and white toilets — one missing its seat. The walls are tiled in white, and the floor is some sort of blue poured plastic. The room smells — of pee and old water — and there is residual dirt in the corners and along the grouting.

A sign above the sinks has some words on it and a symbol of a tap crossed by a red line. She knows what it means, but still she cups her hands under the running water and drinks, then washes her face and armpits with the soap and the flannel.

31

In the ITU, nothing is changed: Julius is still being helped to breathe, still being monitored, fluids are still being pumped in and taken out. At lunchtime when Jeanie is faint with hunger, Bridget buys sandwiches and crisps, and she and Jeanie eat them in the Relatives' Room.

"When Julius is better and home again, I thought maybe he should look for a regular job, something permanent. Learn a trade," Jeanie says, taking a bite of her prawn mayonnaise. She wants to eat it quickly, to stuff it in, but she forces herself to go slowly so that Bridget won't know how hungry she is. Bridget raises her eyebrows at Jeanie's words. "What?" Jeanie says. She's tired of Bridget, even while grateful for her help. The way Bridget considers herself the medical expert. "It's never too late to learn something new." The words snap out.

"It's not that," Bridget says. "Has anyone

talked to you about Julius's prognosis? If he recovers, and God knows I hope he does, there'll be some damage, Jeanie."

"His eye —"

"Brain damage."

"You don't know that, no one knows until he wakes up."

"He has three bullets in his brain." Bridget says it softly as though Jeanie is just learning this.

"Shotgun pellets," Jeanie says pointedly.

"Whichever. They'll have done a lot of damage. Brain damage."

"He'll come home though."

"Where to?"

They look at each other.

"To the caravan?" Bridget asks, her voice a whisper. Jeanie shakes her head; she doesn't want this conversation. "He might be in a wheelchair, he might need lots of help. How is that going to work? There isn't even a toilet out there."

Jeanie reaches for the other half of her sandwich, but she's already eaten it. "I should go back." She picks up the crisps.

"It's a lot to take in, and you're right, who knows?"

Jeanie doesn't like Bridget's patronizing tone and how, whatever she says, her voice

386

sounds like she doesn't think Julius will survive.

Before they leave the Relatives' Room a temporary truce is reached when Bridget offers to look up the number for the local dog warden. When Jeanie gets through, she asks if a whiskery, biscuit-coloured lurcher has been found with a collar although no tag, but no dog fitting that description has been brought in.

Bridget goes into Oxford to do some errands, and as Jeanie is throwing away their sandwich wrappers she sees two plastic bottles in the bin. She takes them out and shoves them into her small carrier bag — she has hidden the large one round the back of the WCs in the village. In the toilet next to the Relatives' Room she fills both bottles from the cold tap. There is no sign or symbol above the sink.

With Bridget not back and no nurses close by in the ITU, Jeanie takes Julius's pyjamas out of her carrier. She pulls the sheet down to below his feet and is embarrassed that the hospital gown is rucked up and his privates exposed. She hurries to scrunch up the pyjama legs, concertinaing them into short tubes, and a memory of a smell comes to her of rosemary cut from the bush outside the cottage's back door. She manages to manoeuvre both pyjama legs over Julius's white and hairy toes. His calves are heavier than she expected and difficult to move. She is dragging the pyjamas over his ankles, first one side and then the other, when Julius's nurse comes and stops her. Calmly he talks about infection control and hygiene, and Jeanie wants to tell him that Julius's clothes are always clean, but she remembers that she picked the pyjamas up off the floor of the disordered caravan that morning and carried them into the public toilets in the village. She lets the nurse take them off Julius's legs and watches while her brother is wiped down with some sort of disinfectant. "You should talk to him," the nurse says, and Jeanie sits in the chair beside Julius's head and tells him that she doesn't know what to do now.

On their way back to Inkbourne, Bridget says she has to go to work tomorrow but that she's arranged for someone from a volunteer transport organization to pick Jeanie up from Saffron's house in the morning and drive her to the hospital and then bring her home, as well as on the other days that Bridget has to work. Jeanie knows this is charity however it's described, but she can't see an alternative, and besides, she's had enough of Bridget and she knows that

Bridget has had enough of her.

While she drives, Bridget talks about Nathan and smokes cigarette after cigarette. She goes on about how Nathan is developing a new relationship with his father.

"You remember that afternoon when Nath and the others went to the caravan?" Bridget says.

Jeanie doesn't reply; how could she forget?

"Well, Nath told me that it *was* Caroline Rawson who asked him to go out there." Bridget speaks like she's relating the storyline of a soap opera. "Nothing to do with the money that Tom was looking for; it was because she felt bad. Can you believe it? Apparently, she sent him to check up on you, make sure you were doing all right. Nath's not working for her any more. Stu's put his foot down. He's looking for a job in a pub or maybe a warehouse. Whatever he can get."

Jeanie zones out Bridget's voice. That Nathan was at the caravan to make sure she and Julius were okay doesn't excuse him, she thinks. He could have stopped Tom from going inside, maybe he could have stopped Tom from returning with his gun. She lets Bridget ramble on until she asks, "Was it all right at Saffron's last night? Shall I drop you there again?" and Jeanie sees that they're nearly in Inkbourne.

"In the village, please," Jeanie says. "I need to pick up some things from the shop."

When she's waved Bridget off, Jeanie collects her large carrier bag from behind the toilet block. Around the back it smells more of pee than inside, and she wonders why anyone would go here and not in the toilets when they're open all day and all night and you have to walk past the doors to get to the back. She sits on the bench on the green. On Wednesday evenings the fish and chip shop is closed, and Jeanie is relieved; she doesn't think she could have tolerated the smell of the frying food without being able to buy any. The lights are off in the flat above, and Jeanie wonders if Bridget or anyone else has thought to tell Shelley Swift about Julius. She opens the tin of baked beans she took from the caravan and eats them surreptitiously with the spoon, hoping no one will pass by. Although she scrapes out the tin, she's still hungry, but decides to wait until it's nearly dark to open the soup with the tin opener. It's condensed cream of mushroom, thick to the point of being almost a jelly; salty and delicious. This soup, which she's eaten all her life, has never tasted so good. Time passes slowly while she's sitting on the bench waiting for the pub to empty, and as it gets colder, she has to stand and stamp her feet and wrap her arms around herself. Finally, when the village is quiet, she returns to the ladies toilets, and under the sinks on the hard floor, with her clothes on, she wriggles into the sleeping bag, using her coat and jumper stuffed inside one of the plastic bags as a pillow. Tiny flies and moths flutter around the fluorescent light on the ceiling, and the husks of their forebears dangle in loops of stringy web.

After an hour, Jeanie is so cold she can't stop her teeth from clacking and her limbs from juddering. She puts on her jumper and coat and crams herself into the corner with her back against the wall. The pain of missing Maude returns and makes her bend over her knees, groaning. She doesn't sleep.

At a quarter to five when it's light outside she uses the toilet. Behind the door when she closes it, the dirt and dust and dead insects run from ceiling to floor down the hinged side. Whoever cleans these toilets does it with the toilet doors open. Jeanie washes, and brushes her teeth, but she feels grubby and worries that she smells. The sinks are too small to wash her hair, and she doesn't have shampoo. She changes her underwear and stuffs the sleeping bag into the large carrier, stowing it again behind the block. She wishes she had saved the soup for the morning. On the walk to Saffron's house her stomach growls and grinds itself against nothing. She hopes the volunteer driver won't go past her in the car, and she tries to time her walk so that she can flag the car down before it turns onto Saffron's drive.

The driver — an ex-military type wearing a tie and a shirt with ironed creases along the arms — doesn't talk except to introduce himself as Alastair. She's pleased he's silent, but she senses that he expects her to thank him, to be grateful for his charity in order that he can feel better about himself, and she won't do it. *You're too proud for your own good,* she can hear Julius saying. Alastair can't stay in Oxford all day, so they arrange for him to pick her up at noon at the hospital entrance and drive her home.

Already the ITU seems normal — the smell of disinfectant, the alarms from the machines, the other visitors who nod at Jeanie but don't want to chat, as she doesn't. Julius is unchanged, although his nurse says they have been reducing the drug that is keeping him asleep and this afternoon they might try removing his breathing support. "We have your number, so we'll call you as soon as we know anything," the nurse says. Jeanie doesn't contradict him; she's not sure whose number they have, if they do actually have one. She imagines Julius's phone ringing in a plastic evidence bag in a cupboard in the police station. A message left on his own mobile to say he's dead.

After Jeanie has sat for an hour beside Julius, trying to think of things that she can possibly tell him, she asks the nurse the way to the cafeteria. The smell of cooking — bacon, chips, toast, and coffee — makes her light-headed with hunger. She finds a seat at one end of a long, mostly empty table, several chairs down from a woman and a man sitting opposite each other and picking at the food they've bought. After ten minutes they get up and leave, and before anyone can stop her or ask what she's doing, Jeanie sits in the man's seat, the moulded plastic uncomfortably warm. She picks up his knife and fork. He has crushed his paper napkin and dropped it onto his plate. Jeanie lifts it off and eats quickly. Half a fried egg, hash browns, more baked beans, and most of a sausage. She drinks the last of the man's lukewarm tea, and then she swaps the trays around and eats what remains of the woman's fruit salad: mostly slices of green apple gone brown. She pockets an unused tiny packet of butter and a miniature jar of jam which has been opened, and then piles up the crockery, stacks the trays, and takes them to the trolley where visitors are encouraged to leave their dirty plates. Here, from someone else's tray, she wraps a half slice of toast and the hard corner of a croissant into a napkin and puts it in her pocket. She would like to take more — there is so much left uneaten — but her heart is jumping and she is sure that at any moment someone will stop her and question what she's doing. She doesn't look around as she leaves.

Jeanie asks Alastair if he wouldn't mind waiting in the car at the WCs in the village before he drops her at the bottom of the lane near the Rawsons' farm, where she arranges for him to pick her up in the morning. She lets him assume that she has to use the loo but collects her large carrier bag from the back of the toilets, and if Alastair notices that she has one more bag with her when she gets back in the car, he passes no comment.

In the five days that she's been away, the garden has gone out of control. The weeds are so vigorous between the vegetable rows that she can't see the carrot tops or the beetroot leaves; bindweed snakes up the runner bean poles, more couch grass is invading from the sides, and the spinach is bolting. She knows she should pick up her hoe and get to work, but instead she pulls up some carrots and collects cherry tomatoes from the polytunnel, and eats them sitting next to her mother's grave, together with the toast and croissant end she took from the hospital canteen. The little square of butter is soft and she licks it from its paper and uses her finger to empty the tiny pot of jam. It's not enough. She thinks again about who her mother really was, to be having this relationship with Rawson for so long. There is so much Jeanie wants to ask Dot now. How was it that first time she left her wedding ring on the scullery windowsill and walked to the farm? Was she attracted to Rawson while she was married, as Bridget suggested? How could she let her children believe Rawson was the enemy, the killer of their father, when she loved the man? She kept Frank's memory perfect and her own secret safe, but at what personal cost?

Jeanie thought she would spend the evening working in the garden, and then she would smash a pane of glass and sleep in the cottage, but when she looks through the scullery window, the place is full of memories and more unsettling than even the public toilets. In the old dairy, she makes a thin mattress from some sacking, cardboard, and newspaper, and gets into her sleeping bag with her jumper and coat on. Thoughts of the message she made Jenks send when Julius was with Shelley Swift swirl in her head. Whatever went on between them, Shelley Swift hasn't been to see Julius or tried to contact Jeanie. She wishes she'd been brave enough to knock on the woman's door that night. Perhaps she would have been invited upstairs, offered a cup of tea while Julius put his boots on. She imagines looking out of the grimy windows and seeing the village from another perspective: the village green, the deli, and the shop all from a different angle. Then Jeanie imagines telling Shelley Swift that Julius has been shot. She breaks down, tearing at her hair and smudging her orange lipstick. Jeanie expects a bitter pleasure from her fantasy, but the emotion that takes her into sleep is sympathy, and in her half dream she puts her arms around Shelley Swift and they cry together.

In the middle of the night Jeanie wakes to the feather-like touch of something crawling over her face — a spider or another night-time insect — and she jumps out of the sleeping bag with a scream, madly brushing herself down and shaking out her hair. She recalls a radio programme about the insects that crawl or burrow into humans while they're sleeping. In the morning she eats more carrots and as many radishes as she can manage before her mouth burns and she has to rush to the privy. Alastair is waiting for her at the bottom of the lane at eight thirty, his blazer hanging behind him on a hook which she didn't know cars had. Jeanie sleeps while he drives and wakes in the hospital car park with saliva on her chin.

In the ITU Julius is paler, his cheeks more sunken. When Jeanie speaks to his nurse he says, "Julius had a bit of a rough night, but he's doing as well as can be expected. Mr. Jones will be around this afternoon and you can have a chat with him." But Alastair can't stay for the afternoons and she doesn't want to ask for a different driver who can. When Jeanie takes a break from sitting beside Julius, she goes again to the cafeteria and this time finishes the end of someone's egg mayonnaise baguette and scrapes out the bottom of a pot of yoghurt. She has to check the picture on the lid to see that it's supposed to taste of cherries.

Back at the cottage in the afternoon she takes the twin-tub out from the old dairy, as well as the trestles and the strips of coffin which Julius split for firewood, and piles it up in the yard. When the room is empty, she sweeps it, destroying any webs she can find and brushing away the spiders. It's cleaner, but in the early morning the cold seeps up from the concrete floor and the air chills through the broken window, and her sleep is fitful with dreams that she can't remember but leave her with an anxiousness she isn't able to shake off. Her joints ache when she first stands up, her ankles so painful she is unsteady, and she goes slowly to the garden tap where she washes and brushes her teeth and rinses out her underwear. She eats a few raw vegetables to keep her going until she can get to the cafeteria. She worries that her clothes smell, that she smells.

In the hospital, Julius looks more gaunt and his skin has a yellowish tinge.

"I thought you were going to take his breathing tube out," she says to a new nurse who has come on duty. The nurse smiles — a practised look of competence and sympathy.

"We tried to remove it yesterday afternoon, but Julius found it difficult to breathe on his own. We'll try again in a day or so."

"Is he going to be okay?" Jeanie knows it's a stupid question, but she wants reassurance.

The nurse smiles again. "Why don't you bring in a book and read to him? Patients often respond well to people talking to them."

"I can't read," Jeanie says, and it comes out spitefully, bitterly, and they both know that she says it to make the nurse feel awkward.

Jeanie thinks she can see the nurse swallow back her retort, but whatever she was going to say is replaced with, "Just a chat then, about the weather, anything."

Over the next few days Jeanie collects things from the caravan and carries them back to the old dairy a few at a time: more clothes and bedding, the radio which surprisingly wasn't taken, saucepans and a frying pan, cutlery, all the tinned food that was left, and her guitar. In the afternoons she works amongst the vegetables and doesn't go to Saffron's; she doesn't want to meet her because she doesn't know what to say. In the evenings she builds a small fire near her mother's grave, boils vegetables, and eats them with whatever she has gleaned from the hospital cafeteria. She thinks about Dot, and Jeanie's new knowledge about her mother and Rawson becomes a slow downward drift of thoughts and emotions which settle into a sediment that she learns to live with. Only occasionally the silt is shaken, and fresh questions arise. How did they get messages to each other when Dot didn't have a phone, and Caroline Rawson would have often been at home? How much did Dot tell Bridget? She wonders what music they played together and wishes that her mother had accepted Rawson's help when she was ill. A new memory surfaces from five years ago or ten: Dot in a fluster, late for an appointment with the dentist, putting on lipstick in front of the small mirror which hung in the scullery. "Lipstick for the dentist?" Jeanie said. Her mother laughed, a quick, embarrassed laugh. "Oh, silly me," she said and wiped it off with a flannel before she rushed out. *A woman with strong opinions and interesting ideas.* Rawson's words come back. Jeanie would like to talk with that woman.

One morning when she is waiting at the end of the lane for Alastair, who is unusually late, a different car pulls up, an old one, and Saffron gets out.

"I only just heard what's happened," she says. "Why didn't you tell me?"

Jeanie ducks to look in the back window;

the car seat is empty.

"Angel's with my mum. Your friend Bridget knocked on my door last night, looking for you. She thought you'd been staying with us. Where have you been sleeping? I found the caravan, but you weren't there. It was a complete mess. And did you know there's a piano on its back in the woods?"

"I'm fine," Jeanie says and folds her arms.

"You look thin, worn out. Come on, get in the car."

"I'm waiting for my lift to the hospital."

"I'm your lift today. It's all been arranged, now get in."

On the way, Saffron says she read about the shooting on the front page of the local paper. There was a photograph of the caravan and another of Julius smiling outside the pub, which they must have got from somewhere, but Saffron had no idea it was anything to do with Jeanie.

"Someone trashed the caravan," Jeanie says. "Went through the lot, after the police probably did the same."

"You're back in your old place, are you? Bridget said you and Julius lived in a cottage at the top of the lane."

"That's right."

"How's Maude?" Saffron says. "Is some-

401

one looking after her?"

Jeanie drops her chin against the memory of Maude's hot breath, the way the dog's eyes followed her around a room, how Maude butted her head against Jeanie's legs when she wanted food or a walk. Jeanie will not cry in front of Saffron. She will not cry. And to keep the tears from coming she makes her trembling anger return by saying, "They stole Julius's fiddle and Mum's banjo." She is certain the thefts and the mess in the caravan are down to either Ed or Lewis.

Saffron glances over. "Have you reported it?" Jeanie doesn't return the look. She likes Saffron but she is from a different world where lost things are found and ill people survive.

"How's the garden?" Jeanie says, to change the subject.

"It's beautiful, you should come and see it. I'm going to order the wildflower plugs for the end of September. You will plant them for me, won't you?"

Jeanie doesn't reply.

"I wanted to ask you something else about the gardening." Saffron speaks quietly, eyes on the road. "I noticed you haven't paid in any of the cheques I gave you. And I wondered, is it because you don't have a bank

402

account?" Jeanie can't help the twitch in her shoulders, the slight turn of her head. "I thought that might be the case. I've got the cash and I can help you open an account if you want, it's not difficult."

"Has Bridget told you everything, then?" Jeanie says, but she's past being angry.

"She said you haven't made an appointment with your GP."

Jeanie thinks Bridget talks too much about other people. "I haven't had time," she says.

Julius is being moved to a side room when Jeanie arrives, and she and Saffron wait in the Relatives' Room. Mr. Jones and Julius's regular nurse come in after half an hour, and Jeanie knows it isn't with good news. She's given more information about Julius and his lungs and his breathing and his temperature which she doesn't take in, but she can tell from the tone of the voices that what she is hearing is a warning, a preparation. Not for anything immediate, but soon.

"Shall I come with you?" Saffron says, but Jeanie shakes her head. The nurse leads her to the room where Julius lies, paler and thinner, if that's possible. He still hasn't opened his eyes, or spoken to her, or told her what she should do.

The nurse checks monitors, wires, tubes,

and says, "I'll give you a moment."

Jeanie sits, holds her brother's hand, strokes his arm, and touches his cheek with a knuckle. She wonders how she will arrange to bury him next to their mother.

"You can go if you want to," she whispers. "I'll manage. I'll be fine."

32

Saffron insists that Jeanie go with her to pick up Angel from her grandmother's house, and then to the bungalow for a cup of tea and to see the garden, even if Jeanie won't stay the night. She cooks pasta with tomato sauce, and although Jeanie says she isn't hungry she eats seconds. They walk the path through the meadow. It needs another mow — Saffron says she hasn't had the time: whenever she's home, she's studying, doing things with Angel, or they're both asleep. They sit under the flowering Indian horse chestnut and eat the cupcakes that Angel and her grandmother have made: blue icing indented with child-sized fingerprints. Angel runs up the grassy path and rolls back down on her side, over and over, veering off into the long grass, running back up, and shouting at them to watch. When Saffron's mobile rings, Jeanie goes cold — this and Bridget's are the numbers she's now given the nurses' station for emergencies — but it's Saffron's mother reminding her to bring a raincoat for Angel tomorrow because it's supposed to be wet.

Saffron takes Jeanie back to the farm lane in the car and asks if she can come up to the cottage.

"I'd love to see where you live," she says.

Jeanie looks into the back where Angel has conveniently fallen asleep in her car seat. "It'd be a shame to wake her."

"Some other time then?"

"Some other time," Jeanie says, getting out.

Saffron puts the passenger window down and Jeanie leans in. "But you're happy for me to come and fetch you, if I get a call?"

Jeanie nods. She has told Saffron that the mobile she first called on about the job was Julius's and that the police must have it now. Somehow she needs to sort out getting her own mobile phone.

She hurries past the farm — she hasn't seen Rawson in the week and a half that she's been sleeping in the old dairy. The grass is long down the middle of the track but now she sees that it has been swept forwards, showing its shiny undersides like the nap on a strip of velour and pointing towards the cottage. Stu's van is parked outside, and with a lurch of her heart she is sure he must have brought Bridget over with news from the hospital. She thinks about turning round and going somewhere else, but she carries on, past the van and its open driver's window. Neither Stu nor Bridget is inside. She knows too that her time is up sleeping in the old dairy — they will have discovered that the cottage is locked and empty, may even have seen her bed made out of the two long seat cushions which she brought from the caravan.

Jeanie goes round the back of the cottage and hears a sound, a yawn perhaps or a cough. Before she is in the yard a dog is running at her, jumping up and making her stagger backwards, a rope leash trailing from the collar. Stu is there, in the yard, waiting for her, sitting on an upturned bucket. He stands and smiles.

"Maude?" Jeanie says. "Is it Maude?" The dog whimpers and pants with excitement, rear end pulled from one side to the other with the swinging of her tail, until Jeanie collapses to her knees and Maude — rangy legs, big head — tries to climb on her lap.

"One of my mates found her," Stu says. "Near Devizes, hanging around an old barn. I brought her straight over, reckoned you could do with some good news. By the look of her, she's been surviving on what she could catch."

"Did you run away?" Jeanie says. "Where have you been, you silly dog? Where have you been?" She laughs and the dog licks Jeanie's mouth, her eyes, and the tears from her cheeks. Skinnier, smellier, dirty fur matted, but without doubt, Maude.

33

At the end of September of the following year, the sun shines for more than a week. It crisps the topsoil and hardens the skins of the harvested squash: Crown Prince and Sweet Dumpling strung like heavy washing on a length of rope between two posts. The light bleaches the wooden planks laid between the vegetable beds and ripens the heads of the couch grass which has burrowed its white fingers under the fencing. The sun turns the tomatoes a deep red, stretching the skins until they split, while its heat dries out the cottage thatch and drives the mice and insects further in, searching for damp shade. There is a tear in the netting of the fruit cage and twice Jeanie has to chase out birds. She needs to repair it. She needs to do a lot of things. She winds her way through the raspberry canes, collecting berries in a bowl she holds in the crook of her arm. When it's full, she takes it and her trug down through the garden. She passes the apple trees, where grass and wildflowers have grown and only a slight rise in the earth shows that anything might be buried there. She passes through the gate into the yard, scattering chickens. Beside the back door, the rosemary bush is leggier and in need of a trim. Maude lies on her side, panting in the narrow shade thrown down by the cottage, raising her head wearily and lowering it as Jeanie passes by on her way into the scullery.

Jeanie puts the trug on the drainer: beetroots, tomatoes — the ugly-shaped ones which Max won't take for the deli — the last of the peas, the first of the leeks. There are voices in the other room, a low, measured conversation. She washes her hands at the sink and calls out, "You okay in there?" There's no response. She takes a few raspberries and goes through to the old kitchen and turns off the voices on the radio. Only the dresser and the range remain from what was in the room when Jeanie lived here last. The grate is clear and the fire permanently out now that there is a boiler and cooker in the scullery, the room she calls the new kitchen. Stu turned up on the day she moved back in, seven weeks ago, bringing a smaller table than the previous one but with a wipe-clean top — the surface chipped and scratched — and three upright chairs from a house clearance, as well as a mattress which he heaved upstairs. She's sure that he saw her makeshift bed on the floor of the old dairy the day he returned Maude, and she thinks that perhaps these gifts stem from an unexpressed guilt at his son's involvement in her predicament. Jeanie prefers to believe this is the reason, rather than pity.

Stu came again the next day too.

"Got something else for you in the van," he said.

Jeanie followed him out to the track. He opened the back doors and inside was her old chicken coop, dismantled, and some of her chickens.

"Five of them's gone," Stu said. "Ed's missus wrung a few necks for their Sunday dinners."

A week after that, Dr. Holloway arrived with a wing-backed chair in his jeep. He carried it into the cottage and put it by the window where the sofa used to be.

Now, Julius is sitting in it, facing the front garden.

"It's too hot for September," Jeanie says to him. "I'm going to have to do the watering later or the leaves will fry. At least you've got a little breeze coming in."

Julius makes a guttural sound, his mouth crooked and working hard.

"Hot, yes." She perches on the arm of the chair. "Look what I've got for you." She holds out her hand and shows him the red jewels cupped in her palm. She puts a raspberry between his lips and watches as he rolls it around with his tongue and crushes it against the roof of his mouth.

A higher-pitched grunt, of surprise and pleasure. His language hasn't returned yet although she can usually interpret what he means.

"More?" She laughs. "Here you are then." She pops in another and another. "That's it, all gone." She shows him her empty hands. "I'm going to make us some lunch. Last night's leftover mashed potatoes fried with leeks and peas, and a bit of scrambled egg? All right?" Jeanie continues to worry about money and bills — the electric, the council tax, how much seed she will be able to afford for next year, the rent which must become due at some point, the rest of the money owing to Stu. Bridget has said she doesn't need to pay it back, but Jeanie's never accepted cash handouts and she isn't going to start now. At least she's caught up on the debt owed to Max and is earning

412

money from the vegetables he sells, and from working for Saffron.

"You've got a visitor coming this afternoon." Jeanie pushes herself upright. "Well, better get on." She speaks as much to herself as to Julius, needing to hear voices in the house, a conversation, even if it is one-sided.

Later, she sits with him while he feeds himself with a spoon and tries not to intervene when he misses his mouth, only wiping with the dampened muslin after he's finished. She combs his hair which has grown back apart from along the line of the scar where the bit of his skull was removed and replaced. This morning Jeanie gave him a shave but she's not good at it yet and she sees a patch of stubble under his jaw, but it's too late to do anything about it now. The three pitted marks across his face have faded to almost the same colour as the rest of his skin, but his bad eye has a temporary eyeball fitted — a watery pink, the colour of the socket. It no longer holds any horror for Jeanie, and an appointment has been made for him to have his artificial eye fitted, but Jeanie wonders whether in the meantime she should make him a patch. It's another item on the long list of things she needs to do which she keeps in her head.

Shelley Swift knocks on the door at five. She's wearing a polka-dot summer dress with a flared skirt, like something from the fifties, and her lips and eyes are made up, and Jeanie wonders if she thinks she's going on some sort of date. A while ago, Shelley Swift sent a note to the cottage addressed to Julius, and Saffron read it out to Jeanie. In it, she said she was sorry to hear about his accident — that was the word she used — and she apologized for not visiting him before but she understood that he would be home soon and she would love to come and see him. Dictating a reply via Saffron, Jeanie tried to warn Shelley Swift about what to expect but who is she to deny Julius a visitor?

"He's in his chair, sleeping," Jeanie says. "Come in."

Maude, inside now, sniffs and licks their visitor's hand and then goes to check on Julius.

Jeanie watches Shelley Swift looking around the old kitchen, holding on to the gold chain of her handbag, and with her orange lips stuck in a smile. If she takes anything in, she would see the wedding photo of Dot and Frank propped up on the dresser beside the bear with the bead eyes holding the ashtray in its paws, and the Toby

414

jug with its handle glued back on, hanging from a hook.

"Pull up a chair," Jeanie says. "I'll make us a cup of tea in a minute. Let me just wake him up."

"Is he all right?" Shelley Swift says, still standing.

"All right?" Jeanie says, pausing to look behind her while she's bending towards Julius. "He's had a good day, if that's what you mean." She turns back to her brother and strokes his arm. "Time to wake up."

Julius makes his moaning deep in his throat, lustful and uninhibited. Jeanie is embarrassed by it and doesn't look at Shelley Swift. She knows that Julius's noises sound sexual even if she has never heard another man make a noise like this. She wants to shush him but she knows it's her problem, this shame, not her brother's. His good eye flickers open and rolls around, trying to get a look at the body it's a part of.

"Shelley Swift has come to see you," Jeanie says loudly. The doctors are unsure how much his hearing has been affected. Jeanie looks back at the woman and sees that the smile has gone and unmasked horror shows on her face — her mouth is open, her eyes are wide. Afraid that Shelley Swift might scream or faint, Jeanie pulls over an

415

upright chair. "Have a seat," she repeats, and the woman plonks herself down. "I'll put the kettle on."

Jeanie goes towards the new kitchen but before she has taken a couple of steps, Julius wails and starts to thrash. His head moves from side to side, elbows bent and arms punching. He slides down in his seat until his bottom is hanging off the edge, and Shelley Swift jumps up, her chair screeching back along the stone floor. Maude, who is under the table, gripes, while Jeanie straddles Julius's waist and puts her arms around his chest, trying to stop him from falling too heavily.

"Help me, will you," she says to Shelley Swift, who looks from one side of the room to the other as though hoping Jeanie might be asking someone else.

"Do you have a cushion?" Shelley Swift says. "A pillow?"

"Next door." Jeanie nods towards the parlour. "On his bed." She lowers her brother to the floor as his seizure starts, cradling his skull until Shelley Swift returns with the pillow. It's over in a couple of minutes and afterwards they roll him onto his side.

"He'll sleep for an hour or so. We can leave him."

On the bench at the top of the garden, the two women drink their tea in silence, and Jeanie remembers being up here with her brother when they were young, no more than seven, sent up the garden because Dot had stuffed an old wicker basket, riddled with worm, into the fire grate. There had been a roaring in the kitchen from up the chimney, and outside she and Julius yelled and danced around the vegetable beds trying to catch the black flakes floating down. Had Dot run to Spencer Rawson to use his phone? Jeanie doesn't remember what happened next, except that disappointingly, as they thought at the time, the thatch didn't catch alight and they didn't get to see a fire engine.

"I don't suppose you'll visit again," Jeanie says to Shelley Swift.

"It wasn't what I was expecting."

They look over the cottage to the wood. A blackbird sings in an apple tree.

"No, I can see that."

"My little brother had epilepsy," Shelley Swift says. "He grew out of it, in the end."

"The doctors are trying to get Julius's medication right, little adjustments, you know. And he's having physio and speech therapy and getting his eye sorted out, well . . ." She trails off, worrying that she

417

sounds as though she's trying to convince Shelley Swift that Julius will get better, when really she needs convincing herself. "The brain's plasticity is a wonderful thing," she says more forcefully. This is one of Bridget's phrases and Jeanie isn't completely clear what it means, but nearly every day she sees a change in Julius. Something he can do that he couldn't do the day before which only she would notice: the way he helps when she lifts him from his chair, that more toothpaste goes onto his brush than in the sink, that he appears to listen to the radio for longer before falling asleep.

Shelley Swift and Jeanie drink their tea. Jeanie thinks about asking whether she and Julius had been planning on getting married, whether he gave her their mother's wedding ring. She hasn't seen it since it was on her mother's finger while her body lay in the parlour. The words are forming in Jeanie's mouth when Shelley Swift says, "Your runner beans are looking good."

"Would you like some?" Jeanie says.

Together, they stand up.

34

A letter comes on the Monday following Shelley Swift's visit, the same day that Jeanie has her doctor's appointment. Very few letters are delivered to the cottage — only bills and appointments really — although the new postwoman will, for the time being, drive up to the door. This letter, like the others, comes in a white envelope with a window and no stamp, only the mark of a franking machine. Absentmindedly, Jeanie leaves it in the new kitchen without opening it.

It's still unseasonably hot for September, and all the doors and windows are open in the cottage to try and catch a breeze. Saffron arrives an hour early, Angel bursting in and her mother hurrying after. Maude is immediately up and dancing, and Angel laughs and pats the dog's neck. The noise wakes Julius and he makes his guttural growl. Jeanie, still embarrassed, has found herself wanting to apologize for his noises to the occupational health woman, the district nurse, the physiotherapist, the man who came to assess Julius for his personal independence payment. Jeanie doesn't feel quite right about Julius getting money from the government: money for a man who never paid any National Insurance in his life. But Bridget says she shouldn't be so silly, how else are they going to afford the things that Julius needs, and besides, Jeanie looking after him in the cottage is going to cost the government a damn sight less than if he was kept in a home. She did agree to let Bridget help in completing the criminal injuries compensation form, but Jeanie isn't sure yet about claiming carers' allowance. Julius is her brother, she doesn't need to be paid to look after him.

Sometimes Jeanie is furious at what has happened to him, to them both. And at others she is stoical, and if not content, then accepting. Just as she learned the terminology of the intensive therapy unit, she has learned the words and phrases used by the police: *criminal prosecution service, on remand, committals,* and *criminal trials.* The police officer in charge of the investigation went to see Julius in his rehabilitation unit, and then perhaps realizing this wasn't helpful for anyone, telephoned Jeanie on her new mobile phone to update her on the investigation. The woman introduced herself as Detective Sergeant Alisha Kapoor and Jeanie recognized the voice of the woman who had interviewed her at the station. DS Kapoor said they were gathering evidence, that the trial wouldn't be scheduled for many months, and that Tom would be on remand until it started. She told Jeanie to expect to be called as a witness, but that they were unlikely to call Julius, given the state of his injuries.

In the year following the shooting, while she was staying with Saffron, Jeanie thought often about Tom and what his life was like in prison; what his life was like after his mother died, and whether one thing led to the other. Bridget's views, though, are firm and vociferous: anyone who takes a loaded shotgun to a caravan in the middle of the night has every intention of using it. And if it hadn't been Julius, it might well have been Jeanie. Sometimes, Jeanie wishes it was.

Months went by after the phone call from DS Kapoor, and then two weeks ago last Friday, just a few days after Julius moved into the cottage and when Bridget was over, the detective came around, bumping up the track in her car. Jeanie hadn't noticed that night at the police station how young the detective was; she couldn't have been more than twenty-five. In the old kitchen, DS Kapoor hovered awkwardly with her back against the dresser, not seeming to know where to put her hands — finally settling on clasping them together in front of her skirt. Jeanie wondered how long she'd been in the job. There had been a programme on the radio about problems with fast-tracking detectives: too green, too naive. She accepted a cup of tea — black, no sugar — asked them to call her Alisha, and sat at the table with Jeanie and Bridget, her hands safely in her lap.

"I've come to tell you that Tom has pleaded —" she said to Jeanie and then, seeming to realize that it was Julius she should be talking to, quickly turned to him and added, "guilty."

Bridget laid her palms on the table and breathed out a long breath. "Oh, that's great news." Jeanie tried to think of what terrible news she must have been expecting.

"You need to speak up," Jeanie said to Alisha. "My brother can understand a lot, but his hearing's not good."

Alisha plucked at her shirt collar with her tiny fingers — no bigger than a child's — and, louder and more slowly, she repeated what she'd said. Julius rocked his head, mashed his teeth and lips together, and made an incoherent noise. Alisha smiled and looked at Jeanie.

"I don't think he thinks it is good news," Jeanie said.

Alisha cleared her throat. "It's good news in the sense that it means there won't be a trial. You won't have to face that stress. You and Julius won't see Tom in court, you won't have to be questioned or relive that night."

"And bad in the sense that . . . ?" Jeanie asked.

"Not bad," she said. "But it means there will be no opportunity to hear an explanation of what happened. I know some victims and their families want this. And your brother . . ." She looked at Julius, looked away. Jeanie wondered if she was actually going to say that they would never be able to learn it from him.

"Surely, Tom will tell you, tell the police?" Bridget said. "Can't you just ask him?" And Jeanie felt a guilty pleasure that Bridget didn't know the answer to everything.

"There's no requirement for him to," Alisha said.

Jeanie had gone over that night in her head many times, imagining what happened between the two men, and Alisha was right — Julius couldn't tell her, or not yet. She thinks that in fact there's nothing much to tell; it's a simple story, even if it is one she holds herself responsible for. Tom was returning to the caravan with his shotgun to have another go at getting the money he believed was hidden there, and Julius was coming home because Jeanie had insisted on it, because Jeanie thought she was dying. Julius, perhaps remembering that Tom had threatened Jeanie, had confronted him, they argued, and Tom fired. Maybe it was supposed to be a warning shot since only three pellets found a target.

"I should also let you know," Alisha continued, "that he's been charged with and pleaded guilty to GBH, grievous bodily harm, and also possession of a firearm."

"Not attempted murder?" Bridget said, and Jeanie put her hand on Bridget's arm to quieten her.

"We don't believe he went to the caravan with an intention to kill."

"No, but —"

"And because he's pleaded guilty," Alisha went on, finally finding her stride, "there has been a plea bargain. The judge has already passed sentence."

"Already? What?" Bridget said. She had to

swallow a mouthful of tea before she could get the words out. Jeanie could tell from looking at Julius that he wasn't following this, it was too fast, too quiet, too much. She would have to tell him later.

"Tom was sentenced to eight years."

"Eight years!" Bridget slammed down her mug and tea slopped over the edge. "Eight fucking years. That's pathetic. Look at what he did to the man." She waved in Julius's direction. Julius moved his head, mumbled again, and Alisha looked at him, then down at her tea.

"I'm sorry," she said.

"Bridget, stop," Jeanie said quietly. She needed time to process this.

"He'll be out in, what, four, five years if he behaves. And then how safe will Jeanie and Julius be out here in the sticks? Eight fucking years." Bridget had shaken her head.

A few times after Alisha's visit, Bridget has brought up the subject of Tom and his sentence, and said Jeanie should at least consider the social worker's offer for her and Julius to meet with Tom. *Restorative justice* the social worker called it, but Jeanie has decided that Tom doesn't deserve any more room in her thoughts and refuses to discuss it. Meeting Tom now, Jeanie feels, would be either too soon, or too late.

425

In the old kitchen, Saffron says, "I brought a couple of Angel's books with me. I thought you could try and read them to her. Can you believe this weather?" She goes into the new kitchen and fills a glass with water.

Jeanie puts a tray on the table and gets out a tin of buttons she bought at a local car boot sale. She seats Angel on a cushion on a straight-backed chair and turns Julius so he can watch. Angel tips the buttons into the tray at the same time as Saffron is speaking from the other room.

"What was that?" Jeanie calls. She likes the noise and bustle of Saffron and Angel in the house — thinking about what treat she can arrange for the child, enjoying clearing up the mess they leave behind — and then the quiet when they've gone.

Angel picks up individual buttons, has them introduce themselves to each other in squeaky voices as she slides them about. Saffron comes to the doorway of the old kitchen with the letter from the white envelope unfolded in her hands. It's Saffron who usually reads aloud the letters that Jeanie receives — the ones with details of hospital and doctor's appointments for her and for Julius — but Jeanie knows that this letter isn't from the NHS, she knows she should have thrown it away before Saffron

426

could open it.

"This is odd," Saffron says, still reading. "It's from the General Register Office in Southport."

"Will you put the kettle on?" Jeanie says, leaning over the table and shuffling buttons around on the tray.

"No," Angel says forcefully to Jeanie, sweeping the buttons away from her. Jeanie stands upright.

"I think it's about your mum. Dorothy Seeder, it says." Saffron frowns, reads again, and looks up. "They seem to be saying that they need part of the burial or cremation certificate. It was never returned by the funeral director or crematorium, although they don't seem to know who that was." Saffron holds out the letter.

"That's the third they've sent. Must be some mistake." Jeanie stands beside Saffron and looks at the page, and although Saffron is teaching her to read, her heart is beating too fiercely for her to take in the simplest words. "What does it say they're going to do?" She tries to ask as though she isn't concerned.

Saffron looks at the bottom of the letter. "Well, nothing, I think. The wording kind of suggests they're giving up."

"I should hope so too," Jeanie says. "Waste

427

of everyone's time." She lifts the letter from Saffron's hands and takes it into the new kitchen where she folds it up and stuffs it underneath the vegetable peelings saved in a pot for the compost.

Saffron stands on the cottage path with Angel, holding on to Maude's collar. "You will go slowly, won't you?" she says as Jeanie straddles her bicycle out on the track. Jeanie bought it cheaply from Kate Gill, whose husband gave her a new one for her birthday. It's much better than the bicycle which used to be Dot's.

"I'll be an hour and a half at most," Jeanie says.

"Take as long as you need." Saffron remains on the path as Jeanie cycles off. It is ridiculously hot and although she would like some breeze in her face and over her body, Jeanie doesn't go fast. She is careful with her heart these days — the thought of what would happen to Julius if she died is too awful to contemplate. For a year after leaving the ITU Julius lived in a rehabilitation unit. Alastair drove Jeanie there a couple of times a week to see him and the improvements he was making: learning to walk with a frame, to feed himself, to use the bathroom. But between the unit and returning to the cottage he'd had to spend a while in a home for the severely disabled: a smelly, worn-down place, desperately understaffed, and his moods swung between anger and depression.

At the GP surgery Jeanie sits on an upholstered chair and waits until her name is called over the tannoy system. Bridget isn't working today. Jeanie put on some lipstick before she left, a muted red that must have been Dot's, hiding at the back of a dresser drawer. She rubs her lips together, feels the sticky slide, and sits up straighter, bolstered by it. Ridiculous, she thinks. When she goes in, Dr. Holloway stands and shakes her hand, invites her to sit on a chair beside his desk. The room is small, and out of the window the sun glares off the windscreens of the cars in the car park. Dr. Holloway goes through the preliminaries, commenting on how well Julius has settled into the cottage, his epilepsy, how there's plenty of possibility for improvement. He says she's doing a great job. Jeanie doesn't think so.

"And so," Dr. Holloway says, "your results."

She expects him to open something on his computer, put his reading glasses on, set the machine to printing — something — but he turns to her and says, "There is nothing wrong with your heart. Everything is completely normal."

Her hand goes to her chest without her realizing, feeling for the thing inside. She's sure it's still there, turning around and around, settling itself inside its shell. "What?" she says.

"The echocardiogram showed no damage to any of your heart's valves, your blood flow is fine, there's no murmur. You don't have rheumatic heart disease."

Jeanie can feel her face folding in on itself, the sting in her nose as the tears come.

Dr. Holloway touches her arm. "It's good news, Jeanie."

"Is it?"

He hands her a tissue and she holds it to her eyes, until she remembers her mother in a similar room, years ago.

"Of course it is."

Jeanie shakes her head. "Did I ever?" she manages to get out. During her first appointment, which Saffron and Bridget bullied her into, she told Dr. Holloway about her visit to the GP when she was thirteen and what Dot said to her afterwards.

"Did you ever have RHD, do you mean?" Dr. Holloway asks. "I went and found your old Lloyd George envelope — we have a room full of them." He leans forwards.

"There's nothing in there to indicate that you ever had a problem with your heart. There was a check-up noted, after your rheumatic fever cleared up, but nothing to say you had RHD." He sits back, picks up a pen, and turns it between his fingers. "And to be honest, if you did have it, or a heart murmur, I would have expected you to be having regular checks, maybe be on some medication. You didn't think that was odd? That you weren't?"

"I just believed her. She told me I had a weak heart and I believed her." Jeanie is suddenly angry. "She wouldn't let me do anything. I wasn't allowed to run or climb trees or get overexcited. I wasn't allowed to have a bloody job! And what, it was all a lie?" She is shouting and she is aware of her blood pumping, heart beating too fast. She is still afraid of it and can't help but take the deep long breaths that Dot taught her.

"I'm sorry," Dr. Holloway says.

"And Julius," she whispers. "She kept him at home too, to look after me." The different lives they might have lived are too enormous to comprehend. She could have had a husband and a child, like Bridget. Or no, not that. A child and no husband, like Saffron. She could have been a proper gardener, a garden designer, a garden

431

designer in Japan, or an engineer. She could have been anything. And poor Julius. If Dot hadn't said she had a weak heart when she was thirteen, would he have been hurrying through a patch of wasteland late one night, returning to a caravan? Is it possible to trace that event backwards?

"Why did she do it?"

Dr. Holloway can only shake his head.

35

On Friday evening, after she and Julius have eaten, Jeanie helps him to the new bathroom. She only needs to be nearby these days in case he calls out for her, and he rarely does, but she hovers in the kitchen wondering how using the toilet, brushing his teeth, and washing his face can take so long. Over the past four months, builders have converted the old dairy and joined it, via a short level corridor, to the end of what was the scullery. The bathroom has a shower without doors or a shower tray, and handrails around the toilet and attached to the walls, in the place where Jeanie once lay down and tried to sleep.

When Julius comes out she follows behind him and his walking frame to the parlour, and it's his slow and methodical shuffling that tonight makes her clench her teeth with frustration. She is envious of Saffron having Angel's noise and energy around her.

In the parlour — now Julius's bedroom — she helps him undress, taking off his slippers, pulling down his trousers and underpants while he stands holding on to the frame. He has lost weight in his legs and arms, the muscle that was there has wasted through inactivity, and he has a little paunch that he never had before. She guides one foot at a time into his pyjama bottoms and tugs them up around his waist. She no longer notices that she can see his private parts. They know the routine well, and Julius positions himself with his back to his bed and lowers himself down, letting go of the frame. Jeanie unbuttons his shirt, takes one arm out of its sleeve and then the other, but he is slow to help her tonight, doesn't move his shoulders or elbows like he normally does.

"Come on," Jeanie says, her irritation showing. "I'm going out, I have to get ready." She hasn't told him that tonight she's going to see Rawson for the second time. "Bridget is coming to babysit." Julius makes his throat noises, twitches his shoulders and gurns.

"Not babysit," she backtracks. "Look after you. I know you're not a baby, Julius, I know. Maybe soon you won't need anyone here when I pop out." The occupational

434

health woman says they need to get him a mobile phone with big buttons which he can learn to use in an emergency. Another thing for the to-do list.

Jeanie starts to feed one of Julius's arms into his pyjama top and he squirms away, jerking his torso and bellowing.

"Stay still," she says crossly. "I can't do it if you won't stay still."

His hands turn backwards, his fingers clench, and his arms flail. One of his elbows catches her in a rib, and with a stab of pain she cries out and then flops on the bed beside him, the pyjama top on her lap. Only now does she remember that on that morning when they knelt over their mother's body on the stone flags, Julius hadn't been wearing a pyjama top; perhaps he's never liked wearing the tops of his pyjamas? How else is he going to tell her except by resisting? She lays the arms of the pyjama top together, folds it in half. "It's too hot for this today, isn't it?" she says.

Jeanie wonders if maybe he understood something of what was going on when she came back from seeing Dr. Holloway and sobbed quietly in the old kitchen while Saffron held her and stroked her hair like she sometimes does for Angel when she's upset. Jeanie still hasn't told him about their mother's lie, just as she hasn't told him about the fact that she wasn't dying when she got Jenks to text him to come home. And now she realizes with a shock that all those times when she thought her heart was beating too fast, all the days she missed of school and lay on the sofa in the kitchen imagining the animal inside her, scared of the pain — there couldn't have been any pain, there was nothing wrong with her. It is hard to rewrite your own history.

Julius lies on his bed and Jeanie pulls just the sheet up to his chest. She fetches her guitar, sits on a chair, and tunes the instrument quickly, knowing that even this will quieten him and steady his breathing. When she first started playing she worried he would be upset by the music, reminding him of what he was missing, but she's found that it helps calm him so he falls asleep more easily after she's played. "What's it to be?" she says and almost begins "Polly Vaughn" but, recalling the lyrics, stops after a couple of notes and instead starts:

"Before our singing is through
And our voices lie broken
Before the silence speaks true
And all the lies we led have spoken
For here we would stay

With all that we borrow
And owe to the day
For holding back tomorrow
Do you know, where then we'll go?"

When he's breathing deeply, she puts the guitar down and goes out to the garden, Maude following. She will not cry, she thinks. Not again.

Jeanie comes out of the bathroom wrapped in a towel, to find Bridget sitting at the table in the old kitchen flicking through a celebrity magazine she's brought with her.

"You're early," Jeanie says.

"Nath gave me a lift. My car's in the garage, ready tomorrow."

"Nathan?"

"He's back home. Jobs, money, I don't know." She rolls her eyes. "He didn't have time to come in. Sends his regards."

"Is he picking you up later?"

"Stu said he'd come and get me about ten thirty. Is that okay?"

"That's good of him."

"He's not a bad husband when he puts his mind to it. He said people were asking after Julius in the Plough. I told him to tell them that they should call in. It'd be good for Julius to have a visitor or two, give you a bit more time off. You could take this dog for a proper walk." She grabs Maude and waggles the dog's head, digging her fingers into Maude's fur.

"I'm not so sure about that," Jeanie says. "Shelley Swift came last week and Julius had a seizure. On the floor, foaming at the mouth, the works."

"She won't be back, then." Bridget turns a page of her magazine. From upside down it looks like a comic strip.

"I don't know. Maybe she will." Jeanie starts up the left staircase to her bedroom.

"Stu told me that Chris from the Plough was wondering if you'd do another gig, when you're ready. Said that some bloke had come in asking about you and your music. He couldn't make it last time. Something about an interview or a recording?"

Jeanie stops halfway up the stairs, where Bridget can't see her. She thinks about the night they played in the pub: Julius's hair falling over his face, the singing, how much fun it had been. Her fingers go to her chest out of habit.

"I don't think I could do it again. Not without Julius," she calls down, her voice lighter than she feels.

"I told him that, but apparently it was you

in particular the bloke wanted to see." Jeanie hears her turn another page and she doesn't know what to think about that.

"Bridget," she says tentatively. "Would you do something for me?" Another page turns. "Would you read me a letter, from Rawson?" She can't get used to calling him Spencer. Jeanie puts her palms on the wood panelling which divides the old kitchen from the staircase. The white paint which she can't remember being done in her lifetime is scratched and marked and yellowed.

"A letter?"

She can hear that Bridget's interest is piqued.

"I've tried, but I can't work out his handwriting."

"Of course I'll read it. No problem."

"Okay. I'll get dressed and I'll show you." Jeanie pushes herself off the panelling and goes up the rest of the stairs. She puts on a clean dress, one she's had for years. It's too hot for tights.

In the old kitchen, Jeanie sits opposite Bridget, the letter in a cream envelope in front of her, her hands placed on top. She knows Rawson has written her name on the front.

"I went to see Dr. Holloway on Monday

for the results of my echo," Jeanie says.

"I know," Bridget says. She's eyeing the letter but clearly trying not to show her curiosity.

"And I suppose you heard what they were?" Jeanie says sarcastically.

Bridget raises her eyebrows, pops a Polo mint into her mouth. "Of course not, that's confidential."

"Do you want to know?"

"Go on then." Bridget sits back, waiting. Jeanie tries to assess from her expression whether she knows about Dot's lies, but it isn't possible.

"All clear. There's nothing wrong with my heart."

Bridget's smile on her big round face is genuine delight. "That's great news."

"Except it's not that I've got better. I never had it in the first place."

"What do you mean?"

"I never had RHD. Not when I was thirteen, not ever."

"But you were diagnosed, weren't you?"

"Mum told me I had it, not the doctor. And I think she made it up. Told me I was ill when I wasn't."

"What? Why would she do that?" Bridget closes her magazine.

"To keep me at home, I suppose. She told

me in the year after Dad died when she was going a bit crazy, before the thing with Rawson started."

All week Jeanie has been thinking about it and this morning finally she decided that it is another simple story: Frank died and in the year that followed Dot realized, or believed at least, that one day she would be alone. Maybe her crying in the doctor's consultation room was not because of Jeanie's diagnosis, because there never was one, it was from relief, or just an outpouring at her husband's death. But at some low point she told Jeanie she had something wrong with her heart in order to keep her at home. The lie grew and could not be undone; Jeanie — and Julius too — would remain in the cottage with her.

"Oh, Jeanie," Bridget says and puts her hand across the table. Jeanie reaches out and touches Bridget's fingers with her own, just for a moment, and then shakes her head at the thoughts of her mother, refusing her tears for a second time that day. Bridget starts to say more, she will want to discuss it, unpick it, and analyze it, and Jeanie can't do that, not yet.

She picks up the envelope, raps it on the table. "This letter then. He gave it to me when I was leaving last time, said he wasn't very good at saying things out loud. I haven't told him that I can't read." Reluctantly, Jeanie hands it over.

Bridget takes the cream-coloured letter out of the envelope; the paper is thick, expensive. She unfolds it. Jeanie knows it has the farm address printed at the top, and she knows it begins with *Dear Jeanie.*

"Dear Jeanie," Bridget starts. "Forgive me for putting this in writing rather than simply saying it to you, but I find that I express myself better on the page, and I want to make sure that what I say is right this time.

"Your mother meant a great deal to me. Perhaps we should have tried harder not to see each other for Caroline's sake, but I refuse to believe that our love was wrong. I miss Dot every day, as I'm sure you and your brother do. I'm also sure that the nature of our relationship must be a shock to you, especially considering the way you have viewed me all these years, but I have always cared about you and Julius and your welfare, albeit from afar, and it is hard to express how devastated I was when I learned of Julius's injuries. Updating the cottage and making it accessible for him was the least I could do.

"And this is why I'm writing. I would like your permission for me to instruct my solicitor to transfer the ownership of the cottage and its land into your and Julius's names."

"What?" Jeanie says.

Bridget holds up her hand and continues. "Dot, as I tried to explain when I came to the caravan, would never let me do this, but I hope you would agree that all our circumstances have now changed. Perhaps next time we meet you could let me know whether this is acceptable to you and your brother. With all best wishes, Spencer." Bridget refolds the letter. "Well!" she says. "Can you believe that?"

"He's giving us the cottage?"

"And the land."

"Actually, I can't believe it."

"I wonder what his wife will make of this?" Bridget scores the paper's folds with the nails of her thumb and index finger.

"I think she's gone for good, she's left him."

"Really? Probably for the best."

They sit silently for a moment, taking it in.

"So, what are you going to tell him?" Bridget asks.

"I'll have to speak to Julius about it."

"But you're going to say yes, aren't you?"

Jeanie takes the letter from Bridget. "I'll

tell him I'm thinking about it." She opens the letter again, scans the spidery handwriting as though there might be some mistake, and then she puts it back in its envelope. "There's some leftover soup in a pan on the cooker if you want it. Julius is asleep. I'm sure he won't wake but if he does . . . well, you know the routine."

"Fine, fine," Bridget says, waving her hand.

"I really appreciate you coming round, again."

"Yes, yes. I'm going out for a fag."

Jeanie's first visit to the farmhouse was awkward to begin with, stilted, sitting in Rawson's white sitting room, drinking tea, talking about the farm and the weather, but Jeanie is sure it will get easier. This time or the next she wants to discuss all the things she has heard on the radio: history and politics and agriculture, and Dot as well, of course. She wants to see what he has to say about her ideas of how to turn the garden into a decent business. Jeanie knows that, like her mother, she is a woman with strong opinions, a woman with interesting ideas.

In Julius's bedroom, she straightens his sheet. He's lying on his left so that the scars and his bad eye, which alter that side of his face, are hidden. She can't help it, she misses the undamaged man: his jokes, his teasing, his crazy ideas. She wanted him to stay with her and not to go with Shelley Swift, she wanted to be back in the cottage, and in the end, didn't she get exactly that?

Jeanie goes out to the yard where Bridget is smoking and sniffing at a twig of rosemary snapped from the bush.

Bridget eyes her. "You make sure you say yes, okay?"

She smiles. "See you later."

Jeanie leaves the garden, goes around the cottage and out the front gate. She turns right, along the track towards the farm, where Spencer Rawson is waiting.

ACKNOWLEDGEMENTS

It takes many people to make a book. I'd like to thank all early readers of *Unsettled Ground,* including Indigo Ayling, Henry Ayling, Dawn Landau, Louise Taylor, and Judith Heneghan, and of course the rest of the Taverners who have given me feedback chapter by chapter, including Amanda Oosthuizen, Richard Stillman, Paul Davies, Beth O'Leary, Emma Scattergood, Claire Gradidge, Susmita Bhattacharya, and Jake Wallis Simons. Thanks also to all The Prime Writers for their unfailing support both online and off. To the amazing Jane Finigan, and to Fran Davies and everyone at Lutyens & Rubinstein, and also to the lovely David Forrer. To the whole team at Penguin and Fig Tree (and beyond), including Assallah Tahir, Natalie Wall, Jane Gentle, and Karen Whitlock, but most especially, Juliet Annan. Enormous thanks to Masie Cochran and everyone at Tin House, including Win

McCormack, Craig Popelars, Nanci Mc-Closkey, Becky Kraemer, Molly Templeton, Yashwina Canter, Diane Chonette, Elizabeth DeMeo, Alyssa Ogi, and Spencer Ruchti, and not forgetting Anne Horowitz and Allison Dubinsky. To Ursula Pitcher, Stephen Fuller, and Heidi Fuller for their love and support. Many people helped me along the way with research and advice, and so thanks go to Jill Kershaw, Paul Ayling, Sam Hodgson, Sarah Kirwan, Caroline Mitchell, Mark Harbord, Lesley Ann Ritchie, Paul Morris, Dave Sell, Olivia Kane, Jane Bartlett, Martin Stallion, Iain Steel, and Enda Gallagher. Thanks to Henry Ayling and Tia Blake for my writing soundtrack.

And my love, always, to Tim Chapman.

ABOUT THE AUTHOR

Claire Fuller was born in Oxfordshire, England. She has written three novels: *Our Endless Numbered Days,* which won the Desmond Elliott Prize; *Swimming Lessons;* and *Bitter Orange.* She has an MA in Creative and Critical Writing from the University of Winchester and lives in Hampshire with her husband.

The employees of Thorndike Press hope you have enjoyed this Large Print book. All our Thorndike, Wheeler, and Kennebec Large Print titles are designed for easy reading, and all our books are made to last. Other Thorndike Press Large Print books are available at your library, through selected bookstores, or directly from us.

For information about titles, please call:
(800) 223-1244

or visit our website at:
gale.com/thorndike

To share your comments, please write:

Publisher
Thorndike Press
10 Water St., Suite 310
Waterville, ME 04901